TRUE LOVE

Artemisia slid to one side of the bench and Alex seated himself beside her. He took her hand in his and played with her fingers. For a long moment they were silent and then Alex raised Artemisia's hand to his lips. Thinking about the coming war, he absentmindedly touched his tongue to the tip of one finger, another, still another. Only when he felt her tremble did he realize what he did. Instantly he dropped her hand. "I apologize."

"Don't."

"Don't apologize?"

She reached for his hands, clasped them tightly. "Don't feel you must."

He wove their fingers together. "It is wrong of me to treat you . . . treat you . . ."

"As a lover treats his love?"

Alex stared into her eyes. "My dear, we haven't the right."

Her chin rose, firming, her lips compressing. Then she looked down at their intertwined fingers. "Alex, I have decided that when I next speak with my father I will tell him that I am sorry to go against his wishes, but that I must. I can no longer obey him when I love you so very much. . . ."

Books by Jeanne Savery

THE WIDOW AND THE RAKE

A REFORMED RAKE

A CHRISTMAS TREASURE

A LADY'S DECEPTION

CUPID'S CHALLENGE

LADY STEPHANIE

A TIMELESS LOVE

A LADY'S LESSON

LORD GALVESTON AND THE GHOST

A LADY'S PROPOSAL

THE WIDOWED MISS MORDAUNT

A LOVE FOR LYDIA

TAMING LORD RENWICK

LADY SERENA'S SURRENDER

THE CHRISTMAS GIFT

THE PERFECT HUSBAND

A PERFECT MATCH

Published by Zebra Books

A PERFECT MATCH

JEANNE SAVERY

ZEBRA BOOKS
Kensington Publishing Corp.
http://www.zebrabooks.com

ZEBRA BOOKS are published by

Kensington Publishing Corp.
850 Third Avenue
New York, NY 10022

All Kensington titles, imprints and distributed lines are available at special quantity discounts for bulk purchases for sales promotion, premiums, fund-raising, educational or institutional use.

Special book excerpts or customized printings can also be created to fit specific needs. For details, write or phone the office of the Kensington Special Sales Manager: Kensington Publishing Corp., 850 Third Avenue, New York, NY 10022. Attn. Special Sales Department, Phone: 1-800-221-2647.

Zebra and the Z logo Reg. U.S. Pat. & TM Off.

First Printing: October 2001
10 9 8 7 6 5 4 3 2 1

Printed in the United States of America

ONE

"... And then I ..."

Artemisia Bigalow clutched her carriage robe and tugged it more tightly around her shoulders against the winter cold. Once she'd closed it against the drafts, she turned her attention to the writing desk on her lap and very carefully extended one gloved hand. She grasped her pencil firmly and set it to the page—only to lift it as the coach wheel slid into still another deep rut. She sighed. Softly.

But not so softly that her father did not hear her. He broke off the flow of his words and glared. "Stupid wench," he growled.

Artemisia lifted her head in time to see her mother straighten her back, to note the slight frown marring her brow. Artemisia, knowing exactly what was running through her mother's mind, spoke first. *"Stupid,* Father?"

"Moaning and groaning and drooping and shedding tears for a man not worthy of your smallest regard!"

"But I was not," said Artemisia gently, her brows barely arched. In actual fact, just at that particular moment, she had *not* been thinking of Alex, Lord Merwin, the man to whom her father referred.

Sir Vincent stared at her, his normally prominent eyes bulging. Then, when she continued watching him steadily, his gaze slid to the side and he harrumphed.

"Well. Well, then. If you were *not* moping about that dratted Tory, then—" He beamed in a particularly annoying fashion. "—you are a good girl after all. Just tired of traveling, are you not?" he added in a falsely jovial voice. "Poor child. But I *did* warn you. You must admit I warned you! But still, you would go! Oh, I predicted just how it would be, did I not? Ha! And have you thought?" He looked pleased. "We have not yet reached Baden—" (The spa was the next decent stopping point on their way.) "—and, therefore, we've still more than two hundred miles before we reach Vienna!"

Again he grinned an unctuous smile, and, inwardly, his daughter cringed. *If only my father were a man more easily respected,* she thought. Melancholy filled her. *If only I did not feel so guilty for not loving him more. If only he were not so . . .*

But here Artemisia's thoughts abruptly took another turn. Even in the privacy of her mind she could not admit her father was rather stupid! Even to allow the unfilial thoughts that had slipped past her guard brought still more guilt to crowd against the sadness. In the previous two and a half years, ever since she'd been forbidden to even *think* of Alex, Lord Merwin, she had discovered that guilt and sorrow were an oddly tiring combination of emotions.

And if it were not for her mother . . .

The coach jounced again, slid sideways, jerked and jerked again as the overworked team pulled it from a deep rut. Artemisia sighed. If the end were not so dearly to be desired, she would deeply regret that her beloved mother had convinced her father to follow where so many others of the *ton* had led. Vienna . . . !

But, at that thought, her mood lightened. *Vienna! Glittering Vienna. Ah! The wonder of it. We are actually traveling to Vienna!* For a moment she felt very nearly light-headed. *Vienna, where Alex, Lord Merwin, is attached to Lord Castlereagh's staff!*

Sir Vincent's voice nudged her consciousness. ". . . so *he* said . . ."

Artemisia instantly closed her ears to the ongoing monologue she could not, while seated across from him in the coach, escape. *How,* she wondered, *has Mother survived his blathering all these years?* And, the thought a conscious thought, she again felt that stupid, idiotic guilt for not believing better of her father.

Baden was still too far down the road, so that day ended at a small town where the hotel was already crowded with travelers. Instead of taking connecting rooms, which was their custom, they had only one. Sir Vincent rumbled and grumbled about the inconvenience, but was ineffectual in changing it. And, discovering the only other hostelry in town was not a fit place to take his womenfolk, he gave it up and settled in to enjoy himself.

Later that evening, Sir Vincent sat in the common room and lorded it over the other men stopping at the same inn. There was no private parlor, so Artemisia and her mother sat near the fire in the bedroom allotted the three of them. Artemisia decided they were very likely more comfortable than if the parlor had been available. Later, her father and mother would share the bed. She would sleep on the floor near the hearth, bundled in bedding brought with them from England.

And, she thought, *I have the best of it.*

She had, while her mother washed away the day's travel, peeked at the linens on the bed. They would replace the sheets, of course, but Artemisia did not like the looks of the coverlets.

If they have ever been washed, she thought, *it has not been for a very long time!*

"Only a few more days, now, and we will arrive," said Lady Bigalow.

Her tatting shuttle flipped and turned and dipped

and flipped and, dropping away from it, an intricate piece of tatting fell into her lap. Her ladyship had begun the work the day they left London, telling Artemisia that she hoped to have enough to trim the new gown she meant to order instantly they reached Vienna. The work was progressing nicely, but Artemisia feared her mother had rather overestimated how much she could accomplish while riding across war-torn Europe. It was true that their well-sprung carriage carried one in reasonable comfort over English roads, but Lady Bigalow had been naïve about the condition of continental routes!

"You will be glad to arrive, I know," continued Lady Bigalow comfortably.

Artemisia felt the faintest of warmth put a glow to her features. "Yes. Do not mention it, Mother."

"Do not mention a certain young man who will be equally glad?" teased her ladyship.

"Alex," said Artemisia, naming names, "has no notion we are coming. When he left London—"

"Under protest, I am sure."

"—for the Congress," continued Artemisia, ignoring her mother's mild jest, "he predicted it would be at least a month, perhaps six weeks, before he returned."

"A month or six weeks which has stretched well beyond that and with no end in sight. I could not bear to watch you declining into a mere wisp of yourself, my dear."

"Is that why you suggested to my father that he missed a great deal by staying in London?"

Her mother smiled a small, sad smile. "It wasn't that which convinced him he should go." Lady Bigalow chuckled softly at her daughter's obvious curiosity. "I merely said that one reason it was taking so long for the Allies to come to agreement was that they needed a few wise heads to point the way."

Artemisia felt her eyes widen. "Mother! You are *the complete hand,* are you not?"

Lady Bigalow blinked. "I am what?"

Artemisia chuckled. "Perhaps I should say you took Father for a flat."

Another blink. *"What?"*

The chuckles turned to giggles. "Is it better if I say you hoodwinked him finely?"

"Oh." Lady Bigalow's eyes widened as she realized her daughter had, if she understood the term correctly, taken *her* for a flat by teasing her in that particular way. "Oh yes, indeed I did. It is the only way to manage him."

Artemisia sobered. "He has been a trial to you."

Lady Bigalow's features became a blank, totally devoid of expression. "He is my husband, Artemisia."

"Still, a rose is a rose is a rose, and your particular rose is full of thorns."

Lady Bigalow sighed. "I will not discuss your father in such terms, Arta. *Our* fathers made the arrangement. I doubt Vincent, any more than I, got the bargain for which he wished." She drew in a deep breath. "But, my dear child, that is in the past. Yours is the future. And I want a future for you in which you may grow and become all you can be. You cannot do that if you are stifled by the sort of man your father would have you wed."

"A man just like himself!"

"Hmm."

"A man like the one who did not allow you to grow and become . . ."

"Enough!" Lady Bigalow could allow only so much. She grasped the arms of her chair tightly and, sternly, said, "He is my husband, Artemisia, and your father. Whatever you think of him, he is the head of our household and it is not proper to contravene his wishes."

"Ah? You have changed your mind and think I should accept Lord Looby's offer of marriage?"

Lady Bigalow choked back a laugh and relaxed. "Lord Loomerbye, Arta. You must not call him by that other name! Someday you will forget yourself and use it in a situation where you should not!"

"But if I am not to contravene . . ."

"Do not play devil's advocate, Arta. You know I did not mean that. Unlike the era in which I was reared, *your* father cannot force you to wed where you do not will it. The other side of the coin, my dear, is that you must not wed to disoblige him. It would be so very wrong."

That thought had Artemisia doing what her father had accused her of earlier that day. She not only drooped, but moped, and even groaned. Once. She did not, however, shed any tears. She had shed all the tears she meant to shed when she was first forbidden to have anything to do with Lord Merwin—and had concluded she must disobey her father's edict.

Merwin was a politically active Tory and anathema to Sir Vincent, who was a rabid Whig. Unfortunately, the baronet had been too late in his recognition of the growing affection between the unspeakable Tory and his daughter. The pair had already fallen deeply in love.

With contradictory feelings, Lady Bigalow had watched her daughter's descent into the abyss dug for her by the fact of Merwin's politics. At the first signs of an attraction between Artemisia and Lord Merwin, she warned her daughter the alliance was hopeless but, beyond that, she had not forbidden the two to meet at balls and soirees.

Her ladyship was indignant but unsurprised by her husband's dictates and, setting out on her first and very likely only rebellion against the man to whom her father wed her, she came down on the side of the thwarted lovers. She would not encourage her daughter to go against her husband's denial of the banns, but she did what she could, within the bounds of propriety, to aid and abet them in their desire to have a modicum of time together—even when all too often that was no more than permitting them to go down a dance together.

Some days later, Alex, Lord Merwin, edged away from a group of men arguing the Polish question. Poland was an important issue to those attending the peace conference in Vienna, but it had been argued to death. Alex had heard every possible variation and, acquainted with the men discussing it here and now, knew exactly how this particular disagreement would progress. He strolled on, his gaze moving restlessly around the ballroom looking for new faces. They arrived daily, especially the English, who had been deprived access to the continent for so many years.

Vienna, or so it seemed to Merwin, who wanted nothing so much as to return to London, was one ballroom after another. The major figures at the conference competed with each other, night after night, to provide the largest, the most glittering, of parties. And if that were not enough, the less-well-known hostesses emulated the great to the best of their ability and as their pocketbooks allowed! All was gaiety, but hidden beneath the surface was a morass of political maneuvering and constant intrigue. The committees and cabals were the serious *raison d'être* for the gathering together of the most glittering members of society from all of Europe.

Alex closed his ears to still another controversy on the subject of Poland, an escalating argument between a young Russian prince and a middle-aged Austrian gentleman. A few paces on he watched a young woman do her best to draw the interest of Richard Trench, Earl of Clancarty.

Alex chuckled softly, sympathetically. The poor creature would need to be far more forward than she was ever likely to manage, well-brought-up young lady that she was, in order to pry the British diplomat's interest from the machinations surrounding the Congress! Clancarty was far too zealous, far too professional, to take up with the shy young lady.

He was also too old for the chit and Merwin wondered, briefly, if she had the notion of using Clancarty to gain an introduction to someone among the dozen or so young men attached to the British Embassy, which, if she could achieve his notice, might actually be a new approach and an excellent notion—so long as he himself was not the man!

Bored with it all, tired of the intrigues, both political and social, disgusted with the eternal spying of one interest group on another, the bickering and the back stabbing, Alex allowed his idle gaze to wander on around the huge, well-lit room.

For a moment his attention was caught by a group of men standing just within the ballroom entrance, delegates from several of the smaller principalities along the Rhine. Oblivious to those around them, deeply involved in still another argument—this one, Alex guessed, was likely to involve riparian rights, the rivers through central Europe of great importance to them all—they impeded the entry of other guests.

His gaze passed on to a group of wives gently fanning themselves but doing little good against the heat of the crowded room. And beyond them . . . Alex stiffened.

Was it? Could it be?

It was. The lovely and unattainable Miss Artemisia Bigalow. Miss Artemisia Bigalow and—Alex glanced all around—Sir Vincent nowhere in sight! Alex smiled. The smile widened to a grin and his heart pounded within his chest. He moved determinedly, single-mindedly, toward her, nodding to an acquaintance here, removing someone's hand from his sleeve there, and, no more often than absolutely necessary to avoid running down some poor innocent, he never took his eyes from the woman he loved.

Loved endlessly, but without hope.

Artemisia hid her mouth behind her fan and leaned toward her mother. "He is here."

"Oh?" Lady Bigalow looked this way and that and did not even pretend she was not searching the crowd for someone in particular. "Where?"

Inconspicuously, Artemisia pointed toward Lord Merwin, who moved gracefully though the crowd that surrounded the floor on which dancers performed a cotillion. "There. He has seen us."

"Oh, excellent, my dear. When he asks you to dance I will go to your father and take care that he does not come into the ballroom until after the second set."

"Mother, you are a jewel. We thank you." Artemisia smiled and held her hand out to Alex, who stopped before her at just that instant. "Alex?"

"Artemisia?"

"Mother?" Not releasing his hand, Artemisia turned slightly on her chair. "You remember Lord Merwin, do you not?" she asked demurely.

Alex flushed at the mild reprimand and turned to Lady Bigalow. "I would apologize for ignoring you, my lady, except that I know you stand our friend. And you know how long it has been since I last set eyes on Miss Bigalow."

Lady Bigalow chuckled. "Indeed I do know. Have I not listened to Arta bemoaning your separation for far too many months?" She nodded her approval when Alex kissed her hand in proper continental fashion and, after a few more words, left her daughter in Alex's care, departing the ballroom in search of her husband. Sir Vincent would not be allowed to interfere in the young couple's enjoyment of the next two sets.

Alex watched her go and then looked down in Artemisia's eyes. "Shall we dance—" He cast a quick glance at their immediate neighbors and lowered his voice. "—or would you prefer to stroll in the conservatory?"

"An excellent suggestion, that! After all, it is *de rigueur* that I feel a trifle faint from the heat, is it not, my lord?" Her laughing eyes caught his gaze and he chuckled, a warm brown sound that sent shivers up Artemisia's spine. "A stroll amongst the flowers would be just the thing to set me up."

Alex offered his arm and, when she took it, squeezed it against his side. "Ah, my Moonbeam," he whispered. "I have missed you so."

Artemisia's eyes darted toward those nearest, a worried frown touching her brow. "My lord! Hush. Do not call me that! You must not!" She cast him a look from the corner of her eye. "At least," she added, smiling, "not in such a public place."

They strolled through the halls. Here Lord Merwin nodded to a lady, there Miss Bigalow curtsied to a gentleman, and far less quickly than either wished, they reached the etched glass doors leading to their host's conservatory. Once within, they moved without hurry along a winding path through the luxurious growth. After peeking into two occupied bowers, they found a third in which they could be private. The instant they were within the dusky grotto, Alex drew Artemisia into his arms. If he was a trifle rough in accomplishing that, he was very gentle when he raised her face to his.

For a long moment they stared at each other. And then, ardently, they exchanged a kiss filled with such longing, such depths of need that, after the first heady moments, it set off another sort of frisson in Artemisia, one that was *not* that of love.

Fearing where such ardor could lead, she pulled her hands from behind Alex's head to push against his chest. He didn't notice. While attempting to turn her face from his, she pounded one fist against his shoulder. Alex lifted his lips from Artemisia's and stared down into her widened eyes. His ardor faded instantly as he realized he had frightened her. He put her aside and turned away.

"I apologize," he said.

"No! I am as much to blame. We have been so long apart." Artemisia sighed softly. She grasped his arm, felt how taut his muscles were, and leaned her head against his shoulder. "Oh, Alex, why must Father be so stubborn? I feel so *guilty* whenever I grow angry with him. Why, why, *why* will he not relent?"

"You might as well ask," offered Alex, his face stark with tension, "why I remain stubbornly in love with you, my Moonbeam, when I know he will not." He lifted his hand and, just barely, touched the pale blond curl falling down over her shoulder in the exceedingly attractive but rather old-fashioned style which was all her own. His tone gentled. "Or why will I not become the Whig he would have me?"

"It would be wrong of me to ask it of you!"

"Not wrong. Very natural, in fact, but I cannot do it. I would come to resent him, perhaps resent you and—" Alex shook his head. "—that would be a hateful thing."

"Truly, Alex, I know how you feel about your work." She put out a hand to touch his, but drew back before he could take it within his own. "We must return to the ballroom, my love," she said sadly, "and join the next set. Mother will ask me how I enjoyed the dancing and it is not in me to lie to her. Not when she understands all too well how it is with us."

"No. Lying to her would be still more wrong than

the kiss we stole. And, although she may ask about the dancing, you may be certain—" He cast her a sardonic look. "—she will not ask about *that*. Come, my dear." He offered his arm. She placed her hand on it and he covered it with his. "Besides, dancing with you is the next best thing to holding you in my arms. Perhaps," he added, forcing a lighter, nearly mischievous, tone, "your father will observe that the waltz is quite the thing here in Vienna and will allow you to have lessons in how it is done."

"So that we may enjoy the dancing and have the embracing as well?"

He cast her a quick impish grin, his elfin features and three-corner smile much in evidence. "One of the reasons I love you, my Moonbeam, is that you are so very quick to understand me!"

"But," she said, falsely demure, "I would refuse lessons in the waltz."

Alex's slanting eyebrows formed a deeper vee. He halted their progress, turning her. "Why will you not be tutored? Please? For me?"

"No." When Alex frowned still more harshly, she chuckled. "It is unnecessary."

"But think of the . . ."

"My dear," she interrupted, speaking softly, "I already know the waltz."

Instantly the frown disappeared. He grinned. "You joined one of those morning waltzing parties of which I have heard, did you not?" She nodded. "But do you yet have his lordship's permission to perform the dance in public?"

She sighed. "No."

"Then my point stands. He will observe that it is the most popular dance in Vienna and his pride will not allow that his very popular daughter become a wilting flower propping up a wall, and he will give you the necessary permission! And then, my dear . . . ?"

She smiled and nodded. "And then we may waltz."

The smile faded. "When he is not there to see us, of course."

Alex sobered as well. "I hate it that we must creep around behind his back."

"So do I, my dear. So do I." She sighed. "We must be very thankful that my mother stands our friend."

They joined a line forming just beyond the door by which they entered the ballroom and, content to merely be in each other's company, enjoyed themselves . . . until the moment the set ended. From long, well-established habit, Alex glanced around the room. Lady Bigalow was still absent so he looked for a chaperone for his love. His gaze lit on Lady Castlereagh who stood near the orchestra chatting with some other women and he led Artemisia to her.

"My lady, you know Miss Bigalow, do you not?"

"Of course." Her ladyship was among the many in the *ton* aware of the couple's difficulties. She sympathized with their problem. "I believe, Miss Bigalow, that I last saw you at Almack's, did I not?"

They discussed last spring's final Almack's ball during which the Season's final scandal had played itself out and, amid laughter from others in the circle who had not heard the tale, Alex faded away. He knew he'd not be allowed near Artemisia again that evening. Not even by her loving mother.

Since he would not be allowed near his Moonbeam, and would suffer envy watching her go down a dance with more favored men, Alex found his host, thanked him for a delightful evening, and, seeing his hostess nearby, congratulated her on providing one of the happiest entertainments he'd attended since arriving in Vienna. He did not, of course, explain that it was Artemisia's presence that made it so.

Alex nodded to an acquaintance he passed in the anteroom outside the ballroom, spoke with another he accompanied down the stairs and while they waited for their cloaks. He waited again for his carriage and

talked idly with several young men who, bored by
anything so tame as a ball, were taking themselves off
to one of the new gaming houses that had sprung up
all over Vienna. Alex begged off joining them and,
after waving them off to their jollification, told his
driver to take him home.

Home. Vienna was overcrowded but his friend,
Jack, Lord Princeton, had been exceedingly fortunate
to lease rooms for himself and his wife not far from
the British Embassy, which was situated just around
the corner on the Minoritzenplatz. Before moving in
with Jack and Patricia, Alex had lived with two other
men in a suburb some distance outside the city walls.
When Jack suggested he join them in their quarters,
Alex accepted. Gladly.

Alex brooded. While traveling along the avenues
crowded with the foreigners attending the Congress,
his gaze wandered restlessly and his straight, dark eyebrows, which grew upward toward his temples, were
more sharply slanted from temple to nose by the depth
of his frown. His teeth worried his lip as he himself
worried about his—he could only call it an attack—on
Artemisia. Parted from her for so long, seeing her so
unexpectedly, he had, very nearly, lost all control.
Worse, he had frightened his love, something he regretted a great deal.

And worst of all—something tightened in his
chest—*might it not happen again?*

Alex, although he understood his love's motives,
wished her sense of right and wrong were not *quite*
so strong. He growled softly, angry with himself.
Artemisia would not be the woman he loved if she
were less true to her beliefs. But still, the conflict
between her love for himself and her feelings for her
parent was putting a terrible emotional strain on the
both of them. It was bad for him, yes, but it was worse
for her because, adding to the strain, was guilt that

she disobeyed Sir Vincent every time she spoke with her love.

The coach pulled up and Alex descended. He entered the large house, which had, for the conference, been divided into a number of spacious apartments, each leased for an exorbitant rent. Alex had offered to pay Jack his share and Jack, not so plump in the pocket as he'd have liked, had accepted, neither offended by the offer nor embarrassed by it.

Jack and Alex were two of a group of schoolboys who had banded together to protect each other from school bullies and to help in other ways. The relationship among the Six, as they called themselves, had only grown stronger as the years went by.

Unexpectedly, the Princetons were in and sitting near a closed stove in the parlor. They welcomed Alex warmly.

"Something is wrong," said Patricia, almost at once.

Alex sighed. "No. Not wrong. Very, very right. Except, of course, it is all wrong."

Jack chuckled. "Trixie, did that make any sense?"

"Oh yes. Miss Bigalow has come to Vienna with her parents. It is wrong that they must pretend to ignore each other whenever her father is anywhere near but wonderful that she *is* here."

"How did you know the Bigalows had arrived?" asked Alex.

"Your world is right but very wrong. What else could it be?" Patricia smiled and Alex grinned ruefully. "Alex, will Sir Vincent never relent?"

"I doubt it."

"Then your Artemisia must make up her mind to go against his wishes or, if she will not, then it is only right she release you from your promise to wed her and only her."

"The promise is not one-sided, Patricia. It is not a question of one of us releasing the other. We love each other." Alex shrugged and, finding it too painful to discuss his dilemma, turned to his friend. "Jack, did you read that letter I received from my source on Elba?"

With this hint that he did not care to talk about the impossible situation in which he found himself, the conversation moved on to a discussion of the suspicion that Napoleon was plotting how he could return to power in France.

When he and Jack said all there was to say about that, they shifted to a discussion of the problems facing the British government. Those were complicated by the maneuvering going on among the Allies, who were gathered in Vienna with the avowed intention of ending the long war with France to everyone's satisfaction. It could never happen, of course. Not when every nation had its own agenda and had claims to large areas of Europe, areas all too often claimed by some other country—or by *more* than one.

Not particularly interested in what was a repetition of all she'd already learned about which sovereign might gain what territory from where at the expense of still another sovereign, Patricia allowed her thoughts to wander to Alex and his ill-fated love for the daughter of a militant Whig. She considered the possibility that Sir Vincent's opposition strengthened the attraction, but the two had been loyal to each other for several years now, which was a very long time if it were merely an infatuation, so very likely it was not.

The love between them had sprouted well before her own marriage to Jack—not that the others of the Six knew at that time that the seeds had been sown. Even Patricia, who was Merwin's cousin and had been his housekeeper before her marriage to Jack, had not guessed the depths to which Merwin had fallen. In fact, it was only after the marriage of Tony, Lord Wendover, another of the Six, that the situation became so obvious anyone might guessed. But there was nothing anyone could do and for some time after Tony's wedding, all their thoughts and concerns were for him since, compromised by the woman he was then forced to wed, he was not a happy man.

In the end, Lord Wendover's scandalous marriage to his Libby had turned out as well as had earlier marriages among the Six but it seemed that Alex's desire to wed the woman *he* loved was likely to be thwarted forever. Patricia regretted that Alex was unhappy.

Worse, that unhappiness was likely to continue for many years. Since Sir Vincent came from a line that lived long lives, the couple's only hope was that Miss Bigalow's father would experience a change of heart—or if *she* did. Unless Alex's love consented to act against her father's wishes, the two would continue to suffer—unless Sir Vincent relented.

Patricia grimaced at such circular thinking and wondered if there was anything she could do to help. Regretfully, she decided there was not. Not, of course, that she would put the problem from her mind and forget about it! She might think of something if she only tried.

Alex, happening to glance her way, met her narrow-eyed gaze. He blinked. Then, realizing Patricia plotted to aid and abet his cause, he grinned. For the first time since leaving Arta's side, Alex thought there might be hope. Patricia, after all, was a born schemer! If anyone could find a solution to the problem, his cousin would take the trick!

TWO

The bridge over the Danube to the Prater was crowded. Lady Bigalow and Artemisia's carriage was forced to a standstill, blocked by those ahead waiting to cross, while still others, attempting to leave the island, filled the span. Artemisia folded her hands and called on all her patience. She hoped Alex would manage to meet her in the park as he'd suggested during their dance the evening before. He had warned her that there was no guarantee he could escape his duties at the embassy, but she was used to his work keeping him from her side.

Usually, Artemisia accepted the situation, knowing that Alex would not be the man she'd fallen in love with if he were the sort who shuffled off his duties when pleasure called. Still, wanting to see him, desperately lonely, needing to talk to him, she had slept badly, both mind and body reliving the first true kiss they had ever shared. On this occasion, she hoped he'd be there for her.

How utterly marvelous that kiss had been . . . and how frightening. Worst of all, perhaps, it was unexpectedly intriguing, rousing feelings Artemisia had never before experienced. *Sensations she wanted to feel again.*

And that was worrying since she knew very well just where such longings led. As had many young women sent off to school for a year or two, the older students had introduced Artemisia to a form of literature to which her parents would have objected. Violently. Not only did it teach her and her friends the facts of life, but some of the well-worn pamphlets that passed from hand to hand included crude drawings that left nothing at all to the imagination!

One girl had sworn she would go into a nunnery before she would allow a man to touch her in such a way. There were some who could not wait for the opportunity to experiment. Artemisia, more intelligent than most, took the printed words with a grain of salt and suspected the diagrams were exaggerated. She neither feared her inevitable future as some man's wife nor did she have any particular desire to hurry that day forward.

But that was then.

Now?

Now, frightening as it had been at the time, she had been gifted with a hint of the glory that might result from the relationship between a man and a woman. She found her mind, to say nothing of her traitorous body, stirring up niggling little thoughts and questions and hopes and fears and raising them to consciousness at the most awkward moments! *What would it be like if Alex were to . . .*

"Ah! At last! We are moving."

Artemisia was uncertain whether to be angry with her mother for intruding on her daydream or to bless her. "Do you think this is the proper hour for visiting Prater Allee? It seems as if everyone is leaving."

"I can only judge by what our landlady said, Arta dear," said Lady Bigalow placidly. "If she erred, then tomorrow we will do differently." Idly, her ladyship looked around. "Arta!" She grasped her daughter's arm, drawing back once she had her attention. "Do look at that bonnet! Am I mad or do you, too, recognize it? Can there possibly be another like it in all the world."

Arta turned in the direction her mother inconspicuously pointed, one finger raised from where one hand clasped the other in her lap. "Surely it cannot be the same. That poor woman is allowed to go nowhere unless she is guarded like a bone between dogs and I cannot see a single one of the Baggett brothers!"

The hat in question turned as the woman wearing it shifted position. A profile was revealed. "Arta! It *is* Edith Baggett. I swear it is!"

"But . . ."

"Yes, I am as surprised as you, my dear. I wonder. Do you suppose—" Lady Bigalow cast a mischievous glance toward her daughter. "—all four of those awful men were taken off by an ague so that she is free to come to Vienna?"

"I would more readily believe Miss Baggett has run away from home."

"Do you think so?"

"Well—" Their carriage drove by the lady. "—it looked to me as if that tall gentleman with the graying side-whiskers was paying her something more than casual attention!"

"I'd have called it rather possessive attention," agreed Lady Bigalow once they were well beyond the couple.

"Mother, is it possible Miss Baggett managed to meet and woo a man who took her away from the brothers Baggett?"

"I cannot see how, but if she did, then I congratulate her. Ah. That must be Prater Allee. Are not the chestnuts lining it beautiful? Even bare of branch, as they are this time of year? Think what they will be like when in full bloom! It is just as Frau Schmidt described, is it not? Shall we walk?"

Lady Bigalow and Artemisia forgot their brief interest in the Baggett woman, whom they knew only slightly and merely because they all attended the same London church. They were too caught up in studying the fashions displayed by others strolling the long, tree-lined avenue to have any farther interest in the woman.

Furs were everywhere and Lady Bigalow made a note to obtain for herself a coat with one of the interesting fur capes and high collars and, for Arta, a fur-lined cloak. And perhaps a muff as well, made from that white fur spotted with darker blotches. She pointed it out to Artemisia.

"A muff would be lovely, Mother, but made of fur it will be too warm when we return to England. I would prefer a bright red, oversized muff like the blue one carried by that woman dressed all in white. I wonder who she might be."

The woman in question sat in a carriage pulled to the side of the allee. She was surrounded by men and held her arm and the blue muff over the side while she talked to a dark man leaning toward her from the back of an all-white horse.

Lady Bigalow took one look, blushed slightly, and ordered Artemisia to turn away her eyes. "She is not the sort of woman you will ever meet," she scolded, but continued in a musing tone, "I agree, however, that it is an interesting muff. I do believe you could carry several small packages in it."

"Very useful." But Artemisia was no longer interested in hats or muffs or even furs. Coming toward her was Lord Merwin. He had seen her and closed the space between them quickly. "Mother . . ." she warned, speaking softly.

Lady Bigalow turned. "My lord," she said and curtsied. Lord Merwin bowed. He even managed to say a few words before turning toward Artemisia and holding out his hand. Lady Bigalow watched her daughter lift hers. It appeared to tremble slightly. Her ladyship shifted her gaze to Artemisia's face and discovered it was suffused with an attractive blush.

Lady Bigalow's brows arched but she said nothing.

Not that it would have made one iota of difference if she'd recited the whole of Lord Byron's latest effusion! Neither Artemisia nor Alex would have heard a word. They were too busy communicating with their eyes, his lordship asking his love's pardon, she giving it, but then questioning him. He responded to her silent query with a rueful look. She dropped her gaze, but only for an instant. Then she met his steadily. This time a touch of red appeared in Alex's neck and ears.

Lady Bigalow, faintly concerned by what she observed, decided the silent communication had gone on quite long enough. Allowed to continue, very soon the two would be noticed and would excite comment, becoming a source of gossip and controversy. She stepped between her daughter and Alex, and grasping an arm of each, set off down the allee at a pace that forced the young couple to think of what they were about.

When her ladyship felt they had had time to recover, she asked Alex his opinion of how much longer it would be before the Congress concluded its business.

"Forever?" he suggested, only half in jest, and then explained. "We've too many strong personalities and several great minds at work here. Unfortunately, each has his own priorities, his own demands, his own reasoning, and his own plan." Merwin sighed. "I doubt Metternich and the Czar Alexander will ever agree on a solution to the Polish problem. England has pretty well managed to protect her interests, but they are far simpler than most. France . . . well, I suspect Tallyrand has the most brilliant mind of any man I've ever met. We are—" His voice took on a tone so dry it was brittle. "—fortunate that his interests lie with England's. At least—" He grimaced. "—they do at the moment!"

"But you foresee no acceptable end to it all?" asked Artemisia.

"Castlereagh is determined there be a balance

among the great powers before any agreement is signed. Tallyrand has the same goal and, if they do not agree on all issues, they work well together on that. Poland remains the largest block to any settlement. Russia claims to want a free Poland, but only if it is firmly under Russia's control. Austria fears Russia." Alex shrugged, but then a thought brought a stern look to his features. "The whole question may be moot." He lowered his voice. "We have reason to suspect Napoleon is planning to leave Elba and return to France!"

"No!" Artemisia stopped and the others were forced to do so as well. "Surely not. Impossible."

"Less impossible than anyone wishes to believe."

"But the French—surely I read that they wish peace."

"Wish it? Yes. They need time to mend and grow. But are they happy with the return of fat King Louis? That, I fear, is something else."

"But . . ."

Lord Merwin grinned. "My dear Artemisia, the call for the king immediately after Napoleon's defeat had not only a rather limited voice but was before the French public realized what it meant to be on the losing side. Think! How many long years was it that Napoleon took all by storm, leading France to victory after victory? Can you not imagine the feelings of—" He waved one hand. "—oh, for instance, the officers released from the disbanded army at half pay. They've nothing left but a great deal of time in which to brood. It is said they occupy their time gambling and picking fights with the English occupation force, pushing duels onto anyone they can in order to prove their manhood!"

"Iniquitous," said Artemisia.

"That England still occupies Paris?" asked Alex, pretending innocence.

"That they find it necessary to prove something which needs no proving!"

Lady Bigalow, more aware of Sir Vincent's plans than Artemisia could be, interrupted to exclaim, "But surely it is impossible that Napoleon leave Elba. Surely he is guarded and kept close."

"Our ships hover around it, but he was given the island. It is his to rule. How, then, can he be kept close?" asked Merwin.

"Do you mean he could return to France, collect a new army, and the war, the horror, could begin all over again?"

"Yes. If he is quick about it, and lucky. And we know he is both!"

Silence descended. Not true silence, of course. Around them were laughing voices—the deep chuckles of men, the flirting, giggling voices of young ladies, one seductive laugh of a mature woman—but little of it penetrated the magic circle surrounding the three strollers. They were in a world all their own.

Merwin was, for the moment, content to have Artemisia near—even though separated from her by her mother. Lady Bigalow was preoccupied with the question of how she might prevent her husband from leaving Vienna for Paris—especially since it could not be kept from him forever that Lord Merwin was in Vienna, knowledge that would make him angry and irrational! And Artemisia was readjusting her beliefs to include the possibility that the long war with France was not yet ended. She sighed softly.

No matter how softly, Alex heard. "I did not mean to distress you," he said quietly, speaking across Lady Bigalow to his love.

Lady Bigalow started, taking the question to herself. "Distress me? Oh no, how could that be? My lord," she continued, firmly changing the subject, "we have just arrived in Vienna. Will you advise me as to where I should take Arta to have new gowns made up?"

The conversation turned to feminine fripperies. Merwin found he must strain his memory for any and every bit of helpful information. Before their stroll ended at the Bigalow landlady's ill-kept carriage, he discovered that somehow, somewhere, he had picked up a surprising amount of knowledge of Vienna's modistes, chapeau makers, mantuamakers, and sources of the finest lace and silks. *And,* most important for Lady Bigalow's immediate requirements, which furrier was least likely to so outrageously overcharge as to bring Sir Vincent's wrath down upon her head!

He watched their carriage disappear among others moving slowly away from the allee toward one of the bridges crossing into the city and was about to walk back to the embassy when a slim, gloved hand caught his wrist, arresting him.

"M'lord Merwin!"

Alex searched his mind. "Ah." He blinked. "Miss Baggett, is it not?"

"Not." Her laugh had a brittle sound. "Most definitely not!" She spoke in a somewhat coy fashion, simpering ever so slightly. "I am Mrs. Marchcomer and here comes my husband." She did not release Alex. If anything, her grip tightened. "Martin," she asked the man who strolled up to them, "are you acquainted with Lord Merwin? He attends the London church I attended."

Marchcomer, although as English as Lord Merwin, had spent most of his life out of England. He bowed from the waist in continental fashion. He lifted his eyes to meet Merwin's utterly expressionless features. "My lord," he said.

Merwin had recognized one of Vienna's more notorious gamblers. He glanced toward Mrs. Marchcomer and back. "I must assume congratulations are in order? I had not heard of your marriage."

"Our passions overcame our good sense," said Marchcomer smoothly. He slid his arm through his wife's and turned a look compounded of satisfaction and wry amusement her way. "We made a runaway match of it, did we not, my love? One knows that such would be unforgivable normally, but her brothers were adamantly against their sister marrying."

"You say they would have objected to any man?" Alex kept his voice innocent or his words might have caused grave insult.

Even so, Marchcomer's brows clashed together. "My dearest Edith assured me it was the only way. They were determined, you see, to maintain control of her income."

"Ah." Alex's tone was dry as dust. "I *do* see."

Marchcomer smirked ever so slightly. "Just so."

"Are you newly arrived in Vienna?" asked Lord Merwin, turning back to the former Miss Baggett.

"We arrived only two days ago."

Merwin recalled rumors that Marchcomer was deep in debt. He also remembered that the man had disappeared from Vienna some weeks previously. It would seem the gambler had taken himself off to find a new source of funds *and* that he had been successful. "Well, my dear," said Alex to the bride as all that ran through his head, "I wish you the very best and hope you enjoy your stay here." He bowed over her hand, wished she would not giggle in that ridiculous fashion—especially given her age, which was very near Alex's own—and turned to Marchcomer. "Congratulations, sir. I know *you* always enjoy Vienna."

Marchcomer chuckled. "Yes, I enjoy Vienna very much. And will do so all the more now I've Edith at my side." He bowed and guided Edith away from where Merwin stood.

Merwin watched them go. He shook his head. "Poor lady," he murmured and then, putting the former Miss Baggett from his mind, set off for the embassy at a rapid pace. He had played hooky for far longer than he'd meant to do, but it had been imperative he find and apologize to his Moonbeam. And she, bless her, had accepted his silent request for forgiveness just as he'd known she would. Now if he could only forgive himself and convince himself there would never again be an occasion for which he must apologize!

But what, exactly, had her last long, sober questioning look meant? Just before her mother interrupted? What had his Moonbeam intended him to understand by that exceedingly intriguing expression?

A tingle ran up Merwin's spine and he looked to neither right nor left as he stalked into the Minoritzenplatz. He was unsure if the sensation was due to anticipation or to fear! Did he dare hope she had found their embrace so enticing she wanted more? And if so, did he fear he must now be on guard for the both of them? In which case, the odd sensation was due to *both* anticipation and fear? Merwin sighed, saw he was about to pass right on by the mansion housing the embassy, and, chiding himself, turned into the building, hurrying up the stairs to the office he shared with Jack.

Merwin stopped in the doorway, all thoughts of Artemisia thrust from his mind. Jack was standing, the crutch he'd needed since wounded in Spain under one arm, his free hand fisted, thrust into the air, shaking violently at nothing at all.

"What is it?" asked Merwin. "What has happened?"

Jack turned. Slowly he relaxed. "Only more of the same," he said ruefully. "The problem is that I do not want my Trixie caught on the continent if Napoleon completes his plans."

"We've had further word?"

He nodded. "The same source."

"He's been accurate in the past."

"That is what worries me. I wish he had been wrong occasionally!"

Merwin grinned, but the smile faded. Jack might worry about his wife, but as her husband he'd the right to protect her. Merwin's concerns were less easily soothed. If he were to go to Sir Vincent and suggest he take his wife and daughter to England, home where it was safe, the man was likely to do just the reverse, perversely unwilling to take any advice, even good advice, from a man he held in abhorrence!

"How much danger is there at the moment?" Alex asked Jack.

"Hmm? Oh." Jack looked down at his desk, chose a particular piece of paper from the maelstrom littering its surface, and handed it to Alex. "Look for yourself. I'd say there is as much as a month before one need feel too much concern. Perhaps longer."

Alex's brows dipped. "You are the military man, but I can't help thinking of all those times Napoleon startled the world by being where anyone of any sense would have said it was impossible for him to have gotten so quickly!"

"This is different. He must send out probes to those who were once under his command and who have gone over to Louis. It takes time for word to travel when it must take secret routes and cover so many miles."

"There is that . . ." Alex's features did not relax. "Jack, if I ask you to leak the word to Sir Vincent at some point, will you do so?"

"Leak secret information! Alex! What are you thinking," he continued in wry tones, "to ask such a thing of me?"

"*Will* you?"

Jack grinned his oddly lopsided monkey grin. "Of course I will. I love my Trixie to distraction, but I am not blind. I can see very clearly why *you* might—for reasons I'll never understand, since she cannot be half the woman my wife is—be *more* worried for the fair Miss Bigalow!"

Alex growled at the teasing, but he could not stay angry with Jack. "You will know when and how to do the deed," he said, feeling better for their conversation. "I will leave it to you."

Artemisia's eyes widened as her mother babbled on and on about how wonderful Vienna's parks and boulevards and shops had appeared that day. Her father grunted when Penelope Bigalow mentioned ordering furs for herself and Arta, but even that news didn't set him off into one of his unstoppable monologues. Arta frowned slightly. Her eyes met her mother's worried gaze and the frown deepened when Penelope redoubled her efforts to rouse her husband from his exceedingly unusual lethargy.

Artemisia could bear it no longer. "Father, are you ill?"

He grunted again, staring into his wineglass.

"Father? You are causing Mother a great deal of concern."

He glanced up. His gaze touched on Artemisia's but moved on immediately to his wife's worried face. "Concern?" he blustered. "For me? Nonsense," he shouted. "One who would go against my wishes to the degree that woman has—" he pointed at Lady Bigalow. "can feel not the least concern for me."

"Oh, oh," muttered Artemisia.

"That woman—" His finger waggled. "—knows exactly what I mean. She has gone behind my back. She has stabbed me to my very soul. She has made a laughingstock of me."

"But Father!"

"She has allowed not only herself but *you,* Artemisia, to be seen in that sorry excuse for a carriage belonging to our landlady. She would neither wait one day until our carriage was free nor until I could arrange for a more suitable vehicle. Oh no. Nor could she bring herself to walk to the shops which are not all that far away—"

"A mile, at least."

"—when she knows how important it is for one to keep up appearances. *Especially,*" he added, shaking his finger so wildly Artemisia feared for the wine bottle set near his place at the table, "when one is in a foreign land. To allow mere foreigners to look down on one! It is not to be tolerated!"

Artemisia relaxed when he mentioned the carriage. It was *not* the discovery that Lord Merwin was in Vienna that had set him off. But how long before the secret was out? Artemisia sighed softly. "Do you escort us to the ball this evening?" she asked.

"No. I am invited to a meeting." He looked from one corner to another and around behind him as if worrying that someone had secreted himself in the room. "There are *some* who remember what a great man he was," he added in a whisper.

"He?" Artemisia looked confused and then, realizing he meant Napoleon, the expression changed to one of horror. "Oh no. You mustn't."

"You will be still," said her father, the finger poking toward her. "You know nothing of such things. Nothing at all."

"I know that no country will tolerate anyone or anything which aids the monster to return to wreak more havoc on the continent!"

"Nonsense," blustered her father. "No such thing," he added. "Merely reminiscing of times past. No one can possibly object!"

Can they not? wondered Artemisia. She glanced at her mother and saw that the older woman feared for her husband's safety.

"My dear, do you think you ought?" asked Lady Bigalow, her tone hesitant.

"Penelope, I will not have you thinking you know better than I. You will say no more."

For once he even managed to project a certain dignity. And he stopped talking, which was even more acceptable. Lady Bigalow and Artemisia exchanged a look. Arta shrugged every so slightly. Lady Bigalow sighed softly. Both refrained from attempting the impossible and both hoped for the best but both were preoccupied with wondering what might be the worst!

Once dinner ended, the family went its differing ways. Artemisia and her mother were actually descending from their disreputable carriage when it occurred to Artemisia that, with her father safely elsewhere, she need not fear being seen with Lord Merwin.

Now if he were only in attendance . . .

THREE

It was late. Lord Merwin hurried toward Metternich's Chancellery on the Ballhousplatz, thanking heaven it was not far from the embassy.

A packet had arrived from London very late that afternoon. It included several questions Castlereagh decreed required immediate response. Half of the less than a dozen young secretaries attached to the embassy were kept hard at work on the less sensitive matters while Merwin labored over a ciphered note. He wrote the final version in invisible ink between the lines of another, quite innocent, report. While the courier, who had managed the long journey from London with surprising speed, slept off his weariness, the bag filled, ready for his return journey.

Merwin's report was finished now. He had done his best to warn of the possibility of Napoleon's escape from Elba, but he feared those in London, most of whom were convinced the Corsican upstart was finished forever, would discount his cautions. The work done, he had returned home and changed. Now, as he hurried along, he sighed. What possible good was he doing here in Vienna when no one listened to him? And worse, while he had wasted his time working on that ciphered secret report, had his Moonbeam given up hope of seeing him this evening?

Not that she hadn't had a great deal of practice while still in London waiting and wondering if he might appear for one or two sets late in the evening! She had had to do that often enough and, too often, had waited in vain. And she had had the patience of a saint, understanding as no other could—or at least *would*—that his work made chaos of any social life he wished to maintain.

But here? In Vienna? Would she expect different behavior on his part? Did she truly understand that his time was not his own? Even here? He quickened his pace. One dance. Surely there would be time for them to share a cotillion or, better, a waltz—if her mother would allow it.

Arriving, he handed his hat and cape to a liveried attendant and moved up the stairs among the press of people who still, even at this hour, attempted to gain entrance to the ballroom. A new fear filled Merwin's breast. Would he be able to find his love among all these hundreds of guests?

"Milord!"

Merwin stiffened. Reluctantly, he turned. "Yes? Mrs. Marchcomer, is it not?"

"You remembered!"

A flush crept up the bride's cheeks, although, at her age, it seemed strange to Merwin that she could still blush. Too, she looked up at him with huge adoring eyes, startling him no end. Merwin cleared his throat. "And Mr. Marchcomer?"

She shrugged. "Off about men's business. I told him to enjoy himself because I—" That simper Merwin found irritating assaulted his ears. "—have every intention of enjoying myself!"

Before he could react, she had attached herself to his arm and beamed up at him. "I will do my best," said Merwin, "to introduce you to interesting people who will help you to that end." She pouted. "But I need no introductions when *you* are available."

Merwin, as gently as possible, disabused her of the notion he was available. "I am meeting my party here," he finished. And, since they'd managed to enter the ballroom at that point, he craned his neck, seeking some clue as to where his love might be found.

". . . so I will join you," he heard.

"Hmm?" He looked down, startled.

"Since I know no one, I will join you," she repeated, clutching him with both hands.

"You must, of course, meet others," he insisted. Running into—very nearly literally—one of the young embassy secretaries who had escaped the work that evening by the simple expedient of having left before the arrival of the courier, Merwin began with him.

He went on to several women he knew, the wives of Congress attendees from one of the smaller German principalities. Mrs. Marchcomer was polite to all, but made it clear she had attached herself to his lordship and wasn't to be dislodged. Merwin discovered she had him outmaneuvered. As a gentleman he could not insist she remain with any of the people to whom he introduced her. That was out of the question. In fact, the only solution was to find Lady Bigalow and hope her ladyship might manage the trick for him while he and Artemisia enjoyed each others company.

He continued on around the room, scanning the crowd for a sign of either Lady Bigalow or Artemisia. Had they gone home already, giving him up? Or had they continued on from here, attending some other function from among the many options one had most any evening?

"Sorry?" he said, realizing Mrs. Marchcomer had said something.

"I merely suggested we were wasting a great deal of very good music," she repeated coyly.

"Are we? Oh. Well, you see, I must find my party."

"But we have very nearly circled the room. Perhaps they have gone elsewhere and not awaited your arrival."

And that was Merwin's fear as well. He sighed. The

set ended and, resigned, he asked Mrs. Marchcomer if she would care to join the next. *As if I need ask!* he thought with only a touch of bitterness.

The two reached the head of their set and Merwin glanced around, still hoping for a glimpse of his Moonbeam. As luck would have it, he saw Artemisia and her mother pause in the doorway, saw his love's color fade, saw her turn to her mother and say something.

Without ceremony, forgetting in the urgency of the moment that he was a gentleman, Lord Merwin grasped Mrs. Marchcomer's arm and led her off the floor. Moving more quickly than his partner approved—something she made clear quite vocally—he eased their way through the crowd.

"My dear, he has seen you," said Lady Bigalow. "You should have more faith in him!"

"But it is that awful Edith Baggett. How could he ask her to dance?"

"Artemisia Theodora Felicia Bigalow!"

"Oh dear. That may have been unforgivable!" Artemisia had the grace to blush, but her anger at seeing her love going down the dance with another surged back. "The thing is, he never dances with anyone but me and has not from the day we realized . . ."

Lady Bigalow interrupted before her daughter could say something she would not want overheard. "You were not here, were you? And Lord Merwin is a kind man. He must have noticed that Miss Baggett knows no one and took pity on her. And here they are." Lady Bigalow beamed a welcome and held out her hand. "Miss Baggett."

"Mrs. Marchcomer!" exclaimed Edith, refusing to release her grip on Lord Merwin's arm even to accept the offered hand. "And you are Lady Bigalow." She shifted her gaze. "This is your daughter?"

"Artemisia, you remember Miss—" Lady Bigalow cast a flustered look toward Lord Merwin, drew in a breath, and finished, "—Mrs. Marchcomer. A recent wedding?"

"Very. Mr. Marchcomer and I made a runaway match of it. You know my brothers." Edith's lips twisted into a grimace. "We do not pretend we were not forced to elope." She took a better grip on Lord Merwin. "I am very glad to meet you, but Lord Merwin was about to take me in for refreshments. Perhaps I will see you tomorrow? In the park?"

The look of consternation on Lord Merwin's face might have made Artemisia laugh if the situation were not so dire. "Refreshments?" she asked sweetly. "What a wonderful notion," she added, just as if she had not, that very moment, returned from eating her fill. "Mother, Lord Merwin will ensure that I am comfortable. He will return me to you soon." She took Alex's other arm and looked up at him, her long, slightly darkened lashes shadowing her eyes. He cast her a quick, appreciative grin, bowed slightly to Lady Bigalow, and directed his charges into the hall and on to the dining room where a buffet offered a wide variety of temptations to the palate.

When Merwin returned to the small table where he'd seated the two young women, he heard Artemisia ask, "And Mr. Marchcomer? Did he not escort you here this evening?"

"We do not live in each other's pockets," said Mrs. Marchcomer, her nose very slightly in the air. "It is not the thing."

Merwin hung back.

"Ah," said his love in rather catty accents, "but if you are so very much in love that you were impelled to elope, surely you cannot bear to be parted for the whole of the evening."

"My dear child," said the older woman smugly, "did I say anything about love?" One eyebrow arched. "I will tell you the truth and I care not who knows it. I became tired of my brothers controlling my every movement. I determined to escape them. Would you care to hear how I managed?"

"Please. Do tell," said Artemisia.

Lord Merwin decided it was time to interrupt what was threatening to become a decidedly scandalous tale. "Ladies? I hope I've chosen well." He knew Artemisia's tastes and had made the same choice for Mrs. Marchcomer. He set the plates before them and motioned to a hovering waiter who hurried up with a choice of wine for the ladies while his lordship moved off to collect a plate of his own.

"Now," said Artemisia with just a touch of humor, "quickly! Do tell!"

Mrs. Marchcomer's eyes lit up. "I like you!"

Artemisia sobered. "I thank you, but until I know you better, I fear I cannot return the compliment."

"Ah! You, too, have it in mind to snabble up Lord Merwin? Is that it?"

"Something of the sort," said Artemisia a trifle ruefully, thinking that for anyone unaware of the situation, it very likely looked that way.

Edith's eyes narrowed. "You'll lose."

"To you?"

"I have the advantage, you see."

"And that is?"

"But it is obvious. I am a married lady with a complacent husband. You, my dear, must maintain your virtue. It is an unfair advantage, of course, but there it is."

"We will see."

Merwin returned just then and Artemisia held out her hand to him. He lifted it to his mouth for a quick kiss before releasing her. And then he seated himself and entered into the most uncomfortable half hour of his life!

He described it to Jack and Patricia later that evening. "I have discovered," he said, "what it is to be the only bone between two dogs . . . not that either woman should be called a dog, of course, but the sentiment still holds! A mouse between two cats, perhaps? Better, except I have never before known Miss Bigalow to show claws. I truly do not understand it."

Patricia chuckled. "But Alex, she was forced to do so. It sounds to me that Mrs. Marchcomer has set her sights on you, deciding you will do very well for the cicisbeo she requires. I am not wrong, am I? Marchcomer is a dedicated gambler, is he not? I thought so," she added when Alex nodded. "She knows you, you see. And you have the entrée everywhere. You are personable and very much the gentleman, so she knows you will treat her well." Patricia shrugged.

"Of course your Moonbeam was forced to defend her territory," added Jack, "but I fear she was out-generaled if you actually escorted Mrs. Marchcomer home!"

"What else could I do? I could not allow her to traipse through the streets at such a late hour!"

"She has no carriage?"

"No. And would not allow me to hire her a hackney."

"Out-generaled all the way!" Jack shook his head.

"But I want nothing to do with the woman!"

"Just out of curiosity," asked Patricia, "did she invite you in?"

"No, she did not." Alex felt heat rising up his throat. "She very likely knew it would be useless since I was a trifle cold to her as we rode out to the suburbs where she and her husband are boarding."

"The suburbs!"

"Yes."

"And you say she has no carriage? How, then, did she arrive at the ball?"

Merwin's eyes widened. "Out-generaled indeed! What a fool I am. Not that I knew where she lived when we first entered the carriage . . ."

"Your Miss Bigalow will not be happy," said Patricia.

Merwin slumped into his chair, his elfin features sagging in a fashion very unlike his usual self. "My schedule tomorrow is full. I cannot send her a note because her father is likely to intercept it. I cannot send her flowers for the same reason. What am I to do?"

"Write the note. I will pass it to her in the park," suggested Patricia.

"Would you do that for me?"

"Why not? I have never liked Sir Vincent. I've no objection to tricking him in this fashion. It is not as if you were an undesirable party, Alex. In fact, you are commonly thought to be a very fine catch! Besides, Miss Bigalow's mother approves."

Jack's lips pursed, but he said nothing.

Patricia glanced at him. "*You* do not approve," she said.

"I admit to ambivalence. I am all for Alex winning the love of his life. After all, *Sahib* would approve," he added with a quick monkey-grin.

"Jason's pet *may* have put his huge paw into arranging the Renwick marriage," said Alex with a touch of sarcasm, "and he *might* have had a hand in yours and *perhaps* did something to straighten out both Ian and Serena and then Tony and Libby, but he is, after all, nothing but an animal, and I do not believe it."

Patricia chuckled. "If you had experienced Sahib's interference, you, too would be a believer. Jack, you truly think I should not interfere?"

"You know it isn't the thing to encourage a daughter to go behind a father's back."

"Perhaps I could give a note to her mother," offered Patricia after a moment's thought. "Will that satisfy the conventions?"

Lord Merwin nodded. "Just the sort of honorable solution one would expect of you, cousin! I will write to Lady Bigalow rather than to my Moonbeam and then everyone's conscience may rest free of guilt. Including my own!" he finished.

He rose and moved to the tall secretary standing against the wall across from the fireplace and tipped down the leaf, opening it. He seated himself and reached for one of the old-fashioned quills he'd brought from England for his own use, checked that it did not need sharpening, and then drew ink and paper to him.

Then he sat running the feather through his fingers and thinking. Finally he shifted, dipped the quill into the ink, and began writing. The fire burnt down in the stove while Jack murmured softly to his Patricia and, eventually, when it looked as if Alex would continue writing all the night, rose to his feet. He offered a hand to his wife, and without saying good night to Alex, led her from the room.

The fire had died to embers and the room grown chill when Alex finally looked down at what he'd penned. A flush climbed his cheeks. There were five closely written pages lying before him. Quickly, he read through it. He shrugged. There was nothing there which was untrue and to whom but his love's mother could he say the things he'd said?

Alex sealed the folded pages and laid them, centered, on the open desk. Then he, too, went off to bed.

A few days later Artemisia and her mother sipped their coffee and went through the invitations that had arrived that morning. "It amazes me that so many of our friends not only know we have arrived in Vienna but know our direction," said Artemisia.

"I wrote a number of notes upon our arrival," murmured Lady Bigalow, frowning over a card she held at arm's length. "My dear, do we know a Mrs. Martin Marchcomer?"

"Miss Baggett, that was," said Artemisia absently. She was trying to decipher the French in which the invitation she held was printed. "Mother, have I ever been introduced to the Duchess of Sagan?"

The question caught Lady Bigalow's attention and she dropped her hands to her lap, one still clutching the note from Mrs. Marchcomer. "The duchess?"

"Assuming I have deciphered this correctly, I believe I am invited to her next salon."

Lady Bigalow scrabbled amongst the invitations still piled between herself and her daughter. She caught one up, opened it, and, letting out a huge sigh of relief, relaxed.

"Mother? What is it?"

"You were not to know, of course."

"Know what?"

"Of the rivalry between Wilhelmine, Duchess of Sagan, and the Princess Bagration. Gossip concerning the two has filled letter after letter ever since the first of our friends arrived here." She bit her lip. "I suppose you had better learn the truth, however wrong to discuss such things with an unmarried woman. If I do not tell you, you may find yourself in difficulties. The duchess is Metternich's mistress. The princess plays hostess for the Czar. There is bitterness and intrigue between the two women that can cause grave social difficulties for innocents such as ourselves. The last thing we wish is to find ourselves caught up in the political intrigues surrounding us!"

"So what do we do?"

Lady Bigalow smiled a mischievous smile. "We, my dear, we ask your friend for advice. *That* is what we do. In the meantime we will lay aside these two invitations." She took the one from Artemisia, added it to the one she held, and laid them aside . . . and looked up. "Ah, there you are, my dear. Should I ring for fresh tea?"

"I ate hours ago. To whom did you refer when you said you would ask Arta's friend for advice?" asked Sir Vincent, his gaze going from one woman to the other.

"Why, Lady Castlereagh, of course," said Lady Bigalow, her eyes opened very wide. "Our daughter and her ladyship had a very long chat just the other evening and I feel she will stand our friend in deciding how one must deal with this rather thorny question."

"What question?" asked her husband, suspicion evident in both stance and tone.

"We have received invitations from both Princess Bagration and the Duchess of Sagan. We would dislike doing anything that might embarrass the embassy, you see . . . or worse," she added when her husband pokered up at the notion his wife worried the Tory-run government might be embarrassed, "perhaps, ourselves."

Sir Vincent was appeased and gave a crack of laughter. "A tricky situation indeed since it is well known those two ladies are up to their lovely necks in intrigue! Difficulty upon difficulty, when you consider they have apartments in the same house and even, I have heard, share a staircase!"

Artemisia was rather surprised by the fluency with which her father spoke, but Lady Bigalow knew it was merely that he quoted someone he had heard discussing the situation. "We will," she said placidly, "attempt to see Lady Castlereagh this morning since it would be unconscionably rude to delay answering these bids for our presence."

Sir Vincent's chin rose and his eyes bulged as he glared down his prominent nose. "You will *write* her.

I won't have you anywhere near our embassy—except, of course, to balls and soirées and that sort of thing where you must be seen. Wouldn't do to insult the Foreign Secretary by snubbing his invitations!"

"But why?" The tension flowed back into her ladyship. Had her husband discovered Lord Merwin's presence in Vienna after all? "Lady Castlereagh's patronage can only add to our Artemisia's consequence."

"When her husband is a bloody Tory! Nonsense! Besides, you know I cannot abide the breed."

Lady Bigalow relaxed. "But my dear, surely we need not ban her ladyship from our company merely because of her husband's politics. After all, what can she do about them?"

"Bah. Stay away from the embassy. Explain your problem in a polite note and she'll send you a polite response. Enough. I've a problem of my own. *I*—" He beamed from one to the other. "—have been invited to a shooting party at the emperor's country estate of Laxonburg. What do you think of that?"

"Why, my dear!"

"Father, that is wonderful."

His expression altered and he cast a hunted look around the room. "Well, yes, but you know how bad a shot I am."

Lady Bigalow hid a smile behind her coffee cup.

Artemisia glanced up, bit her lip, and decided she could not resist. "You might," she suggested with only a touch of sarcasm, "put it around that you made a promise to your grandmother on her deathbed that you'd never fire a gun at anything but a target."

Sir Vincent was far too thick-skinned to hear the mild derision. His eyes widened. "My dear, occasionally I feel that I do not appreciate you enough. Thank you very much. I will explain that I enjoy accompanying those who shoot, but that I myself cannot do so and then I may explain why I cannot." He frowned, pouting slightly. "But *why* did I promise such a thing?"

"Perhaps, if someone asks," suggested Lady Bigalow, "you might say your grandfather died in a duel, which he did, of course. That would explain why your grandmother asked the promise of you."

Sir Vincent beamed at his wife. "Now that is just the sort of good advice I have come to expect of *you*, my dear."

He fiddled, as was his habit, with a button on his coat. Before the day was out he would very likely loosen it and lose it. His valet had quickly learned he must keep extra buttons on hand for each and every coat Sir Vincent's tailor supplied!

"Have you plans for today?" asked Lady Bigalow when it appeared he did not quite know what to do with himself.

"Hmm? Plans? Haven't really thought."

"How was your meeting last night?" asked Artemisia, half curious and half afraid of what she might hear. Her father had been much in the company of the secret society that lauded and, she suspected, supported Napoleon.

"My meeting? My meeting? Oh, ta rah." He waved a hand in an airy movement very unlike him. "Just a little get together of like minded souls, you know." He laughed but it sounded strangely hollow to his womenfolk.

"Father . . . ?"

"I'm off," he interrupted. "Just remembered an important appointment, you know. Can't wait." And, with that, he scurried from the room in a manner reminiscent of a rabbit escaping a fox.

"Artemisia, that was rather strange, do you not agree?"

"Surely he cannot be mixed up in anything . . . traitorous. Can he?"

"Don't say that word aloud!"

"But he wouldn't, would he?"

"Would he not?" There was a touch of bitterness in Lady Bigalow's voice. "I cannot say what your father might do. I have known him capable of rationalizing almost anything—if it is something he wishes badly enough."

"Oh, when it means he can forget some duty or some obligation in order to do something else, yes, of course, but . . ."

"Don't say it!"

Artemisia sighed and looked blankly off into some distant prospect no one but she could see. "If he does and is caught . . ." She gulped back a sob that rose unexpectedly, surprising her. "Alex . . ."

"Oh, my dear child!" Lady Bigalow's eyes widened in horror. "Yes, I see. But my dear, *dear* child, we are merely speculating. We must not jump to conclusions!"

"No, of course not."

But Artemisia tucked away her decision to have a conversation with Lord Merwin on the topic of secret societies and the possibility that one particular society might lead her father into trouble! *It is not so much telling tales as attempting to protect him from himself,* she told herself—and then wondered if she had inherited her father's tendency to rationalize things so that they did not sound so very bad after all!

There was a tap at the door and, when asked to come in, Arta's new maid entered, looked around, and then stared at her mistress with a look that spoke volumes.

"You've been bribed to deliver a message, is that the problem?" asked Artemisia bluntly.

The girl blushed, then glanced toward Lady Bigalow, who smiled gently before nodding her permission. "Come, Fraulein," said her ladyship. "Give Miss

Bigalow her note. I will not insist you be let go without a character, nor will I eat you."

The maid, who had been hired upon their arrival in Vienna some days earlier, cast Lady Bigalow a doubtful look, but did as she was told and handed Artemisia her missive.

"Is it from . . . ?"

"Yes." Artemisia nodded. "It is. Mother, I believe I am in the need of more exercise than I've managed since we began our travels. Do you not agree that a walk along The Ramparts would do me good?"

"The Ramparts?" Lady Bigalow tilted her head. "I don't believe I know anything about any Ramparts."

"Nor do I. Aha!" she said after reading further, "Alex refers to the old city walls. He says it is a common rendezvous."

"My dear," said Lady Bigalow, tongue firmly in cheek, "I have just had the most wonderful notion. This morning we will take our maids and stroll along The Ramparts. If we have our maids with us, then if we were to become separated, each of us discovering someone to whom we wished to speak, why, the conventions would be satisfied, would they not?"

"A wonderful notion indeed." Artemisia reread her note. "Would one-of-the-clock rush you, too much?"

"I must write Lady Castlereagh, requesting her advice on that vexatious social question, but beyond that I've nothing which should interfere in our leaving about one."

The promenade atop The Ramparts was interesting. One could look down on the old city within and at quite different views to the outside where a wide park, the Glacis, was crisscrossed with streets and avenues. They gazed in awe at the Hofburg Palace and, once beyond it, into a jumble of houses and streets, which made for a constantly changing scene.

Lady Bigalow made little "ohs" and "ahs" and "my dear, do look!" sort of comments to an utterly unresponsive Artemisia, who searched among the strollers for one face only. She had very nearly given Alex up when he appeared and, seeing them, picked up his pace. He arrived at Artemisia's side just as Mrs. Marchcomer approached from the other direction.

Alex rolled his eyes. Lady Bigalow, noticing, giggled behind her fingers, but, a resourceful woman, she instantly intercepted Edith Marchcomer, grasping her arm and turning her away from where Alex and Artemisia stood, heads together, speaking softly and quickly.

Artemisia had informed her mother she meant to discuss her father's new acquaintances with Alex and, after a brief argument on the propriety of this, had succeeded in convincing Lady Bigalow that Alex had an interest in the situation. She was determined to ask his advice instantly and was very glad her mother managed to lead Mrs. Marchcomer away.

Edith Marchcomer was not totally devoid of manners so could not instantly think of a reasonable excuse to avoid a conversation with her ladyship. And, after a few moments, was not totally displeased with her present company.

Lady Bigalow got off on the proper foot by telling her new acquaintance that she could not possibly continue to live if she were not instantly apprised of every detail of exactly how the former Miss Baggett had managed to hoodwink her brothers.

". . . My daughter told me you were about to explain it to her the other evening when for some reason—" Lady Bigalow glossed over the reason. "—you were unable to do so. I have been on tenterhooks to hear the whole ever since she suggested there was a mystery!"

Edith, surprised and pleased by Lady Bigalow's interest, chuckled in a surprisingly delightful fashion with none of the simpering disliked by Alex. "Hoodwinked. Oh, I like that. And just exactly what I did! My brothers hadn't a notion of any of it until it was all over and nothing they could do."

"But what did you do?" The original question had been a ploy to keep the interloper from interfering in the *tête-à-tête* between Arta and Alex but now Lady Bigalow was very nearly as curious as she'd claimed to be!

"Once I thought of it, it was quite simple. There are always men looking to wed money. All I had to do was put an advertisement in the papers that I was a woman with money who wished to wed."

"There must have been more to it than that. How did you insert the announcement? And how did you meet the man without your brothers knowing? And how did the two of you manage to wed without their knowledge and—" Lady Bigalow threw up her hands. "—you must tell me every detail!"

Again Edith chuckled that musical and unaffected laugh. "I've one friend where my brothers were content to leave me by myself. The poor lady is bedridden, you see, and can go nowhere, has little in the way of company *none* of which is male, and is otherwise what they think of as safe—"

"Thought of."

"—or, as I was about to say, thought safe! She and I perfected my plan. I wrote out the advertisement, giving Miss Derwent's address. Miss Derwent was concerned about meeting gentlemen with only her maid in attendance, but we managed that by inserting a time in the advertisement when I could be there as well. When I decided upon Mr. Marchcomer I told him to acquire a special license and bring the minister to Miss Derwent's where Miss Derwent and her maid could be our witnesses. We went straight from the wedding to my solicitor who, since we'd our marriage lines, could do nothing but acquiesce in my wishes."

A surprisingly stern look settled into Mrs. Marchcomer's features and Lady Bigalow wondered at it, but only for a moment. The explanation followed instantly:

"I knew what sort of man I'd married. What *he* didn't know is that my inheritance is tied up in such a way that my brothers controlled the income before I wed, but that after, it came to *me*. And nothing but the income. My solicitor explained this sad fact to my new husband."

"And?"

Mrs. Marchcomer laughed still again. "Oh, I am not greedy. Nor am I ungrateful. What I wanted was my freedom. What Martin wanted was money. I have ordered my solicitor to give each quarter's allowance to Martin." She shrugged.

"But surely you have expenses. Will your husband give you an allowance from your own funds then?"

Edith sobered instantly, her eyes narrowing. "I admit that I was remiss in not thinking a trifle farther into the future than the moment only, and I do not know what I will do if I ever need money just for myself. Although—" She brightened. "—I may, of course, change my orders to my solicitor!" She smiled again. "You see, all ended happily. Poor Martin is merely restricted in what he may lose at his everlasting gambling, not forbidden it, and I am *free*."

Evidently the thought reminded her of her current plan for the use of that freedom and she came to a halt. "I believe I noticed Lord Merwin talking with your daughter, Lady Bigalow. He is a special friend of mine—" She smirked. "—and I would not dream of departing from The Ramparts without a word with him. Shall we join them?"

The last words were spoken with such firmness there was no possibility of mistaking them for a request. Lady Bigalow knew when to accept defeat gracefully. She turned, looked back to where they had left the others, and blinked. The area was quite empty of anyone. Anyone at all, known or unknown! "Well!"

"Well indeed," said Mrs. Marchcomer. "I had not thought your daughter so brass-faced she would go off with a man and no chaperon in sight!"

"She was chaperoned by her maid, of course," said Lady Bigalow, her tone much colder than any but the very few mushrooms with whom she'd had to deal would have guessed possible. Her ladyship spoke *just so* only to those who attempted to impose on her—or who dared to insult her daughter!

FOUR

Mrs. Marchcomer was silenced, but not happy. She and Lady Bigalow parted on something less than friendly terms and Lady Bigalow put her mind to where her daughter might have gone. Her new maid, a cousin to Artemisia's, cleared her throat. Lady Bigalow looked around, realized who had made the sound, and asked, "Yes? You've something to suggest?"

"There is a small coffeehouse just across from the gates there." The maid nodded toward stairs leading down to ground level. "It is a pleasant place where one may sit at tables behind large windows and have a coffee and pastries."

"It is permitted that a young lady go to such a place with a gentleman unrelated to her?"

The girl nodded. "Chaperoned, of course."

"And your cousin is with them." Lady Bigalow's lips firmed. "That will do for the moment, but we must join them immediately. Assuming—" She cast the maid a quick glance. "—that is where they went."

As she spoke she led the way to the stairs and down. As they waited near the arch for the traffic to clear, Lady Bigalow looked across to the pleasant-looking shop. Huge windows fronted it, the lower portion covered by crisply starched lace curtains that hung from a polished brass rod. Inside, one could see small, round tables, each with two or three spindly chairs. Many boasted customers and, when they had crossed

over, Lady Bigalow scanned the room for a glimpse
of the truants.

And found them.

Lady Bigalow heaved a huge sigh of relief and entered the coffeehouse. She strode gracefully to the
slightly larger table at which Lord Merwin had placed
extra chairs, one of which was occupied by Artemisia's
maid. A tiered cake dish boasted a variety of delightful
goodies and the coffeepot steamed gently.

"My dears! How very good this looks."

"Mother? You were very quick," said Artemisia.
She spoke both for the ears of anyone who might be
listening and because it seemed to her she had only
just begun speaking with his lordship. She was not
happy. While her maid hovered near them, she'd felt
unable to do more than tell him in the most unbiased
of fashions of her father's new acquaintance. She had
felt unable to ask him the questions she needed to ask
concerning her father's safety.

The maids, using a tray retrieved from a waiter, removed themselves to a table some distance away.
Artemisia decided her mother should hear what Alex
had to say concerning her father's new associates.

"Lord Merwin," she began, speaking softly, "I
mentioned the society my father has joined since arriving in Vienna. What I could not say earlier is that
it rather frightens me. You see, I believe they support
Napoleon. Secretly, you understand." She glanced
around. "I cannot believe anyone would be so foolish," she added on a shudder, just in case someone
was listening.

Alex's mouth straightened and firmed. He nodded.
"I too have heard of such a group. They are, I believe,
closely watched by Baron Franz Hager's secret police."

Both Artemisia and her mother felt the blood run
from their heads.

Merwin glanced around, looked back at Artemisia,

and smiled. "Let us finish our coffee and I will walk you home."

There was a promise in the soft sound of his voice and Artemisia relaxed. She and her mother spoke of nothing in particular until Artemisia remembered that Mrs. Marchcomer had been about to join them. "Mother, I wish to thank you for taking that dreadful woman off and away from us."

"Dreadful . . . oh." Lady Bigalow smiled a smile that very nearly qualified as a grin. "You will never believe the story she told me!" And with that, her ladyship retailed every detail told her by the former Miss Baggett. ". . . so you see, she has not only tossed her bonnet over the windmill, but is, I fear, ready to kick over the traces as well!"

Artemisia, who had smiled often during the tale, sobered instantly. "And it is quite obvious whom she has chosen to join her in that particular harness," she said, speaking in a chilly tone.

"If, my dear, you refer to myself," said Lord Merwin with no pretense of modesty, "then remember that it is very difficult to harness a pair which refuses to go together!"

Artemisia blushed prettily. "I apologize."

"You actually flatter me that you think she is interested in me."

"Alex, she *is*."

Alex chucked. "Nonsense. She is simply enjoying her freedom and is, perhaps, just a trifle outrageous because . . ." He hesitated.

". . . Because she wants to make up for all that lost time when her brothers had her shackled?" suggested Artemisia.

Alex frowned. "My dear . . . !"

She sighed. "I know. I am a cat. I should not scratch and spit simply because Mrs. Marchcomer has the good taste to flirt with the man I love."

Lady Bigalow smiled, but felt it necessary to scold gently. "My dear, you must mind your tongue."

"Not for my sake," said Alex, grinning. "I like it very well when she does not! It is most flattering, you see."

Artemisia blushed. "I will behave, Mother. If for no other reason than that Alex will, otherwise, continue to embarrass me!" She glanced around the table. "Have we finished? I am looking forward—" She stared at Alex, reminding him she wished to know more about Baron Hager's secret police and any possible danger to her father. "—to our walk home."

Their conversation on the way back to the Bigalow lodgings was disrupted again and again by the proximity of people who should not overhear what was said. Merwin, when they reached the house, shrugged. "My dear Lady Bigalow, say no more." He took her hand. "I will have conversation with Lord Castlereagh and explain all. Castlereagh will know how to handle the situation so that Sir Vincent does not find himself in deep waters."

Lady Bigalow squeezed his fingers and released him. "Thank you. I have been so very worried. When Arta said she would speak to you on the subject my heart fell into my shoes that she would reveal my husband's folly, but I see she knew better than I how you could help us."

Merwin grinned. "Do not tell him you've passed on word to me. I doubt very much he would appreciate my interference."

"Very true. Arta, I know you wish a trifle more exercise. You may walk to the end of the avenue and back if Lord Merwin is free to escort you." Lady Bigalow gestured to her maid and entered the house leaving her maid's cousin to chaperon the two.

"Can you explain to me how you think Castlereagh will solve the problem?" she asked hesitantly, checking that the maid walked far enough to the rear that she would not overhear.

"I've a notion, but must discuss it first with the Foreign Secretary. Castlereagh may have objections to which I've no answer. You did say, did you not, that your father seemed a trifle upset? Perhaps it is that he felt he had fallen into deep waters and was unsure how he might swim out of them?"

"Yes. I very much fear he made promises that, now he knows more, he regrets." She sighed.

"We will see. You are not to worry. Or if you find you've a sudden reason to fear for him, then you may tell me and I will see what can be done."

They returned to the house soon after and, reluctantly, the two made their good-byes.

The next morning at breakfast, Sir Vincent was surprisingly jovial. "Such a to-do!" he said, coming into the room in which they ate their breakfast. "You will not believe the gruesome situation in which I found myself involved late last evening."

"Gruesome, my dear?" Lady Bigalow did not look up from perusing the letter she held.

"Exceedingly so. Such events are one very good reason women are forbidden entrance to the gaming houses!"

"I did not know *you* patronized such places, Father." Artemisia filled a cup for him and pushed it closer to him. "Those are particularly good this morning," she said, indicating a plate of rolls. "I like them with the jam, but Mother claims they are very good with that soft cheese."

Sir Vincent frowned. "Is no one interested in my news?"

Both Lady Bigalow and Artemisia instantly stopped

what they were doing and gave him their complete attention. "Do tell!"

"Harrumph." He scowled from one to the other. "You are only pretending interest."

"No, Father. Indeed, we are all ears. If we appeared less interested than you expected it is merely that it is so very early and we are not yet quite awake." Artemisia spoke with great earnestness and, thereby, soothed her parent's ruffled sensibilities. "Please, Father?"

"Well, if you are certain."

"Oh, we *are,*" said his wife, her eyes wide open. It was an expression she adopted whenever it was necessary to appease her husband. It always worked.

"Harrumph. Well—" His frown faded. "—it was this way. You'd not know the man, of course, and I am ashamed to admit he is English, and of course one should never speak ill of the dead, but still it must be said." He looked from one to the other.

Artemisia stifled a sigh. It was obvious every word must be drawn from her father or he would not be happy. "Why are you ashamed he is English? Especially if he is dead."

"He was discovered to be a cheat," said her father sternly. "Not," he added, virtuously, "that that excuses that other man's actions."

"What man is this, Vincent? Surely not the dead man?"

"Of course not. The one who killed him, of course."

"Killed the Englishman?"

"There is only one dead man in my story, Artemisia. Do not interrupt."

"Yes, Father."

"It began perhaps half an hour after I reached the casino with several friends. We were playing a rather rowdy game of whist—not at all the thing, you know—when suddenly a row burst out in the next room. We didn't think anything of it. Having far too good a time, you see. Not for a minute or two, anyway. And then one of our number suggested we go see what was happening. So we did." He beamed.

"So?" Artemisia wanted the story over so she could get back to the newspaper she had been attempting to translate before her father's arrival. "Did you go into the room? What was happening?"

"I'll get to it. Do stop making silly comments!" He frowned until Artemisia hung her head. "There, there," he added, "I did not mean to scold! When we entered the room, we found the two men standing at opposite sides of a small table, the one holding the other by the wrist. A card peeked out from the man's sleeve! What do you think of *that?*"

"What should we think?" asked Lady Bigalow, feigning interest.

"Why, that the man was cheating, of course."

"Ah. I am glad you explained it."

He eyed his wife suspiciously, but she widened her eyes at him and he relaxed. "The cheat was denying everything, of course. And the other was accusing him. Not that anyone could possibly doubt his eyes. And then the one challenged the other to a duel."

"Ah. A duel."

"Yes. And this is what you will not believe. I could not believe it myself. These continentals have no notion of decorum," finished Sir Vincent only a trifle pompously.

"But what happened?" asked Artemisia, her curiosity finally roused.

"Why, it was arranged instantly. Right then and there."

"You mean in the casino gardens?"

"I mean right there in that room *in* the casino!"

"Surely not."

"But it was. They moved the candles around so the light would be fair for both and then the middle of the room was cleared and the two placed back to back. The count was made and then—poof."

"Poof?"

"Marchcomer was dead, of course."

"Who?" Artemisia half-rose from her chair, her hands, placed on the table, supporting her.

"Mr. Marchcomer. I understand he has lived by his wits forever and ever." His eyes narrowed and he stared at his daughter. "You did *not* know him, of course," he said. He made it a statement and *not* a question.

"But we do," said Lady Bigalow, drawing his ire. "We were introduced to him the other day. By his wife."

"His wife? Nonsense. The man never married."

"But he did. Father, do you recall Miss Baggett from our church in London?"

"Baggett? Baggett? The one who is always so closely guarded by her brothers? Well! I see they had reason to guard her if she hadn't any better sense than to wed that outsider!"

"But, don't you see, Father? She is widowed. And a stranger to Vienna. I think Mother and I should . . ."

"You will do nothing. Do you hear? Nothing." Sir Vincent pounded the table so hard the teacups rattled.

"But it is the Christian thing . . ."

"No."

"Why should we not?" asked Lady Bigalow placidly.

"I'll not have it said we are associated in any way to that . . . that . . ."

"But he is dead. His wife, surely, is not a gambler."

"You will do as I say!"

Artemisia sighed, nodded, and lifted her cup. She grimaced at the cold contents, and replaced it in its saucer. "I believe I must go to my room. I've letters to write. Father, will you object if I just mention your news in my letters?"

"No, no. Nothing wrong with gossip, of course."

Artemisia raised her gaze to the ceiling at that example of her father's wisdom, but since she was already leaving the room, her back was to her father when she did so. Once her note was finished, she gave her maid orders to see it was taken immediately to Lady Castlereagh at the embassy. If she and her mother were not allowed to succor the widow, then someone must, and surely it was the duty of those at the embassy to see that all the religious needs and Austrian legal requirements were met.

Half an hour later she joined her mother in their sitting room. Lady Bigalow was finally finishing up the last of the tatting for the special gown she'd ordered for herself. "Did you send a note?"

"To Lady Castlereagh. I feared to send one to Mrs. Marchcomer. If Father were to discover I had done so, he would go into one of his rants and I haven't the energy to soothe him and I see no reason why you should have to do so!"

"I am about done with this," said her ladyship, ignoring her daughter's comment, "and intend to visit our modiste immediately since I have this horrid feeling we will be leaving Vienna very soon now." She glanced at her daughter. "I just wished to warn you, my dear. So that you'd not reveal shock when your father mentions it."

"Why do you think . . . ?"

"My dear," interrupted Lady Bigalow, "your father will soon find himself in difficulties if he has begun frequenting a casino. He is no gambler and, although he will not lose to excess, he will know of no way to prevent himself from going along with acquaintances who invite him to join them there." She shrugged. "The solution will be to leave Vienna and the problem behind."

Artemisia sighed. "Well, I'll have had a bit of time with Alex. I suppose I must be thankful for that."

"Yes, dear, I think you must."

They both sighed.

Mrs. Marchcomer arrived on the Bigalow doorstep after they departed for the shops. When she discovered Lady and Miss Bigalow were out she insisted on waiting. She was still there, wearing a path in the parlor carpet, when the two arrived home after several exhausting hours at their favorite dressmaker.

"Mrs. Marchcomer! What a terrible thing! Do accept our condolences." Lady Bigalow glanced around. "Did no one offer you tea or coffee? Or something more warming?"

The Bigalows' guest waved away the conventional inquiry. "I don't know what to do."

"What to do?"

"I can find no money among my husband's belongings and our landlady swears the rent is paid only until the end of the month and that is barely a week off!"

"You should go to the embassy," suggested Mrs. Bigalow.

"Do you think so? I am no one important."

"No, but you are a British citizen and one function of the embassy is to help distressed citizens."

"It is? I didn't know. I thought of going there to discover Lord Merwin's address because I know he would be delighted to help me, but then, when I set off to do so, I felt a trifle embarrassed." She cast a speculative look from her ladyship to Artemisia. "You seem to know his lordship rather well. Perhaps you could tell me how to find him? If only he knew I was in need of him, he would come instantly to my aid."

"Why do you think any such thing? You only met him here in Vienna, did you not?" asked Artemisia. An instant later she was more than a trifle ashamed she had asked such a rude question. On the other hand, she wished desperately to know the answer so didn't retract it!

Mrs. Marchcomer widened large blue eyes. "But has it never been your joy to discover an instant rapport between yourself and another?" A dreamy expression, unfocused eyes, and a tiny smile played over her features. "Our eyes met and I *knew.*"

"*Knew?*" asked Artemisia. This time she kicked herself mentally upon hearing a faintly dangerous note to her tone.

"So sudden. So special." Mrs. Marchcomer clasped her hands before her bosom. "It was our fate to meet! And now I am a widow." The wide-open eyes opened still more widely. "Oh yes, fate indeed, do you not agree?"

Neither Lady Bigalow nor Artemisia could mistake her meaning. They looked at each other and sighed. "My dear Mrs. Marchcomer, perhaps you are unaware that . . ."

"What my mother would say," interrupted Artemisia, "is that we wish you very well and believe you should apply to the embassy for aid in returning to England."

"Return to England? Now? When everything is going so well?"

"But did you not say you've nowhere to stay after the end of the week?"

Mrs. Marchcomer glanced around the parlor. "I don't suppose . . ."

Artemisia could not believe her ears. *Is that woman actually suggesting we put her up? When she knows I am in love with the man she has chosen as her prey?*

Lady Bigalow interrupted her daughter's rampaging thoughts. "It is uncertain, Mrs. Marchcomer, exactly how much longer we will be in Vienna," said her ladyship smoothly. "If we knew we would be remaining here for any length of time, I would invite you to stay with us until other arrangements could be made for you, but I fear we may be moving on any day now."

Their guest sighed and then grimaced. "I suppose I must steel myself to the embarrassment of applying to the Foreign Secretary for aid."

"Perhaps it would be less embarrassing if you were to tell your story to Lady Castlereagh, who could then make the application to her husband for you. If you will wait only a moment I will write you an introduction to Lady Castlereagh."

Some minutes later Lady Bigalow folded the note and, after a moment's hesitation, sealed it with a blob of wax into which she pressed an impression of the Bigalow family crest. Not, of course, because she truly believed Mrs. Marchcomer would read an unsealed missive . . . or did she?

She handed the note to Mrs. Marchcomer. "I'll have my maid call a hackney for your use," she said.

Mrs. Marchcomer shook her head. "It isn't far. I will walk."

She left and after some moments' silence, the two women spoke as one. Artemisia said, "Very likely she has no money to waste on a carriage," just as her mother asked, "Why did you prevent me explaining why Lord Merwin was unlikely to, er, oblige her?"

Artemisia, staring into the corner, bit her lip. "I've no hold on him, have I? I cannot allow my love for him to stand in the way of the possibility of his finding love elsewhere."

"With Edith Baggett? Mrs. Marchcomer, I mean?" Lady Bigalow cast her daughter such a look of astonishment Artemisia giggled. "Well! Really, dear—" The look changed to one of chagrin. "—it is not polite to laugh at your mother!"

"No, of course not," responded Artemisia, sobering, "But Mother, Mrs. Marchcomer is aware there is something between Alex and myself, so if she is still so certain she can take him from me, then she must have reason for that belief. And if she does—" Artemisia felt tears filling her eyes and blinked rapidly. "—then I wish to know it now and not at some point in the future when . . . when . . ."

"When it is too late," finished her mother gently. "Yes. I see. But I think you do Lord Merwin a disservice, suspecting him of encouraging that woman. Arta, dear, I am more than ten! I assure you I am not guessing when I say she is just the sort of woman to convince herself that whatever it is she wants, that is exactly what she'll get. It is a sort of daydreaming, which is the only sort of life Edith Baggett could have had, living with those brothers of hers. But now she has been married and quickly widowed. I fear the freedom she gained by her marriage, after so many years under her brothers' collective thumb, may have very slightly deranged her!"

Artemisia tipped her head. She pursed her lips thoughtfully. "Perhaps. But he *has* shown her more courtesy than she deserves and there must be a reason for it."

"Lord Merwin's manners are always gentlemanly, Arta. Do not be misled that such simple courtesy is anything deeper or more serious."

A stubborn look settled over Artemisia's features. "We shall see, shall we not?"

Lady Bigalow shook her head, but said no more. For reasons beyond her comprehension, it appeared that Artemisia needed to test his lordship's love for her. A mistake. *Always* a mistake. The loved one could only resent such lack of faith and, very likely, would react in a manner equally irrational! Which would also be misinterpreted and result in still more strain and stress.

Lady Bigalow cast her daughter a sad look, shook her head once more, and picked up a ball of thread and her shuttle. Tatting always soothed her. She began to roll thread onto the shuttle. *I'll start a new collar for my best robe. . . .*

* * *

Lord Merwin stared at Lady Castlereagh. "But . . . !"

"My lord, she was most affecting."

Aghast, Lord Merwin shook his head. "This is all nonsense. I barely know the woman!"

"She was quite insistent that, if you could only be informed of her distress, you would most willingly come to her assistance."

"Lady Castlereagh, the most I ever did for Mrs. Marchcomer was to take her home one evening from a ball. We left at the same time and she was about to set off all by herself on foot for her lodgings. *Afoot at that hour!* As a gentleman I could not allow a lady to walk the streets with no protection. My driver saw her to her door. I did not even get out of the carriage!"

"But you rode all that distance with her, the two of you alone in your closed carriage?" Lady Castlereagh watched him closely.

Lord Merwin's lips compressed. "My lady, I know of no way of convincing you, but any relationship the lady perceives to be between us is a product of her imagination. If that is less than gentlemanly, so be it. When a man's life is about to be ruined by a woman who, it appears, will stop at nothing to get her own way, then that is the time a gentleman may be forgiven for forgetting his breeding! This gentleman, at least! I will not be made a cat's-paw in whatever game she plays!"

Lady Castlereagh hid a smile. "I had something of the same impression. I watched her carefully since Lady Bigalow warned me that Mrs. Marchcomer has a bee in her bonnet where you were concerned. Her ladyship, of course, was worried about her daughter."

Lord Merwin's skin felt tingly.

"My lord! Are you well?" asked Lady Castlereagh, his paleness rousing her concern.

"Mrs. Marchcomer visited Lady Bigalow?"

"She hoped to obtain your address through them."

Lord Merwin's eyes opened very wide. For once his brows rose in such a way they lost every bit of their famous tilt. "That . . . that . . ." He closed his mouth with a snap, the brows dipping to a normal angle.

Lady Castlereagh covered her mouth with her hand but a giggle escaped her nevertheless. "My lord, I believe I can supply the missing word. You need not strain to discover an acceptable substitute."

"Yes, that is all very well, my lady, but—" From being far too pale, Alex now felt far too hot. "—I love Artemisia with all my heart and it is outside of enough that that woman should impose on her in any way!"

"Yes, but we still have to reach a solution concerning Mrs. Marchcomer."

"The embassy has policies for such situations, does it not?"

"Very true, but they require the cooperation of the indigent citizen. Mrs. Marchcomer, when I told her the embassy would arrange for her passage home, instantly denied that she could possibly take such a major journey alone or even under the care of an embassy-approved courier. She insisted her reputation would be ruined."

"Instead she suggested that I escort her?" asked Merwin.

"Which, you would say—" Lady Castlereagh chuckled. "—would *also* result in the ruin of her reputation!"

"In other words, she thinks to force me to wed her." A muscle jerked in his jaw line "I think not."

"Still, *something* must be done . . ."

"If she will not accept the usual aid of the embassy, then she will suffer all she brings down upon her head!"

"Now, Lord Merwin, you do not mean that!"

Do I not? wondered Alex. He struggled with his conscience. "No, of course I do not, but I do not see what you think I can do."

"For the moment, nothing," said Lady Castlereagh, her voice soothing. "And here, if my ears do not deceive me, is my husband. My lord," she added, "do come help us determine what must be done."

Lord Castlereagh was told the whole story. His brows arched. "But my dear, she must return to England."

"Yes, so too do I think, but if she will not go . . . ?"

Castlereagh cast a look toward Merwin, whose brows drew down, his anger roused by the speculation he read in the foreign secretary's glance. "I do not like to reiterate this," said Alex through gritted teeth, "but I am innocent of leading that woman on! My whole heart and life is dedicated to Miss Bigalow. I have no interest in any other woman!"

Castlereagh laughed, but he also apologized. "Your Shakespearean romance is known to everyone, Romeo—as I have heard you called. Behind your back, of course." He chuckled at Merwin's grimace. "Will your personal Capulet ever relent?"

Hopelessness flooded Merwin. "My lord, I cannot say." He had discussed Sir Vincent's association with the Bonepartists and the foreign secretary had said he'd put his mind to the problem. "Gaining his permission to wed does not look promising at this point in time."

Castlereagh nodded and changed the subject. "I will send Charles to talk to Mrs. Marchcomer," he said, referring to his half brother. "You need not concern yourself that he will be taken in since I'll assure myself he fully understands the woman's deviousness. He will charm her into doing what is best. For her and for you."

And then Castlereagh held out his hand. It was dismissal. Everyone knew that he and his wife spent certain times of the day together if it were at all possible, and this was one of them. Alex shook his lordship's hand, bowed over her ladyship's, and departed.

Instead of returning to his desk where a great pile of work awaited him, Merwin found his hat and fur-lined cloak and stalked from the embassy. It did not occur to him to wonder if Sir Vincent would be at home. His only concern was to see Artemisia and ascertain that she had not been taken in by Mrs. Marchcomer.

He was in luck. Sir Vincent was out. Lady Bigalow, all aflutter, welcomed him, but was rather obviously nervous about doing so. Nevertheless, after a very few moments she found an excuse to leave the room.

Alex moved quickly, grasping Artemisia's hands firmly in his own. "Moonbeam, I have done nothing to give that woman the notion I've any interest in her. Nothing."

"I believe you." She smiled mistily. "Many would not, but *I* do."

Alex's features fell into grim lines. "If she has her way, there will be a great number who think I have. She will tell her lies to all and sundry. I am afraid of her, my Moonbeam."

"But if we are true to each other, then why should either of us worry about what the rabble says of either of us?"

A weak smile lit his eyes but her sober mien caught at his heart and he wanted to bring back the smile to her features. "Are you aware the *rabble* already says a great deal?" When her gaze questioned him, he explained. "We are known to all the world as Romeo and Juliet. About a year ago, a cartoon made the rounds of London depicting us in the balcony scene. I am shown climbing a rickety trellis and you, my dear, are letting down overly long hair which is, I presume, to aid my climb up to you."

Artemisia blushed. "But that is awful!"

"No names were mentioned, of course. They never are. But my eyebrows are easy to caricaturize and your lovely long hair is known to all. Those two features were enough to identify us to anyone who knew us and our situation." The brows pulled into a deep vee as he realized he was *not* easing his love's mood. "Should I not have mentioned it? I'm sorry if it distresses you, but, unlike many, the cartoon is not vicious. Not even unkind. Merely making a trifle of fun of our thwarted love." He flushed when she still looked unhappy. "When I return to England I will find the copy a friend bought and gave me. He was amused by it, but also commiserated with me. I assure you, you will not be overly upset by it."

"Only by the fact we are the objects of sport and on everyone's tongues! Oh, Alex, if only . . ."

"My children," said Lady Bigalow, hurrying into the room, "my lord has just come in. He went directly to his room, but I cannot think he will remain there long."

Alex instantly squeezed Artemisia's hands and lifted first the one and then the second to his lips. His gaze locked with hers.

Artemisia felt a frisson pass up her spine. Something in Alex's gaze tugged at her heartstrings but, even more, it filled her soul with longing. Her fingers, lying within his, trembled.

For a moment, his grip tightened, then, knowing he *must* go, he dropped her hands and left the room. The front door closed behind him just as another door slammed. He had been just in time.

Alex crossed the street, musing over his situation. He was almost certain he had soothed any fears his Artemisia might have felt concerning Mrs. Marchcomer, but he had roused other cares by mentioning the Romeo and Juliet bit when he'd meant to do no more than amuse her. Unfortunately, it had not done so.

Actually, now he recalled his *original* reaction, *he* had not been amused either. Not at that time. Alex sighed. He returned to the embassy and the work he'd left behind and, as he walked, attempted for the hundredth time to find a solution to his problems.

Sir Vincent stalked into the parlor, frowning ferociously.

"My dear! Whatever is the matter?" asked Lady Bigalow, rising from her chair and going to him. *Did someone tell him Lord Merwin was here?* she wondered.

"I will not be joining the emperor's hunt," sputtered Sir Vincent, his disappointment obvious.

"But my dear!" Her relief that he had not yet learned of Merwin's presence in Vienna left Lady Bigalow feeling very nearly faint with relief. "Why? What has happened?"

A furtive look crossed Sir Vincent's face and he seemed somehow diminished. But his blustery words were as loud as before as he loftily informed his wife it was none of her business exactly why he'd not be going to the emperor's hunting box for the shoot. "Instead you will begin packing. Immediately. We leave for Paris within the next few days."

"Paris!" Artemisia lifted her head from her book. "Pack? Leave Vienna? But why?" she asked.

Again the baronet looked a trifle flustered. "Never you mind. You've no need to know anything more than that we are going. Just do as I say and begin your everlasting packing. I know how long it takes you ladies to manage that particular piece of work. You get at it now so we need not delay the moment I know . . ." He broke off abruptly. "Never mind," he repeated. "I must see to hiring a second traveling coach since we will not travel alone." He cast a hunted look about the room. "We will have a . . . a proper *courier* who is competent to arrange each day's journey."

Before either woman could speak he scurried from the room. Lady Bigalow looked at her daughter. "What was that all about?"

"I do not know," said Artemisia, "but his demeanor was all wrong and I fear the worst." She frowned. "Oh, but surely he has not involved himself in a plot to return Napoleon to power!"

"Oh no. He could not be so foolish."

"Could he not?"

"Artemisia!"

"I won't apologize. I very much fear the intrigues of Vienna have gone to his head."

"Your father isn't a traitor."

"But would he think it traitorous to support Napoleon?" Artemisia pondered the point and shook her head. "He has verbally supported the emperor for years and was allowed to do so with no one saying him nay."

"Yes, but that was merely stating an opinion, not taking action!"

"Hmm. I dislike suggesting my father is incapable of seeing the difference, but I think it may be so!"

Lady Bigalow shuddered. "Oh dear. Is there nothing we can do?"

"Pack. If we do not, I can see him ordering us into our carriage with nothing more than we might, at that particular moment, be wearing on our backs!"

"Arta, child, you truly must not speak so sarcastically of your father. It is not the thing."

"Then he should behave in such a way he does not rouse me to sarcasm." Artemisia's lips compressed. "Mother, I am slowly coming to the conclusion I may be forced to go against his wishes. I want to marry Alex. He has waited patiently, with great understanding, for several years now. I thought I could bear to wait forever if necessary, but I . . . oh Mother, can you not understand?"

"My dear," said Lady Bigalow, her color fading, "I will not interfere if you feel you *must* go against your father's wishes. It is only that I am selfish. I will miss you so."

Artemisia blinked and then, horrified, she went to hug her mother. "He would *not.*"

"He would."

"No." Shaking her head, Artemisia held her mother away from her and saw tears slipping from the corners of the older woman's eyes. "Surely he would not forbid you to see me."

Lady Bigalow sighed and searched her reticule for a handkerchief. "He told me—oh, when he first discovered Lord Merwin was a Tory—that if you wed without his blessing you would cease to be our daughter. He said he would never give his blessing to—" Lady Bigalow blushed but quoted the words, "—that devil's spawn of a Tory."

Artemisia giggled.

Lady Bigalow smiled. "Well, yes, I suppose it is funny. Especially when your Alex has those odd eyebrows, which *do* tend to give him a rather devilish expression. Even when he *isn't* frowning."

The two women were silent for a long moment. Then Artemisia squared her shoulders, told her mother she mustn't worry just yet, that surely something would happen to change her father's mind, and that if they did not wish to arrive in Paris without a stitch of clothing to their names, they'd best go up and give their maids direction.

FIVE

Lord Merwin listened carefully as his friend, Lord Princeton, outlined Lord Castlereagh's plan for dealing with both Mrs. Marchcomer and Sir Vincent.

That Sir Vincent meant to leave for Paris at any moment was known to the whole of their world. More people than the baronet *wished* to know also knew that he took with him a man pretending to the role of courier. And finally, the dangerous word that Bigalow carried letters addressed to Napoleon for the false courier was known to the embassy if to no one else.

The fact that those papers swore fealty to Napoleon and were meant to continue on to Elba was something of which the baronet himself had been unaware and something which, Jack admitted, shocked the poor man to the core when Charles Stewart, Lord Castlereagh's half brother, revealed it to him.

Mrs. Marchcomer, when it was made clear to her that Lord Merwin would *not* come to her rescue, reluctantly agreed to travel with the Bigalows to Paris where the Paris embassy would arrange her further journey on to England.

When Jack finished describing all that, Alex nodded. "I've only one question. In what way does this plan safeguard Sir Vincent from charges of treason?"

"Charles made it clear when he had his little talk with him."

"So?"

Jack chuckled. "Sir Vincent, I am told, began by refusing to carry the letters, insisting he was no traitor even if he did think Napoleon the greatest man to have graced the world since Alexander. Charles offered an alternate plan. At an appropriate time and place, Sir Vincent is to see the letters are left where one of our men can read them, copying out anything of any importance. The baronet's cooperation in this assures that he'll remain in good standing with our government."

"I presume it was pointed out to him that otherwise he would be charged with treason?"

"The poor man insisted it was not so, but Charles, explaining everything very carefully, managed to convince him otherwise—as least for long enough we can get our hands on those papers."

Alex grimaced. "The man is a fool. If I did not love his daughter so very much, I would suggest we allow him to put his head in the noose, but I do and we must not. Artemisia would feel she could not wed me if her father were labeled traitor!"

Jack nodded. "A problem to be avoided at all costs," he said with a straight face.

It took a moment for the tone of Jack's comment to register. When it did, Alex took a swing at him, deliberately missing, of course.

"A fight!" called one of their friends from the hall outside their open door, teasing them.

Jack laughed and, once again, Alex grimaced. Five minutes of banter was exchanged with the fellow and then, suggesting *they* had work to do even if the other man did not, they shut the door. Alex instantly walked to the window. "Did you ever find a way of suggesting to Sir Vincent that Paris might not be safe for very much longer?"

"I tried." Jack's lips compressed. "The idiot felt I must be exaggerating and that, even if by some wild turn of fate, Napoleon did manage to return, he would, obviously, be pleased to meet an Englishman who has always felt the emperor much maligned, one who wished him well."

"Did you remind him of the Englishmen interned in France from nought-eight until Napoleon's abdication last year?"

Jack frowned slightly. "I'll admit I didn't think to do so. I merely suggested that perhaps it would be safer for his wife and daughter to return to England rather than to make a prolonged stay in Paris."

Alex sighed. "Keep me informed. If word arrives that Napoleon is about to leave Elba I want to know about it."

"And if he does?"

"Then I'll take horse and ride off in classic style, *ventre à terre,* racing to the rescue of my beloved, of course."

Alex spoke in jest but ten days later he was doing just that—although perhaps he traveled a trifle more sedately than suggested by the overly dramatic phrase. As an official excuse for the journey, he carried dispatches from Vienna. His orders were to take them directly to England, but his intention was to go only so far as the embassy in Paris where someone else must carry them on. He would not leave France until he was assured of Miss Bigalow's safety!

The weather that March was bad and Alex was not only exhausted upon arriving in Paris, but suffering from a cold. Feeling exceedingly miserable, he stalked into the main reception room in which he'd been informed he must wait before seeing the *chargé-d'affaires.*

Misery was instantly compounded.

"My lord," sang out a bright and cheery voice. "You have followed me!"

Alex felt himself so tense he trembled. Very slowly he turned. "Mrs. Marchcomer." He bowed. "I'd no suspicion you were in Paris. It was your intention to travel on to London, was it not?" Alex spoke loudly, hoping to counteract, somewhat, any damage done by the lady's greeting.

"But how could you not know? I have written all my Viennese acquaintances that I await you here. Surely someone passed on that news."

"No one said a word to me." Alex was too exhausted to attempt tact. "I fear," he said, speaking more brutishly than he would have done otherwise, "that your acquaintances are not mine. If I *had* known I could have sent word that you should not waste your time here."

Mrs. Marchcomer blinked her eyes rapidly. They glittered with held-back tears and Alex felt guilty for causing such misery. "But my dear . . ." she began.

Guilt fled. "I am *not*," he interrupted, "nor have I *ever* been your dear!"

"But . . ."

"Mrs. Marchcomer, you must cease building castles in the air. You are an attractive lady, but you will never be my lady. Please turn your attentions to a man who can appreciate your many charms!"

Alex didn't wait for her reaction. He turned on his heel and stalked from the room, hunting up the minor bureaucrat who had directed him to the salon and demanding another room where he could wait in privacy. "I am too exhausted to be polite. Until I can sleep, I must be alone," he said by way of explanation.

An hour later he turned over his papers. Half an hour after that he was snuggled into blankets piled on a comfortable mattress in a small room on an upper floor of the embassy.

And much later that evening an acquaintance entered the room, exited hurriedly, and sent immediately for a doctor. For several days Alex's fate hung in the balance. But then, slowly, he began to recover. It was well over a week when he finally lifted himself from the malaise holding him in thrall and asked someone for news.

"We are packing up everything in sight," said his acquaintance. "Napoleon landed some time ago in the south and—would you believe it?—Ney, who promised Louis he'd bring Napoleon back in an iron cage, has committed treason! He has gone over to his old emperor!"

Alex shoved himself up until he leant against the back of the bed. "They march north?"

"Yes!"

"He could be here any moment then."

"He has been slowed a trifle because he is collecting troops as he comes, but, yes, he could arrive at any time."

"At any time! Be a friend!" Alex threw back the covers. "Find me my clothes, my razors, order me hot water, and one more thing—" He grasped the man's arm when he turned to leave "—find out if Sir Vincent has removed his wife and daughter from Paris."

"I'll answer that one instantly. He has not. He tells everyone he cannot give up this opportunity to meet the great man!"

"Lord love him!" Alex grasped his hair with both hands, then rubbed his cheek. "Hot water. I must shave. Oh! One more thing, and I'll owe you my first-born son! Write down the Bigalows' address for me."

Twenty minutes later, feeling wrung out from merely preparing himself to leave the embassy, Alex sat down in his chair before a small fire and closed his eyes. *This will never do. Moonbeam needs me!* And then he drifted into a light doze from which he came awake over an hour later and once again berated himself. *Of all times to be ill!* he thought.

Still, the brief nap had helped and, conserving his strength, Alex made his way to the address his friend gave him. Fate smiled on the lovers and once again Sir Vincent was not at home while Lady Bigalow and Artemisia *were*.

"My dear," said Artemisia, rising to her feet. "You look terrible!"

"You must not flatter me, my love," responded Alex, grimacing. "Lady Bigalow? I find you well?"

"Yes. Except—" She wrung her hands. "—I wish you would tell me if the rumors are true. Has the king fled Paris?"

"If he has not, he soon will. Lady Bigalow, it is imperative that you, too, leave. You and Artemisia must go even if you cannot convince Sir Vincent to do so."

"Oh dear."

"Mother, don't dither! You know you have said that if you only knew how to do the trick, you would take me and go! Alex *will* know. You *do* know, do you not, my love?" she finished, turning to him.

"I will escort you to the coast just as soon as we can be ready and I urge you to hurry. Napoleon could arrive in Paris at any moment and I am concerned he will do as he did before, when the treaty of Amiens fell. He will intern any English he finds still in France!"

Lady Bigalow's complexion took on a pasty look. "My husband . . . !"

"Mama, you cannot force him to do as he should."

"No." Her ladyship firmed her spine. "What is more, my duty is to you, my dear. Lord Merwin," she said, speaking with dignity, "we will be ready to leave tomorrow morning. Early."

"I will have transport for you."

"Bring it to the rear of the house no later than six. There is a gate in the fence by which we will leave."

"Mother?"

"My dear, your father will forbid us to go. I will,

of course, urge him to leave, but if he will not—"
Lady Bigalow's mouth firmed. "—then so be it."

Alex bowed over her ladyship's hand and quietly
said, "You do the right thing even if you do not quite
believe it."

"Artemisia must reach safety," said her ladyship,
nodding her head.

"I will leave you now. Until six in the morning."
Alex turned to Artemisia. He glanced at Lady Bigalow, shrugged, and taking a step nearer, pulled his love
into a quick, warm embrace. "I love you, Moonbeam.
Trust me to keep you safe."

"We do trust you, my lord," responded Artemisia.
Her hands clutched his shoulders, pulled him down.
She put a quick, hard kiss on his lips. "I love you,"
she whispered as she released him. "Now go. Father
must not find you here."

Alex took one long, last look at her before striding
to the door which he pulled open—

A man with thinning hair very nearly fell into the
room.

"—And just who are you?" he asked.

Artemisia came to Alex's side. "He was our courier
but is now my father's secretary," she said, a sarcastic
note unhidden. "It appears he defines his duties
broadly."

"They do not include listening at doors, surely,"
said Alex, rubbing his narrow chin between thumb and
finger.

"It appears they *do*. Did you hear enough or would
you like me to repeat it for you?"

Two spots of color appeared on the cheeks of the
man who had watched over the papers for Napoleon
while pretending to be Sir Vincent's courier. He glared
from one to the other, turned smartly on his heel, and
disappeared up the stairs.

"I cannot like that man," said Artemisia, frowning.
"He is far too weaselly."

"We must hope we spoke softly enough that he could not hear us."

"He will report your presence here."

"And Sir Vincent will forbid you to speak to me again."

"Yes, but that will not matter now." She turned to him. "Alex, are you well?"

"I am recovering from a bad case of the sniffles," he said, understating the seriousness of the illness that laid him low.

Artemisia nodded. "I don't want to let you out of my sight, but you must go."

Alex went.

His next problem was to locate a proper carriage for the journey to the coast. This was more difficult than he'd expected, but, by paying three times what it was worth, he found not only a carriage, but the horses to pull it and—he felt it a major miracle—an English coachman to drive it. They arranged a place to meet the next morning and, exhausted, Alex returned to the embassy.

All he *wanted* was his bed. What he *found* was Mrs. Marchcomer, white of face, hovering in the hallway, waiting to pounce on him.

"My lord, everyone is leaving. The servants have been paid and let go. I don't know what to do! You must help me."

"Mrs. Marchcomer." Alex felt a muscle in his jaw turn over. "How do you think I may help you?"

"But you know! I must leave Paris at once. We must all leave Paris. Surely you know . . . you must have heard . . . oh dear." She wrung her hands.

"You know that Napoleon approaches?" She nodded, her eyes wide with fear. Alex sighed, knowing he could not leave her to her well-deserved fate. "Can you be ready to leave tomorrow morning early?"

"Not today? Now?" she asked. "Shouldn't we go at once?"

Alex closed his eyes. "If you can find another means of traveling to the coast, leave me word here. If you cannot, then we leave this building tomorrow morning no later than five o'clock."

"It is the middle of the night!"

"Bring no more than you can carry. We meet our carriage nearly half a mile from here."

"I must walk? Must carry my own belongings? But I cannot possibly carry all I own . . ." She cast him a speculative look.

"I will be carrying my own," he said smoothly, feeling caddish but unwilling to take baggage space from the Bigalow women.

"You are cruel!"

Alex made no response.

"I think I was much mistaken in you, my lord." When he still made no response, she sighed. "Very well. I will be ready."

The next morning, early, Napoleon was known to have camped just outside Paris, preparing for a triumphant entry.

SIX

Alex and Mrs. Marchcomer arrived at the gate just as Sam Young, the coachman, finished loading Artemisia's trunk. His love was white of face and looking exceedingly unhappy. "Your father?" he asked.

"He was gone already when we awoke. He left a message that he has joined friends who mean to ride out and welcome the emperor back to his city."

Alex's mouth thinned. "My dear, we dare not wait."

"I know." Artemisia glanced at her mother who, if anything, looked still more glum. And then Artemisia glanced to where Mrs. Marchcomer watched the driver stow her baskets and a bundle. "Was it necessary to bring her?" she asked softly.

"Would you have had me leave an Englishwoman, destitute and unprotected, in a city where Napoleon is about to take up arms against the English?"

Artemisia compressed her lips and stared at nothing at all. After a moment she sighed. "Alex, I do not know what it is about that woman, but she brings out the worst in me. Forgive me. I am uncharitable and unkind and a beast."

Alex's gaze caught hers and he reached for her hands, held them tightly. "You are also worried about your father, unsure you do the right thing in leaving him behind, and are equally worried about your mother, who comes with you only because she knows you cannot go alone. My dear, it is understandable that you feel a trifle twitty!"

She smiled weakly at the odd but descriptive word. Alex squeezed her fingers gently and turned away to check that all was ready. The driver nodded and Alex helped the women up and into the carriage. He met his love's eyes, smiling a commiserating smile, and was about to close the door when Mrs. Marchcomer leaned forward.

"My lord! Do you not come with us?"

Alex had decided earlier he could not bear to be closed into a carriage in which Edith Marchcomer rode. Not when she continued to make it clear she still pursued him. "I ride with Sam," he said, and closed the door on the woman's protests before climbing up to the high seat.

Sam flipped the reins and the team moved forward. As soon as they were started, Alex checked the guns he'd ordered placed atop the coach ready to hand. He added his own pistols to those available, covered them with a carriage rug, and then, watchful, prayed they'd get further than the gate by which he hoped to leave the city.

Alex had decided to join the cavalcade headed for Calais and the ferry for Dover for only part of the way. Their route began along the same road but eventually turned off and went farther west. Le Havre was one choice, but if that too seemed unsafe, they would go the much greater distance to Cherbourg. He would decide what he deemed best when he had taken the temperature of the French populace along the way.

Cherbourg was, perhaps, the wiser choice if it became necessary to use unconventional transport across the Channel. Thanks to Miles Seward, a longtime friend, he knew that smugglers abounded along that coastline. If his party could cross to England no other way, he would bribe a smuggler to take them!

Alex's thoughts raced along lines he had thought

out the night before: If he and the driver, Sam Young, shared the driving they should make excellent time with as few stops as absolutely necessary. All his calculations, however, assumed that they could find teams along the way and that was *not* something one could take for granted.

Their arrival at the gate broke into his cogitations. Tipsy soldiers celebrating the return of their emperor manned it. They were not only rude but, alternately, arrogant and belligerent.

Finally, Mrs. Marchcomer lowered the window and leaned out. "But what is the difficulty?" she asked, smiling widely from one soldier to the other, her long, darkened lashes batting prettily. They stared at her golden good looks, bemused. "Have we done something wrong?" she continued with a sweet and, so far as Alex was concerned, unbelievable naivety. "Such wonderfully strong men. Surely you understand that we must go on?"

One soldier gulped, then straightened his spine. He smiled but it wasn't a very nice smile. "Sweet ladies, yes. You may proceed." He pointed toward the driver's seat. "Those gentlemen? *Mais non.*"

Mrs. Marchcomer opened her eyes wide. "But you would leave us with no driver? No protection? No, no, no, you cannot mean it?"

Artemisia joined Mrs. Marchcomer at the window. "Oh, my good sirs," she said in her excellent French, "I am so afraid! Have you not sisters you would do your very best to protect? Do let us all go on together."

Alternately, the two women coaxed, cajoled, flattered, and begged. They even flirted a bit. Finally their passports were stamped and the carriage passed through the gate.

. They were far down the road when Alex had Sam pull the carriage to a stop. He climbed down and opened the door. "I cannot decide whether to praise you, laugh myself silly, or scold you royally. How could you—" He looked from one to the other. "—either of you, have behaved in such an inane fashion?" He sobered. "Such a *dangerous* fashion. We were lucky there was no officer in sight. Very likely anyone with any rank has gone south to welcome Napoleon, but if one *had* remained at his post, he would have clapped us all in the nearest gaol!"

"For flirting with his soldiers?" asked Mrs. Marchcomer pertly.

"For subverting them from their duty!"

Lady Bigalow chuckled. "Arta and Edith did it very well, did they not?" She sobered, casting a glance back through the tiny rear window. "But should we not be on our way? We are still overly near to Paris, are we not?"

Alex nodded. "You've the right of that." He shut the door, still more than a trifle irritated by Artemisia's behavior. *It is quite all right,* he thought, *for Mrs. Marchcomer to act the coquette. She is one! But that my Moonbeam should do so! Outside of enough!*

Alex was, off and on, still scowling over the notion several hours later when the driver pulled up before a small country inn. "Don't suppose the ladies had anything to eat and I know I didn't. Besides, the horses will take us farther if we rest them now and again."

Alex couldn't argue that point, but he wasn't happy. They were still far too near Paris. On the other hand, it was necessary that they keep up their strength. And Sam was right about the horses. The longer they could use this team, the better. With care, perhaps they could take them all the way, although it would slow them far more than he liked. On the other hand, a team found to replace them was unlikely to be sound and would also slow them. For far too many years, horses from all over France and beyond had been requisitioned by Napoleon for his battles. It had reached the point there were few remaining and those few were old or otherwise in sad shape!

Sam looked grim when, half an hour later, he picked up the reins and threaded them through his fingers. "Don't like the sound of things," he muttered.

Alex responded softly. "Nor was I happy with the proprietress's attitude. That settles it. At Mantes we turn toward Le Havre, although I doubt we'll end there. If Napoleon sends soldiers to close the ports, and he very likely will, he'll begin with Calais, but Le Havre will be a close second. We'll find no help there."

"If we can't take the ferry, what will we do?"

Alex grinned. "If I cannot hire a smuggler to take us across the Channel, I can, I think, hire one to carry a message. I've friends who will rescue us."

"Assuming someone doesn't turn us over to the Frenchies before all that to-ing and fro-ing is done!"

Alex sobered. "Yes. That is a distinct possibility, is it not? Well, we'll face the problem if or when it arises."

As their carriage approached the Le Havre turn, a party of soldiers rode past them, the dust raised by the horses' hooves making Alex and Sam cough. Sam slowed the team and turned onto the new road. They had gone no more than a quarter-mile, however, when two of the soldiers returned and ordered them to halt.

Artemisia lowered the window. Of them all, her French was by far the least accented and, imperiously, she asked why they had been stopped. A very young officer rode near to look down at her.

He glared. "We check for English. All such are to be taken into custody."

"You can see we are not English," said Artemisia, again speaking with authority. "We have had word of a sick relative and go as quickly as we can to her bedside."

"Ah! Then all is well. My apologies." The young

officer bowed over his horse's neck, straightened, and
called, "Carry on."

The French was beyond Sam's minimal understanding, but when Alex poked him, he guessed at the
meaning and gave the team the order to start. The
soldiers wheeled their mounts and returned the way
they'd come. When they were out of sight, Alex again
had Sam pull up, climbed down, and opening the door,
complimented Artemisia on her quick thinking.

"I thought we were lost," he said. "I had my hands
on my pistols, but if I'd been forced to use them, we'd
have had a troop on our trail within hours."

Mrs. Marchcomer lost all color and suddenly
swooned.

"Oh, dear," said Lady Bigalow, searching her reticule for her smelling salts.

Edith groaned when the opened bottle was wafted
under her nose. "Surely I dream . . . . a nightmare . . ."
She spoke those words softly, but then her eyes
snapped open. Her voice was shrill when she said,
"No guns! No!"

Quietly, Artemisia suggested Alex get them on their
way. "Mother and I will take care of her."

Alex nodded, shut the door, and they trundled on
down the road.

A dozen exhausting hours after they'd left Paris,
Alex helped the women from the carriage. He had
found a small inn down a side street in a country town.
In its window was the sign of the white feather, indicating a royalist. Alex hired the whole place, which,
even so, was none too big for his party.

"Where are we?" asked Lady Bigalow, grimacing
at the pain in her stiff joints.

"We've reached Lisieux, which is quite well for one
day." He squeezed Artemisia's hand as he helped her
down. "If we can do as well tomorrow, we'll sleep in
Cherbourg."

"Cherbourg," exclaimed Mrs. Marchcomer, half

falling into Alex's arms. She had not recovered from the shocking realization that their party was truly in danger, that the French were truly her enemies and not merely men with whom she could play off her tricks. "But why are we to go to Cherbourg?" she whined as she clutched at Alex's arms. "Why not to Le Havre? In fact, why did we not go immediately to Calais?"

Alex set her on her feet and pried loose her fingers. "The last time Napoleon broke a treaty," he said, speaking sharply, "his first step was to close the ports. Those soldiers who stopped us were part of a troop headed for Calais. Le Havre will be next, just as soon as word reaches it. If we are lucky, Cherbourg is far enough from Paris that Napoleon will not bother and it will have a captain willing to take us across the Channel."

The women, all of them, were suddenly white of face not only because they were exhausted, but from fear. "But . . ." Lady Bigalow looked bewildered. "You mean we might still be forced to remain in France?"

"We will return to England. Do not concern yourselves about that. On the other hand, I may not be able to immediately find a means of doing so. We are in danger from now on." He looked from one to the other, his gaze settling on Artemisia. "Your French is without accent, my dear. Does anyone else speak it fluently?"

"Mine is terrible," said Mrs. Marchcomer instantly, "as you heard. The French laugh at me."

"Artemisia has been complimented on the fact she speaks like a native, but I do not know if that is true or merely the Frenchmen thinking to compliment her!"

Artemisia blushed. "Mother! But it is true that, thanks to a French émigré friend, I speak it reasonably fluently and more or less idiomatically."

"In other words, you do not sound as if you learned it in a classroom. Good. My own is not bad, but it isn't so fluent that I could ever be mistaken for a Frenchman. Sam has barely enough to communicate his needs in the stable and you, Lady Bigalow?"

"I am understood, but," she admitted, very much on her dignity, "I would be known, the instant I open my mouth, as an Englishwoman."

"I am not happy with the notion, but if we again find ourselves in difficulties, it is you, Artemisia, who must speak for all of us. As you did on the road. But that will not be necessary this evening," he said more bracingly. "We are lucky to find a host who supports Louis."

Before departing the next morning, Lord Merwin found an opportunity to hint to the landlord that it might be the better part of valor if he were to change sides—until Napoleon was once again defeated.

Assuming he was defeated.

Grateful for the advice, the landlord gave Alex the name of a cousin in Cherbourg, another loyalist, who would take them in. He also provided a letter of introduction.

The cousin's house was tall and narrow in a row of tall, narrow houses, well located for their needs, but not the sort of accommodations to which the women were accustomed. Arriving late in the evening, they were too tired to make complaints about the lack of luxury. The next morning when they discovered they were in the home of a sea chandler in a good way of business it was a different matter. Lady Bigalow and Artemisia were willing to make the best of things. Edith Marchcomer, on the other hand, not only complained, but insisted something be done. Instantly.

"What, exactly," asked Alex, doing his best to remain polite, "would you have me do?"

"Why, you must find us someplace suitable in which we may await transport to England, of course!

A hotel, or a Frenchman of status who will take us in!"

"And when Napoleon's soldiers appear? When they ask to see your identification papers and you must give them your passport?"

Mrs. Marchcomer bit her lip. She looked around the tiny parlor into which the lady of the house had proudly shown them immediately after breakfast. "But surely . . ."

"Believe me, the hotels will be watched and I have no acquaintance in the neighborhood. Monsieur Champlain, your host, who has put himself into danger by taking us in, has agreed to help me find the captain of a small boat who will take us across the Channel, but he must be careful. If he were to approach someone who reported us to the officials who seek the English—" He shrugged, continuing in a cold tone. "—not only we, but *he* would suffer. You must be patient. Surely, Mrs. Marchcomer, you are capable of setting aside your dignity for a few necessary days."

Edith Marchcomer sighed gustily. It had occurred to her she was irritating his lordship with her megrims and annoying Lord Merwin had no place in her plans. "I apologize. Sincerely—"

Alex believed her.

"—and abjectly."

That he doubted.

"It is merely an irritation of the nerves. I will attempt to emulate her ladyship and remain calm."

"Or you might copy Artemisia's demeanor."

Mrs. Marchcomer stiffened, then smiled a sour smile. "Ah yes. Miss Bigalow is perfection itself, is she not?"

"But of course," said Alex, widening his eyes, which had the effect of straightening his slanted brows into arched wings. "Are you only now perceiving that obvious truth?" He bowed and left the room, leaving silence behind him. For a moment he wondered if he'd also left an enemy, but shrugging, decided he'd too much to worry about without adding that possibility to the rest. Surely the woman had the good sense to see her only hope of returning to England was to behave herself and to wait patiently.

He found his host and the two left the house, leaving behind three women at odds with each other.

Word reached England that Napoleon had slipped his leash. Ian McMurrey, in London on business, read the news and immediately went in search of his wife, Lady Serena. "Alex and Jack are in Vienna, are they not?"

"The Princetons are there, but I've just been reading a letter from Patricia saying that Alex followed the Bigalows to Paris."

"How long ago?"

Patricia smiled. "You will be shocked when I inform you the letter arrived in England by courier, sent on in the official pouch by Lady Castlereagh. Alex left Vienna only one day before the courier!"

"If he had reached England we would know it. Which means he is very likely trapped in France." Ian's lips pursed. "Serena, I think we must visit the Renwicks."

"An excellent notion. But should we not get word to Miles and Tony before leaving London? You see to that and I'll get our packing started so we may be off as soon as may be."

They separated and, worried about Alex, each accomplished his task as quickly as possible. Before evening, there were more worried friends and, late the next day, still more when Miles, Ian, and Serena arrived at Tiger's Lair.

"Actually," said Serena to Eustacia, "I do not doubt

that Jack and Patricia are equally worried. Tony and Libby wished to come but could not leave London just now. The question, of course, is whether there is anything anyone can do."

Miles, entering the blue salon along with Ian and Jason, laughed. "That certainly *is* the question."

"Alex would not sit around waiting for Napoleon to round him up and intern him!" exclaimed Ian.

"No, of course not. But what *has* he done?"

"Isn't the obvious response that he arranged for the Bigalows to reach the coast?" asked Jason.

"That is the sensible thing, of course, but we all know," said Miles, his tone dripping sarcasm, "Sir Vincent is anything but sensible."

"Whatever Sir Vincent may or may not be, Lady Bigalow *is*. She will not allow Miss Bigalow to remain in danger," said Serena.

"I have never met the lady," said Eustacia, "but as a mother myself, I'd feel my first duty was to my children. If a means of saving a daughter was suggested, I'd go along with the plan."

"I agree," said Serena. Her hand went to her nicely rounded tummy. She and Ian were expecting their third child. "A mother's children must come first no matter how much she may love their father and in this case," she added, her voice dry as dust, "I doubt that love for her husband will complicate Lady Bigalow's decision. I believe it was an arranged marriage and neither Sir Vincent nor Lady Bigalow have found it the most satisfying of relationships!"

"Then," said Miles, who had no taste for gossip, "we may assume that, since they have not arrived in England, that Alex is to be found somewhere along the coast. Our next question is *where*. Jason, we need maps. Your study, perhaps?"

The men trooped out as quickly as they'd trooped in. Eustacia, Lady Renwick, shook her head. "Happy as a clam, is he not?"

"Miles? Of course. He is always happy when there is something to be done." Serena's shoulders lifted and fell with the quick, sharp intake of breath. "Now, if *we* are to remain happy, we must be made aware of all the men do so that we may put a spoke in any plan which is too wild!"

The women looked at each other. They sighed. Keeping their menfolk from going off half-cocked was not going to be easy!

One day followed another and Alex began to wonder if he would ever manage to complete the rescue. Mrs. Marchcomer was growing more and more difficult and Monsieur Champlain rather sulky as his fear of discovery increased with passing time. The poor man was probably justified in his pettishness. He had not, after all, expected to house so many for so long. Nor could he, for much longer, put off his curious neighbors with tales of sickness among his visiting relatives.

On the other hand, he very much liked the francs the fine English lord handed him with great generosity.

Alex cast the man a rueful look. "I know we cannot impose upon your good nature for much longer but if you could manage to put up with us for only a little longer?"

Monsieur Champlain nodded. "If you are caught, however, then I too will be arrested. My family will be in grave difficulties."

At the unsubtle hint Alex bit his lip. His pockets were deep but not bottomless and he must have money for whatever bribe the as yet undiscovered smuggler might require. "If only I could get a message to my friends!"

"I have learned of a captain who is somewhat different. I have sent a message."

"Someone who is from elsewhere?"

"North of here. I fear quite a little ways north of here."

Alex sighed. "You neither know how long it will take for the message to arrive, nor do you actually know that it *will* arrive. Why can we find no one who will carry my message?"

Monsieur Champlain chuckled sourly. "Because, my friend, not only are your English coast guard on duty, something our poor traders are used to, but Napoleon has ordered all boats to remain in port. He wants no English escaping his net. And you, my lord, are English."

Alex returned to the small house. Pausing in the entryway, he listened to Edith Marchcomer complain to Lady Bigalow about the morning coffee. "Why may we not have tea? That is the proper thing to drink in the morning. Why can we not leave here? Why may we not, at the very least, walk to the shops? I cannot *bear* to be closed into this room for still another day. I cannot bear it, I tell you!"

Alex gritted his teeth. He entered and Edith smiled immediately. "Why, my lord, what a wonderful surprise. You have come to tell us you have arranged all, have you not?"

"Not."

Her smile faded. "I cannot bear it, I tell you."

"I believe there is no one who can deny that you have told us," said Alex in a soft, dangerous voice. "In fact, you have told us over and over, but you *do* bear it, do you not? We are none of us happy. We are all of us in danger. Including our host. You do not help with your constant whining."

"My lord!"

"I suggest you do as Lady Bigalow is doing." He gestured toward where her ladyship, who sat with her tatting. She had finished the collar and bestowed it on their hostess who, that Sunday, wore it to church.

"But I don't know how to tat."

"There are other forms of handwork."

"My embroidery would shame a girl in the nursery. And I dislike knitting, of all things." She turned her nose into the air and her back on the others and moved to stand before the tiny fire. "And I am cold. It is always cold in this house."

"Add another shawl to your shoulders and you'll be warm."

"I haven't another shawl. You did not allow me to bring my wardrobe." When Edith turned back toward them there were tears wetting her face. "I am so very miserable and no one cares. No one cares at all."

"But Edith," said Lady Bigalow gently, "we are all miserable. Why do you act as if you are the only one?"

Mrs. Marchcomer fell to her knees before a chair, laid her arms on it, and her head on her arms. She sobbed. Although nearly garbled by her misery, Alex managed to hear her say, "I only want to be loved. Is it so terrible to want to be loved?" Alex, a horrified look on his face, backed from the room and moved into the kitchen, where he found their hostess kneading bread dough. He pulled a chair up to the worktable and sat on it, watching her. Her quick smile and calm, continuous movements soothed him; gradually he managed to bring his thoughts away from the pitiful sight in the parlor and return them to their problem.

It had crossed his mind a day or two earlier, when he'd found it impossible to buy a boat, that he might steal one. He changed that to *borrow* before putting his mind to just how he should manage the trick!

He was frowning ferociously when the front door burst open and their host, his heavy boots incapable of gentle steps, pounded down the short hall to the kitchen. He slammed open the door. "My lord! Come at once."

Alex rose and turned, upsetting the stool with a clatter. *"Mon ami!* What is it? The gendarmes have been informed—"

Monsieur Champlain shook his head.

"—of our . . . No?"

"No, no. Do come. I think it possible help is at hand!"

Alex went, following his host down to the harbor and into a tiny café that catered to fishermen. There, not even pretending to hide himself, was Miles Seward, speaking perfectly idiomatic Marseilles gutter French, regaling the other patrons with a story so outrageous many were holding their sides with gusts of laughter.

Miles looked up. His brows rose slightly, but then he turned back to the rough-dressed men crowding around his stool and finished the tale. He then called for a round of drinks and waved a hand toward Alex and Monsieur Champlain, including them in the order.

"All are welcome," shouted Miles in French. "Come, friends," he added. "You are newcomers. You will join me at a table, will you not? I celebrate! I celebrate. Host! Here—" He tossed a purse on the counter. "You keep setting them up until that is gone! Yes, yes, I celebrate!" And clapping an arm around Alex's shoulders, he led him toward the corner.

"You, my friend," said Alex softly, "are a sight for which I've prayed—and worthy of a better celebration than this!"

"As I have prayed for a glimpse of you in every possible—and impossible—place from here to Le Havre! We must lay plans."

"Monsieur Champlain will be happy to see the back of us!"

"You and the Bigalows, am I correct?"

"The ladies, yes, and our coachy and a Mrs. Marcomer, but Sir Vincent refused to leave Paris until he had greeted his hero," said Alex a trifle sourly.

"At which point he found it impossible to leave."

Miles, noticing that the room had become a little too quiet, raised his voice in what was soon understood to be an exceedingly bawdy song. The chorus was simple enough, and soon all were joining in, quieting to hear the next verse. Miles brought the song to a triumphant conclusion and began another, much better known, tune. Soon a chorus of voices joined in and gradually Miles dropped out.

"I fear I have been a trifle indiscreet in my search for you, Alex. We must not linger here. Can you bring the women to the quay just at dusk?"

Monsieur Champlain spoke for the first time. "They will be there." He rose to his feet. "And now we must go."

"Ah, such sadness," said Miles, rising to his feet and looking morose. "To lose you when I just begin to know you." He raised his glass in a toast, drank it off, and herded Alex and the Frenchman to the door. He himself turned back and, before they'd gone a dozen paces, Alex heard Miles's voice raised in still another song. This one was so idiomatic he could not follow it, but the soft, half-embarrassed chuckles Monsieur Champlain emitted suggested it was *not* something one would sing in a drawing room to amuse one's friends. Alex wondered at what point in his adventurous life Miles had learned such lewd verses!

They returned to the house just in time for Alex to join the ladies in a nuncheon. "My friends, I wish to announce that rescue is at hand. This evening the five of us will stroll out together, just as if we were taking an evening constitutional. We will not return."

Mrs. Marchcomer, elated by the thought of rescue, suddenly realized that Alex meant they were to take nothing with them. "But . . . !"

Alex held up a hand. "I suggest you dress in as

many layers of clothing as you can manage. Not only will it be cold on the water, but that is the only way you may carry anything with you."

"But . . . !"

"My dear Edith," said Lady Bigalow sharply, "you may travel to London in our company and may go immediately to your solicitor who will arrange for you to have funds. Think of the shopping you may indulge in if you must purchase everything new!"

Edith shut the mouth she had opened, ready to begin a tirade against thoughtless gentlemen who had no sensibility whatsoever. After a moment she nodded. "I must plan exactly how I may layer what clothing I have so as to take as much as possible. It will be days and days before my modiste can supply me with what will be needed."

Leaving her plate barely touched, she hurried from the room. None of the three remaining said a word for some little time, but there was a general relaxation and, when conversation resumed, it was not only general but, Mrs. Marchcomer absent, it was pleasant for the first time since they'd left Paris.

Unfortunately, once the meal ended everyone began thinking about the dangers attendant on walking through town and onto the quay and tensions rose. Soon it seemed as if everyone was snapping at everyone else.

Alex prayed dusk would arrive soon!

SEVEN

The route suggested by Monsieur Champlain was a trifle complicated and, at one point, Alex was forced to backtrack. Dusk was rapidly turning to dark and he feared he would lose his way altogether, which would mean disaster. Therefore he was greatly relieved to find they had reached the strand. He guided his small party along it, strolling toward the point Miles had said he'd have a boat awaiting them.

But Alex could see no boat. Too, the waves were higher than he'd expected. Mrs. Marchcomer had begun eying them soon after their arrival at the shore. Now she jerked at Alex's arm. "No." She stopped.

"No?" asked Alex, scanning the water for the promised transport.

"I cannot do it."

"Cannot do what?"

"You cannot make me."

Alex looked down at Mrs. Marchcomer. "Cannot make you do what?" he asked, irritated.

"Make me go out on the ocean in such weather, of course. Surely, even if you have no care for *my* sensibilities, you care about Lady Bigalow and Miss Bigalow! No man would be so unfeeling as to force a woman to face such a journey." Her hand rose and fell in a suggestive manner and—Alex peered closely—she did look a trifle green about the gills.

Artemisia opened her mouth but her mother

grasped her daughter's arm, silencing her. Lady Bigalow then pressed Mrs. Marchcomer's arm. "My dear
Edith, are you one who suffers from *mal de mer?* Poor
dear. But do you not understand? We have no choice.
We must leave France and our only chance is to sail,
now, this evening!"

"No. I cannot," said Edith, backing a step away.
She shook her head.

"The boat comes, I think," said Artemisia quietly.

Alex looked seaward. Then, suddenly, a sound
catching his ear, he looked back the way they'd come.
"Moonbeam, my lady, make haste. Sam? Help them
and I'll bring Mrs. Marchcomer!"

Artemisia looked back. "Soldiers! Mother, hurry!"

They grasped hands, and picking up their skirts,
headed for the approaching boat. Mrs. Marchcomer
gasped when Alex scooped her up and rushed after
the two fleeing women, but truly terrified of the sea,
she did not understand the danger approaching from
the rear and struggled to free herself.

Miles stood in the water near the bow of the dory,
spume foaming around his high-topped boots. He
tossed first one and then the other woman into it. A
sailor helped them to seats and when Alex, struggling
with Edith, arrived, Miles reached for her. "Get in,"
ordered Miles. Neither Alex nor Sam argued. "Mrs.
Marchcomer," continued Miles in a loud, firm tone,
"if you do not cease this nonsense at once I shall
knock you silly."

Edith gasped. "You wouldn't."

"I would. I've no intention of spending the next
few years in one of Nappy's gaols!"

Edith allowed herself to be set in the boat and Miles
pushed it into the surf even before she was settled.
Then he lifted himself in and the rowers set oars to
water and pulled.

They were still far too near the shore when the soldiers reached the water line. Miles swore, began

counting cadence for the sailors, and motioned to Alex to get the women to lay their heads down.

Artemisia gasped at the orders she heard shouted in French. And then the first shots were fired. "Mother!" she screamed and threw herself across the older woman's shoulders, protecting her with her own body.

Mrs. Marchcomer fainted and slid into the bit of dirty water sloshing around in the bottom of the boat.

"Leave her. She's safest there," said Miles when Alex leaned down to lift the insensible woman.

A grunt and one of the oars flipped into disarray. Miles instantly moved into position and grasped the oar, pushing the wounded man off his seat. This time he didn't object when Alex stepped into position to see if there was anything he could do for the seaman.

Artemisia, seeing Alex pressing his hand against a spurting wound, tore a wide strip off the bottom of one of her petticoats. She folded it into a pad and, balancing precariously, moved to hand it to Alex.

"Get down," ordered Alex.

"We are beyond range," said Miles and smiled over his shoulder at Artemisia. "You have chosen well, Alex. Your Moonbeam will make a great addition to our growing numbers!'

Artemisia felt her face heat. How dare Alex allow another to know his pet name for her? She sat down, hard, when a particularly nasty wave caught the dory and threw her off balance. Cold, briny water flooded over her shoes and, softly, she swore. *It is going to be,* she thought, *a miserable journey across the Channel if the wind does not drop!*

That thought reminded her of Mrs. Marchcomer, who still lay in the bottom soaked to the skin. She sighed. Once again Artemisia moved to give aid. This time it was unappreciated. Mrs. Marchcomer, when she came to her senses, was in such a panic she became hysterical, threatening to overturn the boat with her antics.

This time Miles did not merely threaten to slap the woman. He did it.

Immediately, Mrs. Marchcomer gasped. She quieted for a moment, but then began sobbing. She would not allow Artemisia to touch her, turning into Lady Bigalow's shoulder and the older woman put her arms around her—but at least she no longer threw herself about in such as way as to endanger others. She was still sobbing when lifted over the side of Miles's ship, the *Nemesis*, and continued to do so even after Lady Bigalow had helped her from her wet clothes and into an overly large nightshirt which must have belonged to Miles. Lady Bigalow quickly tucked Mrs. Marchcomer into a bunk—but minutes later she was forced to help the woman as Edith was sick into a basin. Artemisia, looking into the cabin, was asked, politely if bluntly, to leave.

Artemisia, not displeased that she was unneeded, turned to Alex and smiled.

"What is it?"

"I am told I am in the way and unwanted." She pretended to pout but then sobered. "I should not feel so happy when Mrs. Marchcomer is so miserable and suffers so."

"I have difficulty feeling sorry for her. Her lack of control very nearly meant our capture. I haven't a notion who sent those soldiers after us, but—" A muscle jumped in Alex's jaw. "—I rather wish I'd not left the rest of my purse with Monsieur Champlain. I cannot think who else might have betrayed us."

"I believe you wrong him. A neighbor woman came in by way of the back door shortly before we left. I am very nearly certain she heard Mrs. Marchcomer complaining—in very bad French, of course—before we noticed her. It is far more likely that *she* gave us away. I only hope she did not cause trouble for the Champlains."

Alex nodded. "I, too, hope they are safe."

Sobered by the thought that they might have endangered those who had sheltered them, Artemisia and Alex stood by the rail, clutching it tightly to keep their feet. Eventually, chilled by wet feet and the soaked bottoms to her skirts, Artemisia asked Alex if there were someplace where they could get in out of the wind.

Alex, unhappy that he'd not thought of his love's discomfort, led her, lurching with the tossing waves, an arm about her waist to keep her safe, into the captain's salon. Since the captain was busy elsewhere, they were alone. As naturally as if she'd a right to do so, Artemisia turned into his arms. Alex's arms closed around her and he dipped his head to meet her offered lips.

Alex's heart and mind fought a furious battle—and his mind won. After a long moment he very gently set her away from him. "You are freezing. Let me find you some blankets. It would be a shame if you were saved from Napoleon only to succumb to an ague!" He smiled. It was a rather sad smile and said far more than any words he dared speak.

Reluctantly, Artemisia moved away. "You are, as usual, more than correct. May I say that I rather wish you had thought of a different way of warming me?"

Alex stiffened. "No."

"No?" She turned.

"No, you may not say it. Do not even think it!"

It was Artemisia's turn to smile one of those weak but revealing smiles. "You cannot order my thinking, Alex," she said softly. "All else you may order, but not that."

He reached toward her but his hand dropped. He turned and rather abruptly left the room in search of the blankets he, too, wished had not entered his mind.

How, he wondered, *am I to retain control of myself if Moonbeam is losing hers?* The grim look about his mouth and eyes stopped Miles in his tracks.

"What is it?" asked Miles.

Alex frowned. "What . . . ?"

"Why do you look like that?"

Alex tipped his head, then grinned. Not a happy grin. More that of the death head pictured in old-fashioned macabre, woodcut prints. He grimaced. "My Moonbeam is cold." His brows straightened, fell back into their usual faintly satanic lines. "And I do not trust myself to stay in your salon alone with her—which is a nuisance since there are far too few times in which we may be alone together. I'm seeking blankets for her comfort."

Miles didn't ask why Artemisia was not in his cabin, which he'd turned over to the women. He simply ordered a passing crewman to find the blankets and take them to the salon at the same time as he took Alex by the arm and turned toward the helm where the first mate stood, legs straddled, his hands fighting the rudder which fought back, the high winds doing their best to force their ship off course.

"Just got a report a good-sized ship is bearing down on us from the northwest," said the mate.

Miles headed for the rail, lifted a small spyglass, and then, swearing softly, headed for a mast, which he climbed with the agility of a monkey. Alex, warned by his friend's tension that something was not right, waited impatiently.

Miles dropped back to the deck, orders already spewing from his lips. Sailors scurried in all directions. More sail was raised. The gun emplacements were opened and the ship's two guns run up. Several sealed chests were unlocked and weapons distributed. Finally Miles returned, spyglass raised, to watch the distant ship still bearing down on them, although far less quickly.

"What is it?" asked Alex when Miles appeared to have looked his fill.

"One of the few French ships that can outrun mine," said Miles with a grim look. "What exceedingly bad luck they happened to be cruising these waters."

"How far are we from safety?"

"I'll put it gently by saying that England may be just a little too far for us to count on the protection of a harbor."

"Let us not. Say it, I mean. Damn and blast, we've women aboard!" Alex's fear for Artemisia sent chills up his spine. "What can I do?"

Miles gave him a glance, noting the pistols tucked into his trousers and the sword slung by an old-fashioned baldric across his shoulder. "I'd say you've done about all you can do. Or perhaps you could warn the women."

"Not yet. Not until the danger is nearly upon us. There is no sense in their worrying before the need to do so is here!"

No more to be said, the friends stood shoulder to shoulder by the railing, watching the slow approach of the enemy. Watching the ship grow gradually larger and larger. Watching the tiny, hurrying dots become tiny figures and, very gradually, watched those figures become individuals with the grinning, expectant expressions of men eager to come to grips with an enemy.

"It is time to warn the women," said Alex.

"Yes."

Alex turned and went first to the cabin where a distracted Lady Bigalow answered his knock. "My lady, we've trouble approaching. A French ship of the line draws near. I very much fear there will be a battle and I cannot guarantee that we will win it."

Lady Bigalow nodded. "Is there anything we should do?"

"At the moment, no."

"Then I will continue to occupy myself with Mrs. Marchcomer. She is so very ill that I rather fear for her."

"Sea sickness is like that. When——" He emphasized the word ever so slightly. "——we reach shore you will see how quickly she recovers." Alex smiled, nodded, and turned to go.

The instant his back was to Lady Bigalow, his frown returned. Artemisia! How he hated that against all odds he had put her into deeper danger than if she had remained in Paris where she would have been treated no more badly than any other English person detained in France. He entered the salon to find his love wrapped in blankets, seated in a wooden-armed chair set so the light coming in the window fell over her shoulder. A rather heavy tome lay open on her lap.

"Is it interesting?" he asked.

"It is only a trifle less boring than sitting here alone with my thoughts. Have you come to entertain me?" Her gaze went from the sword to the pistols to Alex's eyes and she answered herself. "No, I don't believe you have. What is it, Alex?"

"A French warship approaches. Miles's ship is known as one that prevents the smuggling that enriches the French war effort. That captain will receive a reward if he manages to capture Miles and his men." Alex put from his mind what capture would mean for captain and crew. Death would very likely be a blessing! His gaze fell on the woman he loved. "Capture will mean *your* capture as well." The grim look changed so that a white ring appeared around Alex's lips. "Artemisia . . ."

She threw off the blankets and came to him. "No. It is not your fault. Do not even think it."

"It is." He drew her gently into his embrace and she adjusted her position so that the pistols did not poke her. "It is my fault that in my arrogance I assumed I could rescue you and keep you safe. If anything happens to you——" His arms tightened. "——my dearest love, I will never forgive myself."

"Just be certain that when it is over you are alive and can blame yourself all you want. What I will not forgive is if you are . . . hurt!" She couldn't even *say* the word *dead.*

"Stay here. I don't believe they will harm you women, but . . ." He put her away from him and looked down into her face. Suddenly he pulled her close and, lifting her chin, kissed her. Thoroughly. "I cannot stay. I must do what I can to help. Oh my God, Artemisia, if anything happens to you . . . !"

He kissed her again—a quick hard kiss—then released her and went out without another word.

When Alex returned to the deck, he found a disciplined and trained crew, grim of feature but ready and willing to defend itself. The French ship was only a few hundred yards behind and to one side. Miles approached him.

"Will they fire a broadside?" Alex asked. "Will we sink?"

"I think they want to capture the Nemesis and are enough larger that they feel they can. Spoils of war, you know."

Alex swore softly. "But there is no war! At least I do not believe it has been declared, so why do they chase you down?"

Miles looked thoughtful. "Revenge, perhaps. I am rather disliked by the French Navy! Whatever their reason, it is clear they are about to attack."

Silence fell. The enemy continued to gain, but only a bare yard at a time. It would be another fifteen or twenty minutes, perhaps more, before battle commenced. Alex felt chills at the thought. He was no warrior and he hoped his courage would not fail him. A vision of Artemisia filled his mind, the faith she had in him vividly writ upon her features. He straightened.

"The first moments are the worst," said Miles softly, understanding Alex's unspoken fear. "Then you find yourself far too busy to worry about abstract things such as courage or failure."

"You are a mind reader."

"No. It is only that I know how you feel. Every battle is the same. No matter how many one endures."

After a long, tense silence, Alex said, "It won't be long."

"No."

Again silence fell, the tension so thick one sensed it as a fog, a miasma all around . . . and then, suddenly, a gasp went up from the waiting sailors. Miles straightened, stiffened, and exclaimed, "What the devil!"

Alex's frown drew his brows into a narrow vee. "But they were within twenty yards of us! Why . . . ?"

A halloo from the other side of the *Nemesis* drew everyone's attention. "Ahoy! In need of help there?"

The gruff British voice was such a surprise that Alex blinked and Miles swore. They hurried around the deck to the far rail.

"Just had this little thought you might be in difficulties," roared the captain of the other ship.

"Not anymore," retorted Miles with a grin. "Come aboard! I've a devilish fine port you might enjoy. Or if something stronger appeals, I'll break out the grog! May I send over a bottle for your men?"

A huzzah from the British sailors on the warship looming over them answered that question. The captain, a grizzled old man who was realistic about discipline, grinned. "A reward, you would say? But what did my men do that they deserve a reward?"

"They managed to have your ship in the right place at the right time. I'd say that is deserving of a reward!"

"Hmm. Well, perhaps."

Another huzzah followed that and again the captain grinned. "Very well. I'll set my first mate to doling out your contribution to the downfall of British discipline. And I'll join you in half an hour."

Alex was amazed by how quickly Miles's crew had their vessel shipshape again. He was equally amazed by the rapidity with which Cook produced a meal of princely proportions. Miles, it seemed, did not believe in ship's rations!

The meal was served in the salon by two of the crew. Lady Bigalow had, regretfully, declined the invitation to join the diners; reluctantly, she had given permission for Artemisia to partake without a vestige of a chaperone, and, of course, Mrs. Marchcomer continued to be far too ill to care a whit what went on about her.

Artemisia discovered that although she enjoyed the meal and the company she was uncomfortable as the only woman in the room. This rather surprised her since it had never occurred to her she would be so missish. Then, toward the end of the feast, she realized the strange captain was not quite comfortable, either. She finished her pudding, rose to her feet, and, smiling around the table, excused herself.

Alex dropped his napkin beside his plate and followed her from the salon. "My dear, where will you go?"

"I will join Mother. Or perhaps I might relieve her. She has had the sole responsibility for Mrs. Marchcomer and must be exhausted."

Alex offered his arm and they proceeded toward the cabin. Again he knocked, but this time he heard Lady Bigalow call out that she could not oblige by coming to the door. Artemisia pulled it open and entered. And recoiled. The stench of illness pervading the room was overpowering.

Alex was proud of his Moonbeam when she

straightened her shoulders, firmed her jaw, and went on in, gently closing the door behind her. He heard her speaking softly with her mother and, a few moments later, Lady Bigalow walked out.

"Oh!"

"Artemisia suggested you rest, did she not? I waited to see if I could be of service."

"Thank you." Her ladyship nearly fell when a rather large wave shifted the deck under her feet in an unexpected manner. "Oh!"

Alex offered his arm. "Come along. A stroll around the deck to clear your head and then we will see to finding you a place where you may rest."

"I cannot be long. Mrs. Marchcomer—"

"—will be just fine. Artemisia will see to her."

Lady Bigalow allowed herself to be persuaded.

The visiting captain, now grimly serious, had returned to his ship after being apprised of Napoleon's latest antics, which, being at sea for so long, he'd not heard. Alex suggested they see if Miles had returned to the salon. He had, although he was about to head back to the helm where he spent most of his time when at sea.

"My lady," he said, "make yourself at home. Have you dined? Should I order a tray brought for you?"

Lady Bigalow's hand went instantly to press against her stomach. She looked a trifle green. "Please, do not mention food. I have not been ill . . . but truly, I dare eat nothing."

"Ah. A mild case of *mal de mer,* is it? I will have a composer sent in to you which aids sufferers such as you. You drink it down, my lady, and I promise, you'll feel much more the thing. No, do not grimace so. I assure you, what I say is true." He patted Lady Bigalow on the arm and went out.

Not long afterwards a young seaman knocked and handed in a glass full of an ill-looking liquid. Alex

took it, looked at it doubtfully, and took it to Lady
Bigalow. "My lady . . . ?"

She, too, stared at the liquid with a suspicious gaze.
"Do you think I should . . . ?

"I'd trust Miles with my life, my lady, but this is
not a decision I feel I can make for you!"

A weak laugh was her response and, taking a deep
breath, she drank down the draught. She cast a rather
surprised look at the empty glass. "Well. That was
not half so bad as it looked to be." She pressed her
hand to her stomach and a still more surprised expression crossed her features. "I cannot believe it."

"Do you feel better, my lady?"

"Much. In fact—" The surprise deepened. "—I believe I am hungry after all. I would," she added dif-
fidently, "like toast, if that is possible? And perhaps
a pot of tea?"

"I'll see what I can do."

Once she had eaten her frugal meal, Lady Bigalow
returned to the cabin, sent her daughter out and into
Alex's care, and shut the door.

Alex and Artemisia stared at each other. "Moonbeam, I do not dare go with you to the salon. Alone
with you . . . well, I cannot trust that I will remain
the gentleman."

"Nor I a lady." She smiled wanly. "Shall we . . .
walk?"

They walked. Or, since the waves remained high,
perhaps it was more true to say they lurched! Finally
they stood at the rail looking toward where England
would appear. After a time they walked again. And
talked. And talked some more. It was the longest
stretch of time the two had ever had together.

And it was not enough.

Miles found them in the stern, their hands clasped,
staring out over the water. He put a hand on each
shoulder, getting their attention. "We'll enter the harbor at Portsmouth within half an hour," he said.

* * *

Soon after they passed the breakwater where the waves stilled to next to nothing, Mrs. Marchcomer felt somewhat better. "Land," she breathed. "I will never again leave it once I set foot on it. When do we debark?"

Lady Bigalow bit her lip. "I fear you are laboring under a misapprehension, my dear Mrs. Marchcomer. It was an exceedingly difficult crossing and took far longer than expected. The men are tired so we stay here until tomorrow when we leave with the tide."

Edith Marchcomer's features distorted. "No!" she cried.

"But my dear, if we do *not* leave we will be placed under quarantine. Do you wish to remain here for two weeks or perhaps more, unable to leave ship?"

Edith bit her lip. She frowned. "But surely they know we are not ill. Surely they will allow us to go ashore?"

"There is a rule."

Mrs. Marchcomer began to cry. Soft, large tears rolled down her cheeks and she looked so forlorn Lady Bigalow felt like chuckling. And then she *didn't*. She could sympathize with the woman's fear of returning to sea and she could understand why remaining on board was also unacceptable. She herself would have liked to be taken to the nearest inn where she could order up the bath and plenty of hot water and soak away the stench of the sickroom along with her aches and pains.

"My dear, it will be a short day. We sail up the coast to where we will take to carriages for Lord Merwin's friend's estate. Tiger's Lair is not so very far inland and Lady Renwick is a kind soul. I am certain she will find us fresh clothing and treat us all to hot baths. We will be fed and cosseted and cared for."

Cosseted and cared for! Who is cosseting Sir Vincent?, wondered Lady Bigalow, thinking of her husband for the first time since finding Edith in such dire straits.

"Tiger's Lair? Where a great white tiger is said to roam free?"

Lady Bigalow nodded. "I have never visited the Renwicks, but have heard much of them from my daughter. Lord Merwin visits often and Artemisia has told me tales."

"I cannot believe it is safe!"

"Artemisia insists it is, that the tiger is quite tame."

"She has met the beast, of course?" asked Edith, scornfully. Her white face was gradually regaining color and evidently reviving emotion was indicative of reviving strength, for she pushed herself up until she leant against the head of the bunk. "I doubt it, or surely she'd not be quite so trusting!"

Lady Bigalow's mouth thinned. She had had quite enough of Edith Marchcomer and wondered how soon they could be rid of her. *Enough,* thought Lady Bigalow, *is enough.*

"My brush is in my reticule," said Edith, breaking into Lady Bigalow's less-than-Christian thoughts. "Fetch it for me."

Her mouth a grim line as she repressed her feelings about having been given orders as if she were a maid, Lady Bigalow did as requested and then, after watching for a few moments, sighed and took the brush back into her own hands. Very gently, she did what she could to return Edith's hair to neatness. "Shall I braid it?"

Edith Marchcomer looked horrified. "Good heavens, *no.* When I left my brother's roof for the last time I swore I would never again wear braids. I care not what you do, but no braids!"

Her ladyship, thinking neat braids would look far better than anything else she might contrive, wound the hair into a nob to one side of Edith's head and put pins in to hold it. "There. That is the best I can do."

"Is there a mirror?"

"No." *Which,* thought her ladyship, *is just as well.* "If you are feeling more the thing, I will leave you for a time."

Edith shuddered. "Do not be so cruel as to mention what thing!"

Lady Bigalow found her daughter and Lord Merwin leaning on the lee side rail and watching the activity in and around the port. "My dears, are you not chilled?"

"Mother! You are freed from duty?" Artemisia turned and leaned back.

Lady Bigalow grimaced. "Until we leave the harbor. Mrs. Marchcomer practically fell into hysterics when she discovered she could not reach shore instantly, but I believe she is resigned. And you, my dear? Is all well with you?"

"Like everyone aboard, I could use a goodly amount of hot water and fresh clothing, but of all of us, I'd say I'm in the best shape."

Alex glanced at her and quickly away. *The best shape indeed,* he thought—and felt heat running up his neck and into his ears. "We will soon enough be able to supply you with your needs. My lady?" he finished, really looking at Artemisia's mother rather than at Artemisia. "Are you, too, ill?"

She shook her head. "It is nonsense, of course, but now that I am no longer preoccupied with Mrs. Marchcomer, I cannot help wondering about poor Sir Vincent, how he does, where he is . . ." She drew in a deep breath. "There is nothing to be done so I will not repine."

Alex nodded. "If Napoleon behaves as he did previously, any English he finds will be under a form of house arrest but not ill-treated otherwise."

"Then I will truly cease to worry," said Lady Biga-low bravely.

Alex could see she *would* worry, but he could not see what he could do about it. At least at the moment . . .

EIGHT

Alex and the others, excepting Sam, arrived at the Renwicks' toward evening of the next day. Sam had relatives living nearby and, thanking Alex and Miles for getting him out of France, he set off on his own. A courier, sent with a message as soon as Miles dropped anchor, had prepared Lady Renwick for their arrival. His lordship, however, had gone off to visit his solicitor and was not at home when his guests arrived.

Mrs. Marchcomer, still feeling down-pin after her ordeal, was taken straight up to a bedchamber and left in the care of a maid. Lady Bigalow, who had nursed the poor lady while on board, was very nearly as exhausted and not long behind her in seeking her bed. Artemisia, on the other hand, had no intention of leaving the fascinating company in which she found herself.

Lady Renwick was immediately her friend. They spoke no more than a dozen words when each knew that she had found a like-minded person in the other.

Besides her hostess, a Renwick cousin was visiting and his faintly foreign air and even fainter accent roused Artemisia's curiosity. Then there was a tall, dark-skinned youth and the boy's tutor, a brother to Alex's friend Ian McMurrey. Artemisia was intrigued by the colorfully dressed lad. She demanded the story of who he was and where he came from and was as-

tounded to learn he was a prince in his own country
and, a child at the time, the indirect cause of Lord
Renwick's blindness.

Other friends were in residence. The McMurreys
had stayed on, awaiting Miles's return with the refugees. And Miles himself, now he was no longer re-
sponsible for crew and passengers turned into a flirt
who kept the ladies in a continual but not uncomfortable state of exhileration.

Best of all, it was exceedingly pleasant to know
Alex was at her side, watching over her.

And, icing on the cake, there was the anticipation
of meeting Lord Renwick and his companion, the
white tiger. The two entered together shortly before
the tea tray came in, and the tiger, upon perceiving a
stranger, moved just in front of Lord Renwick, pressing him back.

"What is it?" asked his lordship.

"We've company," said Lady Renwick, rising and
going to his side. She stood on tiptoe and touched her
lips to his cheek. "Sahib," she continued, putting her
hand on the tiger's head, *"friend."*

The tiger looked toward Artemisia who, involuntarily, clutched Alex's arm. The animal took a few steps
and stared up into her face. He made an odd chuffing
sound.

Lady Renwick, who had followed, said, "That is
the same as a purr in a cat, Miss Bigalow. He is telling
you he likes you."

Artemisia hesitated a moment and then held out her
hand as she would to a dog to whom she was being
introduced. The tiger stretched forward and, politely,
sniffed her fingers, then looked up into her face.
Artemisia smiled. "I like you, too, Sahib." The tiger
opened his mouth wide in a silent roar, startling her.
"Well," she added after gulping, "I *think* I do."

Lord Renwick, who had followed, his long cane tap-
ping the floor ahead of him, chuckled at her tone.

"Sahib can be a trifle intimidating, but I assure you, you need not fear him. He wishes all our friends only the very best of all things and, you will discover, does his feline best to see that all have it."

Lady Renwick glanced from Artemisia to Alex and back again before looking down at Sahib. "Hmm," she murmured. She turned her gaze to Alex. "Do you think perhaps . . . ?"

He grinned. "I not only *think*, I *hope*."

"Hope? Hope what?" asked Artemisia, mystified.

"Never you mind!" said Alex, laughing. "But do pay attention to our furry friend here. If he tells you something is the thing to do, then you do it. He is never wrong, you see."

More confused than ever, Artemisia glanced at Miles who, never far from the center of things, had joined them. "Do *you* know what he means?" she asked.

Miles laughed. "I've a clue, but I don't think I'll pass it on to you. You just do as Alex says and pay close attention to Sahib. He's been a very good friend to four of us and now it is Alex's turn. And then he'll have done his duty by us and can rest on his laurels."

"But there are six of you, are there not?" asked Artemisia. "You mention only five."

Miles's smile faded and his expression grew very slightly wary. "Well, yes, of course we are Six, but I am a lost cause and Sahib is much too intelligent to waste time on lost causes."

Sahib lifted his muzzle and roared. He did so with some volume and Artemisia jumped very nearly behind Alex, clutching him and peering around him. Alex himself stiffened. Lord and Lady Renwick frowned, but Miles, not even wincing, stared down into the tiger's hotly glowing eyes.

"I am not a lost cause?" asked Miles politely.

The roar was repeated.

"Well, if you say so, but I fear you are wrong."

There was a third roar and Sahib turned his head to stare up at Lord Renwick. The big cat moved until he could press against his master. Renwick reached down, found the beast's head, and rubbed it. The cat made that sound Lady Renwick had said was like a cat purring. Slowly everything returned to normal except that Prince Ravi had joined the group.

"Sahib is a magic beast, Mr. Seward," said the boy earnestly. "He will not *have* to give up on you. He will see you, too, have . . ."

Alex interrupted him. "Have all you want and need, Miles. Prince, forgive me, but I think we will not discuss Sahib's propensity—"

Artemisia watched the boy carefully mouthing the word.

"—for interfering in the lives of Jason's friends!"

"Yes sir." He bowed. "Excuse me."

Artemisia watched the prince ask his tutor a question and listen carefully to the answer. She suspected the lad had just learned a new word and, since the men had begun discussing Napoleon's return to power, she turned to Lady Renwick and asked.

"Oh yes. Prince Ravi is insatiable. He soaks up words as if they were sweets and he a boy let loose in the bakery!"

"He is a delightful lad."

"Hmm." Her ladyship grinned. "He is at the moment. Try crossing him and see how charming he can be!"

"In other words, he is a growing boy."

Lady Renwick cast her guest a thoughtful look. "I'd not thought of it in quite that way. You see, when he first arrived he was spoiled to the point we could do nothing with him. He is far more sensible now, and, for the most part, cooperative. But there are times when he can act the despot right royally."

"Which, if I understood correctly, is exactly what he is."

"A royal despot? Why, how true. I keep forgetting that!" The two women shared a laugh and, the tea tray coming in just then, they linked arms and moved toward Lady Serena, who had been talking to Mr. Renwick, Lord Renwick's cousin.

Much to Artemisia's disappointment, the delightful evening ended immediately after everyone finished drinking their tea, but once she reached her room, which connected to her mother's, she discovered she was tired. In fact, now there was no longer the stimulation of new company, exhaustion washed over her like a wave. She couldn't stay awake even to brush her hair, but merely slipped into the shift Lady Renwick had loaned her while her own was washed and fell into bed, asleep almost before she'd pulled the bedding up around her shoulders.

The next morning the whole household met at breakfast. Sahib, of course, was present and Edith Marchcomer, who had not previously encountered the beast, screeched and, as if she'd seen a mouse, scrambled up onto her chair. Naturally, Sahib found this behavior rather odd and, equally naturally, he approached to find out what was wrong.

Edith screeched again and, the stranger next to her having risen to his feet, she threw herself into the man's arms, screaming for him to save her.

Trey Renwick, a distant cousin to Jason, found himself clutching an armful of curvaceous woman. A quick wit, he instantly removed her from the breakfast parlor, Lady Renwick on their heels.

"Someone tell me what happened," ordered Lord Renwick, breathing a sigh of disgust. He discovered Sahib was not at his side and called the cat. The scene was explained to him and he dropped his hand to Sahib's scruff. "I must write up Sahib's history and see that a copy is placed in each guest room. This is not the first time someone has been ignorant of Sahib's existence and been frightened by him."

"He is rather unsettling, even when one is *not* in ignorance," offered Artemisia. Alex, seated beside her, put his hand over hers where it rested, fisted, in her lap. She instantly relaxed. "I know it is silly. I find him intriguing and quite beautiful, but I cannot help feeling a trifle wary of such a huge beast!"

Lady Bigalow nodded from her place across the table. "I, too, find him oddly beautiful, my lord, but a quite shocking guest in a lady's salon." She continued in a wryly humorous tone. "Not that I wish to complain, of course, but you will admit it is not every household which allows such freedom to such an exceedingly alarming beast!"

Lord Renwick chuckled. "I don't suppose I'd keep him by me if he were not so very important to me. When Prince Ravi's father gave me Sahib I was newly blind, ill from infection, and the only Englishman for a hundred miles or more. You see, I was left there by the others when they had to return to Calcutta. I was exceedingly depressed and he saved my sanity, did you not, Sahib?"

The tiger, which had pushed himself up onto his haunches early in the exchange, opened his mouth in the nearly silent roar that was his characteristic response when spoken to.

"Yes, I knew you would agree," said his lordship, his tone serious but his eyes twinkling. "I wonder. Should I take him out and properly introduce him to Mrs. Marchcomer? It will not do if she is to behave as did an easily frightened guest some years ago. Every time that young lady encountered Sahib, she fainted. We were forever having to have her carried up to her room and Reeves complained that it interfered with the footman's regular duties!"

Lady Renwick entered on the words and, hearing them, said, "Don't go, Jase. Not just now. Trey has taken her into the conservatory to speak to her about Sahib. He asked Reeves to bring them a pot of coffee and a plate of scones. Jase," she continued earnestly, "for the first time since he arrived, I am glad of your cousin's presence!"

"He did act quickly, did he not? I wish I could have seen his face when Mrs. Marchcomer hopped into his embrace!"

Since Lord Renwick spoke the words with no hint of self-pity no one felt it, but Artemisia happened to glance toward Eustacia, Lady Renwick, and saw a shadow pass over her features and disappear. Later, when the two women were alone together, she asked about it.

Eustacia smiled a trifle sadly. "When first we met, I became Jase's eyes. I would describe the world around him so he could see it in his mind. It seems lately that whenever I should do that for him, it would be too terribly impolite and I do not dare!"

"I see the difficulty. Describing what *Edith* looked like at just that moment would indeed be impolite! Or perhaps merely tactless?"

"Tactless in the extreme although I believe Jason would have been amused by a description of his cousin's expression!" Lady Renwick chuckled softly as she recalled the man's raised brows and downward curving mouth. "I go up to the nursery at this time each day," she said. "Will you come to be introduced to our daughters?"

They climbed two flights of stairs and walked down the hall. As they approached the little girls' dayroom, they heard childish laughter and a deeper voice neighing like a horse. Eustacia grasped Artemisia's arm and put her finger to her lips. The two tiptoed nearer and peeked around the door and into the room. Immediately, they ducked back, their hands over their mouths to suppress giggles, their eyes twinkling. Then, forcing their expressions into soberness, they entered the nursery.

"My goodness," said Lady Renwick. "I believe one

of the horses has escaped from the stables. Artemisia, whatever do you think we should do?"

"Hmm. Order a stable boy to come for him?"

"Or perhaps, since he has so royally entertained Liza, have him brought an extra ration of oats?"

At the first words, Alex stiffened. His ears turned bright red and, carefully, he helped his goddaughter from his back. Then he sat on the floor and pulled her into his arms.

"Horsy!"

"Elizabeth," said Lady Renwick sternly, "you must ask politely."

"Horsy?" said the little girl, patting Alex's cheek.

"Later, my dear. This horsy has worn itself out. And—" He glanced at Artemisia and flushed a brighter red. "—seems to have embarrassed himself terribly."

"Why? Because you show yourself capable of loving a child?"

"Is that how you see it?"

"I think it wonderful." Artemisia chuckled. "I think Elizabeth does, too."

The little girl scrambled up and hugged Alex. "Horsy?" she asked in a pleading voice.

Her fond mother shook her head. "She is so small, but she loves to see the horses and ride with someone holding her. I believe I must allow her a pony. Our head groom is a quite wonderful teacher. I can trust him to take good care of Elizabeth."

The adults spent another twenty minutes in the nursery, Artemisia holding Anne, the baby, while Lady Renwick and Alex played with Elizabeth and then they returned to the ground floor all together. Alex went off to find Jason and Eustacia and Artemisia watched him go.

"I didn't think I could love him more than I did," muttered Artemisia.

"They do surprise one now and again, do they not?" asked Eustacia.

"So they do." Artemisia tried to straighten her sleeve. It had been badly crushed during their adventures and washing and pressing had not removed all the creases. "I wish he'd surprised me by rescuing my wardrobe along with the rest of us," she said a trifle ruefully.

"Ah. Now there is a problem for which I've the solution!" Eustacia asked if Artemisia and her mother would care to drive into Lewes and order a few items of clothing from the modiste there. "I assure you the woman is really very good for a provincial seamstress. I am not certain how she manages to keep *au courant* with London styles, but she is never far from what is right up to the knocker."

"She sounds quite the thing. When may we go?"

"Anytime." Eustacia sighed. "I suppose," she said, "that I must ask Mrs. Marchcomer as well."

Artemisia also sighed. "It would be grossly impolite of us if we did not."

"Ah well," said Eustacia after a moment, "what cannot be cured must be endured."

"Yes."

They were silent for another long moment and then, together, sighed. Catching each other's eye, they giggled. Eustacia put her arm through Artemisia's and the two went in search of the other women. Lady Serena meant to drive out with her husband but Lady Bigalow and Mrs. Marchcomer decided they could be ready to leave for Lewes very nearly immediately.

A number of hours later, four satisfied women returned. Some of their order would be sent out to Tiger's Lair by messenger on the morrow—gowns Mrs. Climpson, the mantua-maker, had had on hand for one reason or another and which could be quickly adapted to the ladies' needs with only trifling alterations. The rest of their order would be sent out as it was finished.

The quality and the styles surprised them and the Bigalow women, mother and daughter, ordered several new outfits.

Mrs. Marchcomer, excited by the thought of new gowns, had chosen two dress lengths before remembering she lacked funds. Her face flamed with embarrassment. Artemisia noticed and, remembering the woman's revelations concerning her lack of money after her husband was killed in the duel, came to her rescue so Edith, too, would soon have a basic wardrobe she could call her own!

They returned home and, after washing up, the four met in the blue salon, Eustacia's favorite, for refreshment. Lady Serena and the men joined them there. The Wendovers, Tony and Libby, had arrived during the women's absence, and now were introduced. Trey Renwick gravitated to Mrs. Marchcomer's side and drew her off into an alcove where they sat on a satin-covered sofa talking softly right up until Reeves announced dinner. Eustacia noticed their long *tête-à-tête*, but said nothing.

Artemisia was not so reticent—although she waited until she and her mother retired some hours later. Artemisia knocked and, at her mother's invitation, entered through the door to the adjoining rooms. "Mother, did you observe Edith's behavior with Lord Renwick's cousin? I wonder if he knows she is a recent widow?"

"You, too, noted how she spent every moment she could with him?"

"She is such an *odd* widow, do you not agree?" When her mother laughed, Artemisia attempted to explain. "It is just that she never seemed married in the first place. Somehow." When her mother chuckled again, she grimaced. "You know what I mean. The way she behaved around Alex, chasing after him, and quite obviously wishing to make him her cicisbeo—"

Artemisia's expression turned a trifle grim. "—if not *worse*."

"Artemisia!"

"Well," said an unrepentant Artemisia, "she made no secret of the fact she was determined to have him!"

"But that seems to have gone off, does it not?"

"I think someone told her he and I are the next thing to engaged."

"I wonder who would have done such a thing . . . ?"

After a moment Artemisia caught her mother's hint and scowled. "Mother, it was *not* I."

Lady Bigalow smiled. "I did not *really* think it was. Would Lord Merwin have lost patience with her and said such a thing himself?"

Artemisia colored up. "I do not know. It would not have been the gentlemanly thing to do, since Father has never given his permission, and Alex is, above all else, a gentleman, but perhaps he simply could not put up with any more of her exceedingly *un*ladylike behavior!"

"Yes," said Lady Bigalow judiciously, "it was unladylike. In the extreme. As is her current demeanor toward Mr. Renwick." She bit her lip, a frown creasing long, thin lines across her forehead. "Arta, dear, has Lady Renwick said anything about the gentleman?"

"Only that he has lived for many years in Naples, but returned to England for a visit when Napoleon was sent to Elba. Is there some particular reason you ask?"

"I seem to recall—" Her ladyship chewed a bit at her lower lip and then shook her head. "—but no. It will not come to mind. Perhaps if I sleep on it . . ."

"Gossip, Mother?" asked Artemisia, joshing her.

"Well, yes, but exceedingly ancient gossip, which is why I am uncertain I've the right man in mind."

"Hmm. You sort it out, Mother, and then you be sure to tell me," she teased, but then grew thoughtful herself. "The gentleman is about of an age with Alex and Lord Renwick, is he not?"

"A few years older, perhaps." Lady Bigalow's frown deepened.

"Why do I have this notion that what you are attempting to recall is not particularly favorable to Mr. Renwick?"

"Arta . . ." But Lady Bigalow changed her mind and shook her head. "No, it would be very wrong of me to speculate when I am unsure. It was, you see, far too many years ago."

"Shall I ask Eustacia? I am sure she would tell me."

"I think it better that you not. It is possible she has never been informed."

"Very well. I shall ask *Alex.*"

With that, Artemisia shut the door between their rooms and chuckled at the words of protest she cut off. It was such fun teasing her mother. Why, she wondered, did she not do it more often?

Downstairs, those of the Six who were in residence had settled in Jason's study, glasses of a very fine burgundy in hand. But then Jason's cousin and Miles left to go to the game room while the other friends continued their discussion of Napoleon's return to power. The conversation had gradually faded to silence and no one spoke for some time.

Finally Jason sighed. "Eustacia told me, just before going to our room, that your Mrs.—"

"Do not, please, call her mine!"

"—Marchcomer spent a great deal of the evening talking with my cousin."

"Now you mention it, I believe she did. I didn't particularly notice at the time, but—"

"Yes," said Jason, his tone dry. "You understand why I mentioned it."

"—she is only recently widowed. It—"

"That is *not* the reason!"

"—has been less than a month. What is the reason?"

"Think back. My cousin's history."

"I had forgotten that," said Ian lazily.

Tony raised his quizzing glass to look at Jase. "I warned my Libby she was to be polite but not forthcoming. The man is *not* accepted even now."

Alex's mind, however, was on the lady. "So new a widow should not flirt with anyone. It isn't done. However, this particular lady will not be guided by . . ." He broke off, swearing softly.

"You have remembered, have you not?" Then Jason asked, "Will not her widowhood stop her from setting up a cicisbeo?"

"From what I know of the lady it will not! Jason, does your wife know your cousin's history?"

Jase was thoughtfully silent for a moment. "It has never crossed my mind that she would not, but it is unlikely she ever learned it. A vicar's daughter, you know, and growing up in an isolated village. I have always believed a man should be given a second chance, so I've not thought to discuss it since he arrived."

"Do you suppose I should inform Mrs. Marchcomer?"

"As you pointed out, she is a very recent widow. Surely she would not take it into her head to bestow hand and wealth upon still another fortune hunter? Not instantly?"

"She is a very odd woman, Jase. She seems to have little or no comprehension of what is right or wrong or knowledge of the conventions by which we live. It is as if she wants what she wants right now! Which, when you think on it, is not so odd after all. Before her elopement, she was kept so close by her brothers that I wonder if she was allowed to do so much as choose the style of bonnet she wore!" Alex pondered whether Edith Marchcomer might possibly have become so twisted by her brothers' treatment as to believe she had earned the right to what she wished, having put up with their control for so long. "Still, I find it hard to believe that anyone can be so totally self-centered."

"I, of course, can only judge by what I am told of her."

Alex squirmed in his seat. "Must we waste our time thinking of her? I've no patience with her. She did her best to come between my Moonbeam and me and I cannot forgive her for that so I am likely to be too harsh in my judgment of her." Alex scowled into his glass, then sipped it. He shrugged, settling his coat more comfortably. "To my relief she does seem to have stopped her more blatant behavior in that respect. I don't know why. I can only be thankful for it."

"You may thank me," said Ian in his deep, rumbling voice. "I found an opportunity to let fall the information that you and your Moonbeam will wed just as soon as her father could be contacted to give permission."

"So she thinks it is only the gentleman's absence which interferes with an immediate wedding?"

"I fear—" said Ian rather pensively, "—that I may have given her that impression. Inadvertently, of course."

"Oh yes, of course!" Alex laughed. There was relief in it. "Have I ever told you how much I admire your habit of never telling a lie?"

"It is a knack. One need only pick and choose what truth one would tell."

"Just not the whole truth?"

"Nae! Never say so!"

"Ah."

"It is," said Ian, smiling, "a trick a good politician might find useful."

"Hmm. I believe I know some who have perfected the way of it. I admit I, myself, have some difficulties with the picking and choosing. I appear to be an all or nothing sort of man."

"Yes, I know how it is with you."

Tony, Lord Wendover, had been listening quietly. Now he asked, "Alex, what do you think is the future of your all-consuming love for Miss Bigalow?"

Alex rubbed the edge of the glass against his lower lip. Then, again, he sipped. "I don't know. Her mother, of course, is our friend, but Sir Vincent has that stubbornness born into some men who know they are not quite so bright as those around them. He must have his good side, however."

"What gives you that notion?" asked Tony, startled into dropping his quizzing glass.

"Since we left Paris, I have observed Lady Bigalow when she is unaware anyone watches her. She frets."

"She is concerned for that idiotic man?" asked Ian.

"He is her husband."

"Yes, but from what I have heard," argued Tony, "there is no love lost between them."

"No, not love perhaps, but a lot of years together, and Lady Bigalow, unlike Mrs. Marchcomer, is the sort who lives with and within the conventions. She will have given her loyalty to her husband not because of the worth of the man, but because it is proper in a wife to do so and it would shame her to do less than she ought. So, now he has placed himself in danger, she cannot help but be concerned for him."

"And his daughter? She feels the same?" asked Jason a trifle dryly.

"Moonbeam loves her mother very much. She would not hurt Lady Bigalow for the world. Her primary reason for refusing to wed me out of hand is that it would hurt her mother to see her daughter behave so undutifully as to marry without her father's blessing." He looked thoughtful. "On occasion I have had a suspicion that there is a trifle more to it. I fear that Sir Vincent is the sort who would forbid his wife to have any more to do with their daughter if she and I were to elope."

"He is so vindictive?" asked Ian.

"Not vindictive. Merely stubborn. He has decreed that she'll not wed me and if she were to do so, then he must prove he was right."

"And he would do so by denying he has a daughter who would do such a thing." Jason let his hand dangle over the arm of his chair. His fingers combed the hair at Sahib's nape, idly scratching the huge cat. "How can we help?"

"I don't know, Jase. I sometimes doubt there is a solution. I fear we are at an impasse."

Tony and Ian commiserated, then said they were going to the billiards room to see if Miles had won his bet with Trey Renwick.

Once they were gone, Sahib pushed himself up onto his haunches and stared at Alex. He looked up at Jason and back to Alex. Then he slid back down to the floor, his great head cushioned on his front paws. For a long time the cat stared, unblinking, into the fire and then sat up again. He looked from one man to the other and then toward the door.

"Does Sahib wish to go out?" asked Alex, swirling the dregs of his wine around the sides of his glass.

"Probably. Will you join us?"

"No. I think I'll see if Miles and Renwick are finished knocking the balls around."

"Very well. I'll see you in the morning."

"You won't join us?"

"Not tonight." Jason grimaced. "If my cousin is in the billiards room I won't go near it! Ever since he arrived I have done my best to avoid any possibility he can corner me for the discussion I believe he wishes to have with me." He rose to his feet.

"Jase?"

Jason shook his head, waiting for Sahib to rise. When the big cat pressed gently against his side, he added, "Trey has said nothing. It is merely that I cannot think why he came here if he wants nothing!"

"An annuity to take himself off again, perhaps?"

"Perhaps, but I see no reason why I should subsidize his life abroad. I don't wish to discover his particular problem, so I avoid him."

"Perhaps you should suggest to Reeves that he organize a subtle war against the man. Damp sheets? Or a smoking fire? Or tepid water for his shaving? Or any of the dozen or so tricks a butler can design to make a guest uncomfortable?"

"It may come to that, but I dislike the notion. We are known for our hospitality and I hate being rude to anyone." He grimaced. "Even a hanger-on like my cousin!"

Alex chuckled. "Perhaps it would be best if we do *not* mention his history to Mrs. Marchcomer. If you are lucky, perhaps *she* will decide to subsidize him. It is, after all, what she did for her first husband."

"Assuming she *knows* that is what she does and that she does it *consciously,* then I'd have no objection. It is if he tricks her into marrying him and then strips her of her fortune and I have done nothing—*that* I would find distressing."

"I believe her fortune is wrapped up so that the funds are protected. She only enjoys the income." Alex had a sudden horrified thought. "On the other hand, I wonder what becomes of it if she dies . . . ?"

"Yes," said Jase, his tone exceedingly dry. "It was never satisfactorily explained, was it, the death of my cousin's first wife?"

"You suspect foul play?"

"No, I don't, but the shadow of it hangs over him. If it cannot be proved he killed her, then *he* cannot prove his innocence."

Alex was silent for a long moment. "Perhaps," he said, "I will set Lady Bigalow to discover, if she can, just what happens to Mrs. Marchcomer's fortune when she, er, has no more need of it."

"An excellent notion," agreed Jason with false heartiness. He'd little interest in his cousin and even less in Mrs. Marchcomer! "Good night, Alex. Sahib and I are off for our evening stroll."

NINE

Alex strolled to the billiards room where Miles and the Renwick cousin still played. Alex joined Ian and Tony and the three watched. Both players were very good. The advantage passed from one to the other and back again as game followed game. The fire fell to embers and, softly, Reese came in to build it up. Having done so, the butler moved to a corner and he, too, watched as the contest between the two, their cues sliding smoothly, snapping balls firmly, continued on into the wee hours.

Alex yawned, his mouth widely agape and his eyes squeezed shut. He was patting his mouth with the back of his hand when he heard a snarled oath. He straightened, flicking a look toward Miles, who stood quietly to one side and then toward Trey Renwick. Renwick glared at the table and then, throwing his cue to the floor, glared at Miles. Alex stiffened.

Finally Renwick's cousin relaxed a trifle. "I fear," he said, "that you must wait a few days until I write and draw funds from my account."

Miles nodded. "I am in no hurry."

Trey turned on his heel and left the room. In the corner, Reeves heaved an un-butlerish sigh and, taking a huge square of white linen from the pocket in the tail of his coat, patted sweat from his forehead and then mopped back over his balding pate. He tucked his handkerchief away and left the room without a word. Silence remained.

"Phew," said Tony, his quizzing glass trained on the cue. "I wondered there for a moment if he would throw *you* down next, Miles."

Miles shrugged, went to put up his cue, and turned, his hands stuffed into his pockets. "There was nothing to choose between us," he said.

"What happened there at the end?" asked Alex. "My attention wandered at just the wrong moment."

"I don't know." Miles took his hands from his pockets and stretched and then worked his shoulders to relax them. "He was doing fine and then he came very close to missing an easy shot. His next spun round and very nearly didn't drop. I saw his hands shake as he checked his cue. Then he set up that last shot . . . and missed. As I said, I don't know why. It was a far less difficult lie than some he'd made with ease earlier in the evening."

"Shaken, perhaps by the near-misses? Or simply tired?" Alex gestured at the clock.

"Nearly four? I'd no notion it was so late." The knowledge of the time had Miles yawning. Alex followed suit. Then the two laughed. Arm in arm they went out and up the stairs to their rooms, Ian and Tony following after.

"Check that I am up when you greet the morning, will you?" asked Miles as, separating, they each approached their own door.

"Hmm. You might do the same for me if you rise first," said Alex. "What, by the way, did Renwick lose?"

Miles grimaced. "His shirt, I fear."

"Seriously."

"He bet me a thousand. Whoever first got a spread of five points won."

"Five! That is nothing!"

A smile flickered over Miles's features, then faded.

"We had played previously and discovered how well matched we are. Good night, Alex."

The men opened their doors and disappeared inside.

"Moonbeam," said Alex softly. It was mid-afternoon when he found his love sitting in a small, rose-covered arbor not too far from the house and now stood before her looking down at her. "What is wrong, my love?"

"Wrong? What could be wrong?" She smiled up at him, but there was a touch of rue in it.

"You are concerned for your mother, are you not?"

Artemisia sighed. Softly. "She worries."

"About your father?"

"Hmm."

"I have written to London to see if there is any word about the English caught up in Napoleon's web," said Alex. "I thought to wait until I'd news before I told you, but if you think she'll feel better, knowing I am attempting to get information for her, then please tell her."

"When do you expect to hear?"

"With the chaos brought about by Napoleon's return to power driving everyone in London to madness, I cannot say. I addressed my question to several men, any of whom will be directly involved in such things and who, I believe, will *not* be drawn into the effort to raise a new army, but into the diplomatic side. Unfortunately, I cannot know for certain who will be assigned to which departments."

"Alex, should you not be in London?"

"Very likely, but I am not returning just yet and refuse to worry about it."

"I will worry for you. You must be needed."

"I know I could be useful, but I am not such a very important cog in the wheels of government that I'll be missed. *A promising young man in the party* is what you will hear from those who are kind to me, but that is all."

Artemisia slid to one side of the bench and Alex seated himself beside her. He took her hand in his and played with her fingers. For a long moment they were silent and then Alex raised Artemisia's hand to his lips. Thinking about the coming war, he absentmindedly touched his tongue to the tip of one finger, another, still another. Only when he felt her tremble did he realize what he did. Instantly he dropped her hand. "I apologize."

"Don't."

"Don't apologize?"

She reached for his hands, clasped them tightly. "Don't feel you must."

He wove their fingers together. "It is wrong of me to treat you . . . treat you . . ."

"As a lover treats his love?"

Alex stared into her eyes. "My dear, we haven't the right."

Her chin rose, firming, her lips compressing. Then she looked down at their intertwined fingers. "Alex, I have decided that when next I speak with my father I will tell him that I am sorry to go against his wishes, but that I must. I can no longer obey him when I love you so very much."

His hands tightened around hers. "Moonbeam, if we wed without his permission, what would be the consequences? To you, I mean?"

A tear traced a line down her cheek. "Very likely my mother would be forbidden to speak to me."

"That would hurt the both of you."

Artemisia straightened her spine. "Yes, but it hurts even more that we are kept apart."

"You might come to resent me, the cause of separating you from your mother."

Artemisia shook her head. "Never. I swear it."

Once again Alex raised her hand to his lips. "My dearest love!"

"You do not believe me."

"I believe *you* believe it. The problem, of course, is that time changes one. As the years passed and assuming we were lucky and had children, you would wish your mother to see them, love them, have a part in their life. And you would remember that it is because I am who I am that she cannot."

Artemisia sighed. "It is possible, of course, but I think I am not so weak minded. The blame would be my father's and I would—I *will*—resent his edict, but I could not blame you for *my decision* to go against his wishes."

She turned and, freeing one hand, touched his lips. Her hand dropped to her lap, the tips of her fingers tingling where his tongue had touched them. She sighed and leaned against his shoulder. For a very long time they sat there, silently, staring into the rose garden into which their bower faced. Only the muted sound of the distant dinner gong, the warning it was time to dress for dinner, roused them from their reverie.

Artemisia sighed. At that very same moment, Alex sighed.

They turned their heads to look at each other and smiled. It wasn't a smile of pleasure, merely one acknowledging that their thoughts were in tune. Alex rose, helped his Moonbeam to her feet, and, together, they strolled into the house. Once changed, they met in the blue salon and awaited the other guests who trickled in, one after another, until finally Lord Renwick and Sahib entered.

Reeves followed on Renwick's heels and, after clearing his throat so that his blind master would know he was there, announced that dinner was served.

Late that evening, once the women had gone up to bed, Alex rose to his feet. "I need a forum," he said, looking around at the others.

Miles instantly collected the cards with which he and Tony had played at cribbage. Ian set aside the newspaper he'd not managed to read earlier in the day.

Lord Renwick rose to his feet from the chair near the fire where he had been sitting, letting the bright firelight tease the bit of sight he had in his left eye. "Let us go into my study," he said. "I asked Reeves to set out a decanter of a rather nice port he recently acquired and I'd like your opinion of it. We'll taste it while we discuss Alex's problem."

Sahib paced beside Renwick, and the others followed. They crossed the entrance hall and entered the Renwicks' wing. None spoke until they reached Jase's study and the door closed behind them. Once all were settled, a glass beside each of them, Jase spoke again. "Alex? Has it to do with Miss Bigalow?"

"Indirectly. Lady Bigalow frets, so Artemisia worries about her."

"And you, therefore, worry about your Moonbeam," Ian finished for him, his deep, rumbling voice soothing.

"Yes."

"Well then, for what do we wait?" asked Miles. He held his glass to his nose and sniffed the delicate aroma.

"Wait? Are we waiting?"

Tony's expression suggested confusion but a hint of a smile played about Alex's mouth. "We await information concerning the whereabouts of Napoleon's English prisoners, of course," he said.

"You wouldn't!" Jase's head turned blindly from one to the other. "Oh, yes, of course you would!" He sighed at the notion of his friends risking their necks on French soil only to rescue a man they didn't even like! "Do you think it will be a new location? Someplace other than last time?"

"I don't know, do I? And going into France will be

dangerous enough that we needn't add the problem of searching the country from one end to the other."

"It hadn't occurred to me before that it was something any of us would need to know, but I'll see if I cannot get word from one of my contacts," said Miles. He went to Lady Renwick's desk and sat down. Very soon he had written out orders for those among his crew who, on rare occasions during the late war, had gone into France to return with information needed by the government. "There," he said, the folded and sealed note to his first mate in his hand. He moved to the bellpull and rang. A footman arrived promptly. "Ask my valet to come to me here, please," said Miles.

"You don't mean to send him off tonight?" asked Ian.

Miles's brows arched, revealing his surprise. "Why not?" He received no response. "The *Nemesis* must sail down the coast to where we keep a rather ratty-looking fishing boat moored. Three of my men, whose French is at least as good as mine, will cross the Channel to a certain village where they are believed to be French smugglers from farther down the coast. Since they are generous, they are taken in and their comings and goings ignored."

"You think they'll discover what we need to know?" asked Alex.

"We?" asked Miles with a lazy grin—the only thing lazy about him. "Surely, Alex, you do not think I'll risk my neck in France with *you* at my side! I will change my mind, of course, if you can prove to me you know even *one* ditty and can sing it in idiomatic French."

"You know I cannot, blast you." Alex scowled. "How can I ask you to go into danger that I do not face myself? Especially when it may very well be a thankless task. I cannot guarantee that Sir Vincent will want to return to England! But if he *does* wish it, there will be the impossible task of making *him* appear French for the duration of your escape to the coast!"

Miles smiled a rather wolfish grin. "Another reason for you to remain in England! You need never know how I manage that trick."

Alex eyed his friend. "Miles . . ."

"Don't ask, Alex. I assure you, you do not wish to know!" A comical expression lightened the situation. "Not, of course, that I know myself at this point!"

Alex turned to the wisest among them. "Ian, have I made an error? Is this going to compound my problems with Artemisia and her father?"

Ian looked at Jase, who reached over the side of his chair for Sahib, who rose up to stare from one man to another and then up at Lord Renwick.

"Uh-oh," said Alex softly when Ian did not instantly reassure him.

Ian grinned. "I am thinking."

"Thinking how to warn me that Miles will likely make things worse?"

"No. Thinking about how I would manage the trick if it were me." Ian stared into space. "I would," he said dreamily, "very much like to know what you have in your pharmacopoeia, Miles."

Miles chuckled. "I have traveled widely and am rabidly curious. You are correct to guess I've collected medicines no English doctor has seen. I have *seen* things no English doctor would *believe*. I had not thought of dipping into my supplies to facilitate this venture, but perhaps I will—" His lips pursed as he searched his mind. He shook his head. "—but only as a last resort."

Alex groaned. "Ian, now you've done it. I am lost!"

"But Sir Vincent will be angry with *me,* not with you," laughed Miles.

"Will he?" Alex continued in the driest of tones. "Why do I doubt that?"

The other men chuckled. "You must keep in mind

that your future wife's mother will be happy," said Miles.

"Yes, and if she is happy, then Artemisia will relax."

"There is one thing you have not mentioned, Alex."

"Yes?"

"If Sir Vincent is returned to England," said Ian, "then you will once again have no access to Miss Bigalow's company. Are you certain that is what you want?"

"What I want is irrelevant, is it not? Her happiness *is.*"

The men sat silent, sipping their wine, each contemplating their own separate thoughts.

Alex, for instance, had *not* previously considered how Sir Vincent's presence would interfere. He had enjoyed having Artemisia where they could walk and talk and he could be alone with her. And if their being under one roof put a strain on his willpower, it had proved that a life with his Moonbeam would be just as wonderful as he'd always dreamed.

Miles plotted and planned. He discarded several ideas before settling on one he was certain would work. Now—an almost silent sigh escaped him—he must wait in patience for information concerning Sir Vincent's whereabouts. Miles was ruefully aware that patience was not among those virtues that could be counted to his credit!

Ian and Tony were, secretly, thinking of their beds and Jason, feeling a trifle guilty, was thinking how nice it would be if his friends took themselves off to their rooms so that he could go to his own. To his bed where his lovely, wonderful Eustacia was already snuggled under the covers and, if he were lucky, still awake, waiting for him to join her.

Sahib, looking up and studying Jason's set features, rose to his feet. He nudged Jason, turned his head and snarled slightly at the other men, and then nudged

Jason again. Alex, startled by Sahib's grumbly noise, frowned. Then, deciding that the big cat had had enough of their company, he smiled. "I think I will take myself up to bed now. Are you coming?"

Ian and Tony rose with alacrity but Miles grunted.

"I said *are you coming?*"

Hearing Alex's tone, Miles blinked. Then he, too, noticed Sahib's expression. "Coming? Of course I am. If Sahib says it is time for bed, who am I to argue?"

Jason, not quite certain what was happening, rose to his feet. "Is Sahib making a nuisance of himself?" he asked.

"Heavens, no," said Alex. "The boot is on quite another foot. Or feet. It is we who are the nuisances." He yawned, surprising himself. "What is more, Sahib is correct. It *is* time to go to bed."

The next morning Alex's first thought was of Miles's offer to go into France to rescue Sir Vincent. His friend was right to refuse to take him, but, as he lay in bed thinking, Alex felt more and more concerned. Miles would go into danger and for what? To rescue a man they weren't certain wished rescue! A man who was such a fool he would *increase* Miles's danger even if he were *cooperative!*

Alex rose, pulled on his heavy silk robe, and checking that no one was in the hall, went to Miles's door. All in one motion, he gave a quick knock, opened the door, and entered.

Miles lay on his side, his chest and shoulders bare, a very small pistol pointed at Alex's chest.

"Confound it, Miles, what in the name of God are you about?"

Miles lay back, one hand caressing the pistol held by the other. "Alex, if I have never warned you, I had better do so now. You must never come in on me unexpectedly. I have lived a life where all too often action comes first and thinking later. Don't startle me into rash behavior."

"Waking you from a sound sleep startles you?" Alex felt his heartbeat settle to a more normal rate.

"Hmm. You are lucky I was not so *very* sound asleep!" Miles rose in one smooth movement, hid his bare skin under a robe even more garish than the one worn by Alex, and put the pistol in his pocket. He stretched and yawned. "Now," he said, "what was so important you almost got yourself shot?"

"I cannot let you go into France. It would not be right."

"It would be right for you to do it?"

"No. I would fail."

Miles grinned. "You have that right. Do we have any notion how many men were caught in Napoleon's web? And if anyone important is among them?"

"Not yet."

"Blast." Miles sighed. "I'll just have to wait until we know more."

"Didn't you hear me? I cannot let you do this! For all we know, Sir Vincent will try to buy Napoleon's good will by abetting your capture!"

Miles laughed. "Alex, I wish you had more faith in me. I have thought of that possibility. And countered it. I have thought of *everything!*"

Alex sighed. "You *want* to do this, don't you?"

A tight grin and sparkling eyes answered that question.

"I will never understand you. You *enjoy* danger!"

Miles shrugged. "Perhaps it is that one feels more alive when one knows death is just around the corner."

Alex shuddered at the thought. "I could never live by that philosophy! And if anything were to happen to you . . ."

". . . *On my head be it!* Come Alex, this is the sort of thing I have done all my life. A little adventure of this sort is bread and butter to me. In fact, life has felt rather flat ever since my usefulness to the government ended with Napoleon's abdication. Sailing to

France to bring you back only whetted my appetite and I have been dreaming of finding an excuse to return to my ship!"

"But this will be far different from merely chasing after smugglers who are unable to defend themselves to any great extent. You could have the whole of the French army on your trail!"

Miles laughed. "Why? When I will be French and *part* of the army?"

Alex blinked rapidly several times. "Part of . . ."

". . . the French army." Miles's grin was infectious. "I have a plan, you see."

"I have a feeling I don't want to know!"

"Which is just as well since I never discuss my plans. Now go away. I hear the maid who brings my hot water." He rubbed his chin, a raspy noise the result. "If she has followed her usual routine, yours will already be in your room. Unless you like shaving with tepid water, you'd best go use it!"

Alex went.

And spent every moment that he could manage of the ensuing days with Artemisia, both before and after Miles departed from Tiger's Lair. A mild touch of desperation was added to their relationship now. Both knew it could end at any moment.

One day a white-faced Libby came into where her husband played chess with Lord Renwick, one of the few games he could still play. "What is it?" Tony asked his wife, rising so quickly he tipped the board.

"I've a letter from Willy," she said, speaking as she went to him, her hands outstretched. "His regiment is off to Belgium within the week."

"You wish to see him before he goes."

"Please?" Libby stepped on a pawn, picked it up, and realizing what had happened, begged Lord Renwick's pardon for interrupting the game, but then turned back to Tony. "I know you are worried about Miles, Tony, but I am so afraid for Willy."

"Miles has been taking care of himself for years now. Willy has not." Tony grasped his wife's hand. "My dear," he said, "the solution is simple. The English who did not go to Vienna seem to be leaving for Brussels in droves. I see no reason why we may not go as well. And then you can see your brother whenever he isn't occupied with his duty!"

The Wendovers left the next day.

And the day following, Ian and Jason came into where the women sat. "We've had word," said Ian.

"Is everything all right?" asked Lady Bigalow, grasping her daughter's hand.

"All is well and about two hours from now Miles will arrive. There will be a rather large group of men and a few women in the party." Jason grinned. "I suppose one might have expected Miles to rescue the whole lot of them!"

"My husband is one of them?"

"Sir Vincent is, of course, one of them."

Artemisia clasped her hands tightly. "Mother . . ."

"Hmm? Oh, my dear!" Lady Bigalow's happy smile faded. "I had not thought!"

"I had."

Lady Bigalow smiled again but it was one of sympathy. "Off with you."

"He was headed," offered Lord Renwick, knowing for whom Miss Bigalow would be searching, "for the billiards room when last I spoke to him."

Artemisia felt heat rushing up her throat, but she smiled, nodded, and then thanked his lordship aloud for the information when it occurred to her that he could not see her silent appreciation. Her skirts swished softly as she moved through the halls to the game room. Once she reached it she stood in the doorway, one hand pressed to the jamb and watched Alex make his shot.

Prince Ravi marked it up and turned. He saw her. Artemisia raised a finger to her lips and he nodded, grinning. Alex made his next shot as well. And the next. Then he missed. He moved back from the table and, from the corner of his eye, saw Artemisia's skirts. He turned.

They looked at each other for a long moment and then Alex handed his cue stick to Ravi and went to her. He took the hands she offered him and held them tightly. "What is it, my love?" he asked.

"They will arrive soon. My father will . . ." She fell silent, biting her lip and staring at him with widened eyes.

"Will," he finished for her, "very likely be exceedingly angry to find you under the same roof as I." Alex nodded. "Should I go?"

"Go?" She frowned. "No, of course not."

"I have thought about it. If you think it would ease things, then I will do so."

She squeezed his hands. "No. You must not leave. The Renwicks are your friends and they have been kind to us. If anyone leaves, then it should be my parents. And—" She sighed. "—myself."

"Sir Vincent will wish to do just that."

"Yes."

"I have enjoyed having you near. It has been quite wonderful to be able to walk with you and talk with you. To—" His voice lowered still more. "—steal a kiss and not fear discovery."

Artemisia glanced beyond Alex, and he looked over his shoulder. Prince Ravi had moved to the far end of the room, but watched them, his curiosity obvious.

"Come, love. Let us walk in the garden once more."

They didn't walk for long, but found one of the several rose-covered arbors set here and there among the flowerbeds. And once hidden among the sweet-smelling flowers, they turned into each other's arms and, for a while, it was enough just to hold and be held. And then they talked. Seriously. And kissed.

Far too soon they heard a cavalcade of carriages

turn up the drive to Tiger's Lair. Alex pulled Artemisia close, held her head to his shoulder for a long moment, and then set her away from him.

"I will tell him as soon as I can," she said.

"You are certain you wish to do this?" he asked.

"Quite certain. Mother understands. I have discussed it with her."

"Then I am a very happy man. I would be even happier if I were certain *you* would not regret it."

"I will be sad that I am forbidden communication with my mother, but it is more than time that you and I were married. My father is not a bad man, but he isn't very wise, I think. I cannot allow him to ruin three lives."

"It is an exaggeration to say your mother's life will be ruined by our wedding, is it not?"

"I am her main support."

"Perhaps," suggested Alex, "she might have a lady to live with her, someone to take your place?"

"She will say it is impossible that anyone take my place, but I agree that she should hire someone to keep her company. I will discuss the possibility with her."

After a moment Alex, reluctantly, said, "We must go in."

After another long moment, Artemisia responded, "I know."

With neither saying a word, they came together for one more mind-drugging kiss.

The English refugees from France had, for the most part, remained in their rooms but a few joined the company for dinner. Miles, of course, was their hero and could not avoid their constant praise and thanks. After the meal ended, he found Lord Renwick.

"I cannot bear it."

"That they are conscious of what they owe you?"

"It isn't that so much as that, once an adventure is ended, I find it ridiculous to go over and over it. I am leaving. I wanted to tell you so you'd not worry."

"I understand. Whether those you benefited will do so is another question entirely."

"What *they* think is irrelevant. Only we Six and your wives are of concern to me. Beyond that I care not a jot what is said of me. But since you understand, then I won't worry that you'll be insulted when I sneak away. You will explain to the others, of course?"

"Oh no, I will let them wonder and comment and carry on . . ."

Jason grinned when Miles reached out and gave him a friendly shove—immediately followed by a hand steadying him when the unexpected thrust moved him off balance. Sahib immediately stepped between the two and stared up at Miles.

"Sorry, Sahib," said Miles. "I didn't think."

The big tiger growled softly.

"Yes, of course, I will remember in future."

Jason sighed. "Sahib becomes more protective the older he grows. I do worry about how he will behave when he is old and cross!"

Sahib rubbed gently against Jason's legs.

"I believe he is telling you that you need feel no concern, Jase," said Miles.

"I will try to believe it. Now, will you at least come to the salon for the remainder of the evening?"

Miles grimaced. He sighed. For a long moment he dithered, making Jason laugh. Miles sighed again. "I suppose I must," he said.

They entered just as Sir Vincent was, for the umpteenth time, telling how Miles had arrived with several "soldiers." " . . . his men dressed in French uniforms, you know." A heel-clicking officer to the bone, Miles had handed over orders that the prisoners, all of them, were to be moved to a chateau farther south.

"Did you guess what was happening?" asked his wife, knowing her role in her husband's story-telling efforts.

"Not a notion of it, don't you agree, Masterson?"

"Hmm? Oh yes, Sir Vincent. We were all exceedingly surprised when we reached the coast and were herded into boats and rowed out to the *Nemesis*."

Sir Vincent pouted. He was not pleased to have his tale cut short in that manner. "But," he said, "hadn't you guessed something was odd? I mean, we rode on and on in that rough farm cart, with very few chances to stretch our legs or even to eat properly."

"We were prisoners of war, Sir Vincent," said the man he'd called Masterson. "One does not expect the best treatment when one is a prisoner." Masterson turned away and joined several other men who had gathered in one of the window alcoves overlooking the drive.

"My dear, it must have been terrible," said Lady Bigalow before her husband could work himself into a passion of one sort or another. "Were you badly fed the whole time?"

"No. Merely while we traveled."

"You will recall," said Miles, speaking near his shoulder, "that I and my men ate no better."

"Should have planned our escape better. Should not have had to starve us as well as jounce us along in that cart and keep us in the dark as to what was happening."

"Well, as to that last, I was afraid to let you know you were being rescued!"

"Afraid? Nonsense. Didn't we all wish to escape? Didn't we all gnash our teeth daily and rant and rave and swear that Napoleon should roast over coals for incarcerating us?"

"I couldn't know that. And you, Sir Vincent, have made no secret that you support the monster. How was I to know that you would not give us away to any passing French official?"

Sir Vincent blustered without really saying anything for some moments. Finally, red spots appeared high on his cheeks. "Admit it. I was wrong. Not a great man at all!"

Lady Bigalow blinked. She glanced at her daughter, who sat nearby, her hands in her lap and a sad expression marring her looks. The two locked gazes. It was the first time *ever* that either had heard Sir Vincent admit to being wrong!

"Didn't know he was so stupid. Nor that he was so . . . so . . . *little*. Why, I think my daughter has as many inches as Napoleon!"

"Perhaps not quite, but no one ever said he had great stature, did they?"

"Don't know. Didn't pay any heed. Made up my mind and that was that. Always make up my mind in a hurry. Quick that way. And never wrong."

"But you have just admitted to being wrong about Napoleon," said Artemisia softly.

"Eh? Eh? Oh, that. Well, but I didn't know, did I?"

"Didn't know what, Father?"

"That the man would throw my—"

His wife, daughter and Miles began speaking all at once and rather loudly, drowning out the rest of what was said.

"—offer of help in my face," he finished.

"I think, my dear, it would be best if you forget you ever made such an offer," said Lady Bigalow softly, her hand on her husband's arm. "It might be interpreted as treason by those who think of such things."

Sir Vincent blanched. "But . . . but . . ." he sputtered. He glanced at Miles, who nodded his agreement with Lady Bigalow. "But . . . but . . ."

"You had best forget it. I will do so for the sake

of my friends," said Miles, and turned on his heel and walked away.

Sir Vincent appeared to shrink. "I'm tired," he whined.

"You have had a difficult time of it. I think we should go up to bed," said her ladyship in soothing tones. "Lady Renwick will chaperone our daughter."

"Harrumph. Chaperone."

Sir Vincent's eyes narrowed and he scanned the room but didn't catch a glimpse of the man he was almost certain he had seen sitting far down the table from his own place. But surely not. Surely his wife would not have gone against his wishes and allowed Artemisia to live in the same house as that blasted Tory who had the nerve to wish to wed her! No, of course his wife would do no such thing.

"Yes, let us go up. I am very tired indeed." He didn't offer his arm to his wife, but allowed her to trail in his wake.

Prince Ravi, noticing, thought it was the first time since arriving in England that he had seen a wife showing proper respect for her husband. Most insisted they walk at their man's side. In the East such arrogance in a woman would be punished. It was good to see this Lady Bigalow had a proper notion of her place!

He said as much to his tutor and as a result endured a lecture on the notion that women were not merely necessary animals in the scheme of things. He was ill pleased by both the scold and the notions his tutor wished him to consider.

"It is not thus in my father's kingdom," he said with all the arrogance of his future position as a hereditary and tyrannical ruler. *"You* would have me begin a revolution when I go home." And, having made his point as he thought, he turned on his heel and left the room.

Prince Ravi went directly to the billiards room,

where he found Lord Merwin alone, idly playing a game of billiards against himself. "My lord," said the boy, "Sir Vincent has taken himself up to bed. Your Miss Bigalow was, I thought, looking exceedingly forlorn. Perhaps you should go and see to making her happy again!"

Then the prince took himself off to his own bed, quite pleased with the mischief he'd wrought. He had, after all, been warned that Sir Vincent would not approve of Lord Merwin coming anywhere near his daughter!

TEN

Two days passed and Alex, walking in the garden with Artemisia, was confused. His Moonbeam's father should have been seething. He should have been ranting and raving. He should have been insisting that he and his wife and daughter leave Tiger's Lair on the instant.

Sir Vincent did none of those things.

"Moonbeam, have you spoken with your father? Is that why he has not yet landed me a facer or taken you off and locked you in a nunnery?"

Artemisia blushed, shaking her head. "Mother asked me to wait until he had recovered some before throwing myself on his mercy."

"Which means you have not been disinherited and your name crossed off the family tree. So why does he act as if I do not exist? Why has he not torn you from this tainted house?"

Artemisia smiled. "I asked Mother if she had spoken to him. She says not."

"Then I do not understand it."

"Nor I. I merely count my blessings. We have had two more days together than I thought we would manage. I cannot look beyond the wonder of that."

"It certainly is a wonder! Ah well, I too will count my blessings. There come some of the men rescued along with your father. Shall we turn down this path and avoid them or should we join them?"

"Turn."

They did and, just beyond the next hedge, wished they had not. "Mrs. Marchcomer," said Alex, bowing slightly. "And Mr. Renwick. Out enjoying this wonderful weather, I assume?"

"It is quite wonderful, is it not?" said Edith Marchcomer. She took a firmer hold on Mr. Renwick's arm and smiled up at him. "Really a marvel. We have had such wonderful weather ever since arriving here at this delightful estate. And it is said we may enjoy still more sun and warmth and . . ."

"Hush, my dear," said Mr. Renwick softly, gently.

Edith pouted but she ceased her gushing.

"We have discussed the possibility of going up to London," said Lord Renwick's cousin when he was certain her tongue was stilled. "Several couples leave tomorrow and we thought we might join them. I would not wish dear Mrs. Marchcomer to suffer the indignity of traveling without a chaperon and there will be two other women in the party."

"I *must* see my modiste, you see," said Edith. She cast such a roguish look at Mr. Renwick that no one could avoid realizing there was more to their journey than that.

Mr. Renwick sent a quick look toward Alex, noted his expression and, on a sigh, suggested, "Shall we continue our walk? Together?"

Somehow he maneuvered them so he strolled with Alex while Artemisia and Edith walked on ahead. When the two pairs were separated by a stretch of path, Mr. Renwick spoke softly. "I have told Edith of the old scandal. I would not woo her and leave her in ignorance of what is said of me."

"I believe she is safe enough with you—even if what is said is true. Her fortune is tied up in such a way that at her death it goes to a religious organization of which I've never heard but which I was informed sends missionaries to the heathen. You will protect her, I am certain, from any possible accident."

Renwick's lips tightened. "I am innocent of those old charges but cannot prove it. Have you any notion what it is to live with suspicion? With the fear I see in some eyes, the horror in others, the knowledge I am thought a murderer?"

"I can believe it is exceedingly unpleasant."

"It is the primary reason I live abroad. Edith and I will reside in Naples."

"The devil you will!" said Alex, startled into swearing. "Have you informed her?"

Trey cast him a look of curiosity. "We have not yet discussed it."

"Are you aware the lady is extremely susceptible to *mal de mer?* If she discovers you expect her to board a ship, she will turn tail and run from you as fast as she can."

"Ah. She has mentioned that she was very ill when returning to England. I must discover if she suffered crossing to France. Perhaps it is the size of the boat which caused her difficulties."

"Perhaps. Shall we join the ladies? I will be quite honest that I much prefer my love's company to yours. The worst of it is that I expect, every moment, to be deprived of it, so I am spending as much time as possible with her."

"Deprived of it?"

"Her father disapproves of me."

Mr. Renwick turned disbelieving eyes on Alex.

"I am a Tory, you see," said Alex.

"So are many. If I were anything I suppose I'd be one!"

Alex laughed. "Yes, but Sir Vincent is a Whig. He doesn't want his family contaminated by my politics."

"Ah! I see. Well, I wish you the best of luck."

"But you don't see a happy ending."

"Frankly, no."

"Then you see why it is important that we waste none of our opportunities." Alex bowed slightly and, picking up speed, joined the ladies. "Miss Bigalow," he said, offering his arm, "I believe Lady Renwick said something about a riding party. Will you join me?"

"Of course."

She took his arm and, after saying all that was polite to Mrs. Marchcomer and Mr. Renwick, she and Alex turned down a path that might have taken them to the house . . . but did not. "I haven't a riding habit, as you well know," she half scolded and half teased. "What is more, Edith knows I have not! Could you think of no better excuse for parting from those two?"

"No. Was she very tiresome?"

"Very," was the dry response. "I noticed you and Mr. Renwick got on rather well."

"Oh, very well indeed. He hinted that he and Mrs. Marchcomer are to wed and I communicated that her fortune was tied up in the odd way of which you told me and he said he was exceedingly tired of the suspicion surrounding the death of his first wife. That he was innocent."

"Do you think he is?"

"I haven't a notion. But I believe that Mrs. Marchcomer will be safe—unless her inane conversation bores him to the point he murders her merely to stop her tongue!"

"She told me they mean to live in London."

He lowered his voice. *"He* means them to live in Naples."

"She will never agree. It would mean a sea voyage!"

"I warned him, but I suspect there is more to Lord Renwick's cousin than we know. He will manage the trick somehow."

"Then she must have a maid with her! One who will *not* suffer when on the water!"

"I am glad *you* do not." He glanced down at her.

She, looking up, met his quizzical gaze. "You've a reason to feel glad?"

"If we wed," he countered, "do you think you would care to visit the United States of America?"

"Ah. I see. Still another sea journey. I have never given a thought to visiting our old colonies. Why do you ask?"

Alex sighed. "We've heard the war there is over. Which means peace talks. It is possible the meetings will be in London, of course, and the journey unnecessary. I have been recommended as a junior member."

"Recommended, were you? What that means is that they want you and your excellent handwriting, someone trustworthy to act as scribe to secret discussions!"

Alex laughed. "Very likely. You have not said if you would come with me if I accept their offer."

"I would go with you to the ends of the earth. You know that."

Alex glanced around. He had—rather deftly, he thought—led them into a glade where a spring bubbled up and a rill burbled away over stones. They were alone and private. He pulled her into his arms and drew her head up. Her lips met his eagerly. The kiss deepened and his arms tightened.

Finally he lifted his head. "Ah, Artemisia. My life, my dearest love."

Artemisia laid her head against his chest. "I must have that little talk with Father."

"Yes." Alex drew in a deep breath. "I very much fear you must." His arms tightened still more. "I don't want to let you go."

"I don't want you to let me go," she responded softly.

Her words brought Alex to his senses and, reluctantly, he released her. "We'd best be getting back to the house. Where there are other people."

They smiled at each other. Their gazes locked, their

smiles faded and, their emotions still more than a trifle overwrought, they moved back into each other's embrace.

"Vincent, I cannot understand what is the matter with you. You say you are not ill, that you need no more rest, but you do not eat properly and you mope around in corners and seem to only want to be left alone." Lady Bigalow took his hand between hers but he turned his head away and freed himself from her grip. "Will you not explain?' she coaxed.

"That Mr. Seward."

"Yes. We bless him for rescuing you and the others from that awful man."

"From Napoleon." His shoulders hunched and the hands he held clasped between his legs tightened. "But I only wanted . . . !"

"Yes dear?"

"He . . . he . . ."

Lady Bigalow nodded. "The monster had you arrested just like any other Englishman," she said, sympathy in her voice.

"He . . . he . . ."

"Yes, dear?"

Sir Vincent hung his head, his hand coming to clasp his wife's. "He wanted me to vow allegiance to him. To France! How could he be so stupid?"

"He . . . !"

Sir Vincent looked up, tears glistening in his eyes. "Why didn't he understand, Penny?"

Lady Bigalow felt a slight shock. It had been years since Sir Vincent had called her Penny.

"Why?" he repeated.

She spoke slowly, carefully thinking about her choice of words. "Perhaps, my dear, he is a man who must have everything. All must bow to him, to his wishes. He can never be satisfied with a partial victory, or dictating to *most* of Europe. He must have it *all*."

Sir Vincent raised shocked eyes to lock with his wife's. "You mean *England*?" She nodded. "But that's not right."

"I agree."

"But . . . but . . ."

"Yes, dear?"

"But *Napoleon*. How can he . . . he . . ."

". . . be other than perfect?" suggested Lady Bigalow.

Two spots of color appeared high on Sir Vincent's cheeks. "You would say no one is perfect." He pouted.

"I fear we are all human, Vinny."

"Don't call me that!" He scowled and released her hand. "You know I dislike it of all things."

"Do you, dear? You used to like it." She smiled at him, a rather coy smile.

Sir Vincent's features twisted one way, then the other. Then he giggled. "I did, didn't I?"

"Hmm."

"Oh well." He tipped one toe and wiggled it into the carpet. Then he cleared his throat. "Oh well, but that was a very long time ago. You—" His brows drew together. "—are trying to distract me!"

"Is it working?" she asked, as innocently as she could.

He laughed. "Well, maybe." The laugh faded and he sobered. "My dear Lady Bigalow, have I ever told you—" A blush reddened his ears. "—you have been a very good wife to me?"

"No." Her eyes widened and this time she was not pretending. "Never."

"Well, you have. I am glad you escaped with Artemisia and I am very sorry I did not stay in Paris and go with you! You will never know how bad it was. Always watched. The food was . . . was . . ."

"Very French?" she suggested.

"Yes. You know I cannot stomach all that strange stuff, all those sauces covering stuff up so you don't know what it is! And the accommodations! We were crowded into a small chalet. Everyone was forced to share and—" This time one tear escaped and ran down Sir Vincent's cheek. "—I did not like it at all."

"No, of course not. Is it not a good thing—" She paused and then, firming her chin, continued. "Lord Merwin realized I was fretting. Worrying about you? He talked to the others and Mr. Seward laid a plan for rescuing you."

"Yes, well, as to that!" Sir Vincent scowled. "Do you know we were within a mile of the coast before he told us he was English and that there was a ship awaiting us?"

"You sound angry."

"He didn't trust us!"

"Perhaps he could have trusted most of you, but *all* of you had to act as if you were still prisoners and what if there was someone among you who was unable to pretend?"

"Oh." Sir Vincent mused about that. "Didn't think of that," he added after a moment. Again silence fell. Then he asked, "Did you say Lord—" He swallowed and tried again. "—Lord . . ."

"Lord Merwin. He saved *us* and then, *thanks to him,* you were saved."

"That's what Mr. Seward said," said Sir Vincent morosely. "Said I had him to thank."

"Him?"

"Lord . . . Lord . . ."

"Lord Merwin."

"I don't *want* him to marry our Artemisia! He's a . . . a . . . one of those unspeakable sorts," he finished in a low tone and pouted.

"He is a good man and he loves our Artemisia with all his heart."

"Love. Love is not so important. Other things are far more serious. Like a man's politics!"

"My dear, I dislike suggesting that, occasionally, even when his politics are the right sort, a man may be wrong. You see, I cannot help thinking of your experience with Napoleon!"

"I still say he is a great man. Misguided, of course, but the man Europe needs to set it to rights. Why will they not recognize it?"

"Vinnie, do you think that perhaps Napoleon *was* that man *at one time,* but that perhaps his successes went to his head and he has changed from a man of great ideas into a . . . a *despot?"*

"No." Sir Vincent looked shocked. "Not possible. Couldn't have." He shook his head back and forth. "Impossible."

Lady Bigalow just looked at him.

"Surely it is impossible?" he asked a trifle wistfully.

Still Lady Bigalow said nothing.

"Not?"

"Not at all. Quite possible. Power often turns a man who would, otherwise, live a decent life into—" Calling Napoleon a monster, she decided, would be going too far. "something else."

Sir Vincent sighed. "He didn't seem such a great man when I saw him. Rude and caustic and . . . and really quite nasty. To *me!"* He pointed to his chest, his outrage obvious.

"Very shortsighted of him, dear. I am so very glad you are returned safely and out of his power."

"You cannot know what it was like! Why . . ."

Lady Bigalow had already heard the tale several times and expected to hear a great many versions on a great number of occasions in the future. She did as she always did when listening to her husband. She turned her mind to planning the rest of her day.

When she heard the tone that indicated Sir Vincent

was at the end of his monologue, she looked up. "Yes, my dear," she said, "but that is all in the past. It is the future we must consider. You *will* say all that is proper to Lord Merwin, will you not?"

Sir Vincent shuddered. "You suggest I must be polite to one of those unspeakable . . . unspeakable—" His voice dropped to a whisper. "—Tories? That I am in debt to the man who wishes to steal away my Artemisia!"

"Yes."

He slumped. "That's what I feared you meant."

"So?"

"You won't make me—" He glanced at her and quickly away. "Will you?"

"You will make yourself," she said, her tone firm. "You would hate yourself forever if you were less than a gentleman."

"Would I?"

"Of course you would."

He sighed. "Well, all right then. I will do it."

"When?"

"When?"

"Yes. When?"

"Er . . . soon?"

She stared at him. He ducked his head, then peeked at her. "Very well, Vincent," she said. "Just be sure it *is* soon." She turned on her heel and left him scowling into the small fire Reese had had built in the Bigalows' room.

ELEVEN

"Well," said Lord Renwick two days later as he groped across the bed for his wife, "they have all gone." Hours earlier they had waved off still another carriage.

"Not quite. Ian and Serena are here," said her ladyship, snuggling into him.

"They don't count."

"And the Bigalows appear to be settled in for a long stay."

"Ah. The Bigalows. And for Alex's sake, we must not hint them away?"

"Exactly."

"I wonder if Alex knows what he owes us!"

"I think he is cognizant of his debt," laughed Lady Renwick. "He apologized to me this morning. That was after he rescued me from Sir Vincent, who had gone on and on and on until I thought I would scream."

"Exactly how did he manage to get you away from the old bore?"

"He told me there was an emergency in the kitchen and I was needed. And then, poor soul, he remained in my place, listening to that idiotic man talk and talk and say nothing at all. Or, if he ever manages to say something interesting, he repeats it until one goes mad. How has Lady Bigalow lived with him all these years?" She pulled the comforter up over her shoul-

ders and Lord Renwick's and yawned. "I would have
gone mad within the first year."

In another bedroom, up a floor and in the other
wing, Lady Bigalow poked her husband. "Vincent."
He snored. "Vincent I know you are not asleep."

He sighed and rolled onto his back. "What is it?"

"Did you do it?"

Silence.

"Well, did you?"

"Did I do what?"

She gritted her teeth. "Did you thank Lord Merwin
for saving you from France."

"He didn't save me."

Lady Bigalow could almost hear her husband pouting. She drew in a deep breath and let it out through
her nose.

"Miles Seward saved me."

"My dear Vinny, you know exactly what I mean.
Were it not for Lord Merwin, Mr. Seward would never
have thought to go into France. I know you are a big
enough man that you can do what is proper and thank
him."

"Big enough man, hmm?"

"Of course. You have always been the epitome of
a gentleman and it is the part of a gentleman to thank
his benefactor, so you, Sir Vincent, will thank Lord
Merwin."

"Well . . ."

"You will uphold the values bred into you for gen-
erations."

"Well . . ."

"You will prove to the world that the Bigalows are
worth a dozen of any other family."

For a long moment there was only silence. And
then, mumbled in a voice barely to be heard, he said,
"Oh, all right."

"You will do it?"

"I will and as soon as I do, then we may leave. We

can go home. And our daughter will cease sitting in that devil's pocket."

"Not a devil. Your benefactor!"

Sir Vincent growled.

"But, Vinny, he *is*."

"But I don't want him to be anything at all to me."

"What you want doesn't change what is, does it?"

Sir Vincent had no answer to that and, after a moment, Lady Bigalow turned on her side and fell asleep. Sir Vincent, however, lay there wondering how he had come to be in a position of being in debt to a dratted *Tory*. Finally he, too, fell asleep.

And downstairs in the conservatory, a nearly full moon giving just enough light so they needed no other, Miss Bigalow and Lord Merwin stood, one on either side of the potting table, talking softly.

"So you have not found a proper time to tell Sir Vincent we are to be wed?"

"Oh, Alex, I feel such a fool. Every time I decide that I will do it, I have glimpsed my mother and remember his threats to keep us apart. Alex, what am I to do? I cannot bear to think of never seeing her again and yet I need you so desperately. Is there no solution?"

"Do you remember when we first arrived and I would not tell you what we were discussing about Sahib?"

"You said something about hope?"

"Yes. Hope that Sahib would do something to solve our problem."

"Sahib? You suggest the *tiger* will help us?"

Alex nodded. "Sahib helped the others."

"Renwick's tiger has . . . ?" She stared. "But what can an animal do?"

Alex chuckled. "You would be surprised. Shall I tell you what he did for my friends when their affairs were not going well?"

"You mean your married friends? I recall that Miles

said it was hopeless to try and help him and Sahib roared."

"So he did. You see, Sahib has put a paw into the arrangement of each marriage." He came around the table and led her to a bench where he seated her. Pacing in front of her, he told her stories of how four of the Six came to be happily married.

Artemisia listened, laughing softly now and then, and, when Alex finished, nodded. "I see. Yes, it is clear now. We need Sahib!"

"If he has not yet returned Sahib to his proper place, I will speak to Jason in the morning. When there are many strangers about, Sahib resides in his cage, but now we are alone again, why, there is no reason at all that he not return to Jase's side!"

"None whatsoever."

They looked at each other and their gazes locked. Artemisia giggled. Alex laughed. They joined hands and Artemisia rose to her feet. Alex dropped his grip, clasped his hands behind his back, and stepped away two paces. "It is late, my love. I'll escort you to your door."

Artemisia just looked at him.

Alex shook his head.

She nodded hers and stepped forward.

Alex stepped back.

Artemisia moved quickly, putting her arms around his neck and leaning into him.

Alex's arms came around her but still he shook his head.

"Just one?"

"No."

"Why?"

"Because I cannot stop with just one. And it gets harder and harder to stop at all." His arms tightened. "Artemisia, don't make it impossible for me to remain a gentleman in my own eyes."

She stared. Finally she dropped her gaze and

sighed. "Very well." Her hand on his chest, she pushed gently, only to find his arms did not loosen. She looked up. Slowly a smile spread, making her eyes sparkle in the moonlight. "Is it too late?" she asked.

A mild groan escaped him. "Far too late," he said softly. "Far, *far* too late!"

"Sahib? Why not?" asked Lord Renwick the next day. "I'd have gone for him yesterday, but thought that perhaps I should wait until the Bigalows were gone. But I've missed having him where I can touch him whenever I wish. Visiting him two or three times a day is not the same. If you think it all right, then we shall go get him."

Jason and Alex strolled out to Sahib's huge cage. The big cat either smelled them or heard them coming. He roared and was waiting at the entrance when they arrived. Once out of the cage he was very like a kitten, rubbing against Lord Renwick on one side and then on the other. From his throat came the odd chuffing sound that was a tiger's purr.

"How does he know we have come to take him into the house?" asked Alex when Sahib headed down the path.

"I haven't a notion, but, somehow, he knows."

"He is halfway to the door. Shall we go as well? I cannot wait until Sahib meets my Moonbeam's father!"

Lord Renwick chuckled. "You will ask Sahib to convince the man you should wed Miss Bigalow?"

Sahib waited for them and, at those words, looked at Alex, but then turned back to Renwick. He rubbed very gently against Jase and then, bumping Jase's hand, he opened his mouth in one of his nearly silent roars. Alex and Jason took the hint and immediately started on to the house and breakfast. Unfortunately, from Alex's point of view, he and Jase finished eating before Sir Vincent and his wife came down. Nor had Artemisia shown her face.

Jase went to his study to put in an hour or two working with Lady Renwick, who acted as his scribe. Alex decided that since Sahib was unavailable to do whatever it was he would do, if he could do, then he, too, would not wait for the Bigalows. He took himself off to the stable where he ordered a horse saddled so that he could go riding with Ian.

Artemisia, looking out her window, saw them ride down the lane. Her long hair, which she had risen early to wash, was finally dry and now that she was ready to go down, what had happened? She sighed softly. She was in a fit state to join him but her love took himself off and out of the way! Artemisia went down to breakfast and discovered her parents were the only ones eating.

"Good morning," she said. She hesitated, wondering if now would be a good time to tell her father she meant to wed Alex, with or without his blessing. After their *tête-à-tête* the preceding evening, she knew it was more than time she did so. Lost in thought, trying to decide how she should phrase what she had to say, she merely nodded when her mother asked if she'd like a cup of tea. She accepted the plate with her customary dollop of shirred eggs, small piece of ham, and breakfast roll that the footman set before her without her usual smile of thanks.

"What is it, dear?" asked her mother, a frown creasing her brow very slightly. "Why are you so preoccupied?"

"Preoccupied?" asked her father with a sneer. "Lovesick, you mean. It is disgusting. A *Tory!* When will you understand, my dear child, that love is of all things the *least* important when it comes to choosing a husband? Of most importance is whether the man will fit into our family, whether he will enhance our prestige, and, last but not least, whether he will add wealth to our coffers!"

"Perhaps he will not fit with *one* member of our family, but you must admit he is a good—" Tears slipped from her eyes. "—man and he is certainly wealthy, which *you* find important. In fact—" She rose to her feet, leaning forward with her hands supporting her, "—he is one of the very best matches in the. *ton* and he is *mine*. I mean to marry him. Soon." Artemisia stood up and pointed at her father. *"You* object to him because you dislike admitting you are ever wrong. But you *were* wrong, were you not?" When her father glared, she added, "About Napoleon?"

Her father's glare faded and he seemed to shrink slightly. "Is it not possible you are wrong in this case, too?" Artemisia stared at him for a moment, but he didn't respond. She gave a weak laugh and left the breakfast room.

Sir Vincent toyed with a finger of toast. "It is too bad of you, Penelope. You say I must thank that . . . that . . ."

"Lord Merwin?"

". . . and my daughter insists she means to marry him. What have I ever done that I have been put in this truly awful position?"

Lady Bigalow considered explaining exactly what he had and had not done, but decided it would do no good. Sir Vincent was not a man who could be changed by something so simple as the truth or by mere logic! "Perhaps Artemisia is not entirely in the wrong, my dear. Have you not thought what a coup it would be if our daughter were to wed one of the young lions of the *ton?"*

"A coup?" Sir Vincent's eyes bulged. "To marry a *Tory?"*

"The *ton* doesn't worry so much about a man's politics, you know. It is his lineage and his fortune and whether he is good *ton*. Lord Merwin has everything to make him a particularly excellent *parti*."

Sir Vincent glared at her. "A wife is supposed to support her husband. You are doing your best to undermine me."

"No, dear. When we are private I sometimes point out to you things you may not have considered. That is all. I would never, ever, do anything to undermine your authority. That would not be a wifely act and you yourself told me I had been a good wife to you." She smiled, her eyes opened as wide as she could manage. When he didn't respond she went so far as to bat her lashes at him.

For a long moment he eyed her, suspicious. "Harrumph. Things I hadn't considered, hmm?"

"Yes, dear."

"A coup?"

"Oh yes."

"I'll think about it."

"But first you must remember to thank Lord Merwin for his part in setting forward your rescue."

"Drat it, Penelope, do you have to spoil my enjoyment of this really excellent breakfast? Can you not let a man eat in peace?"

"Oh dear. I wouldn't care to think I had destroyed your appetite. Since I have finished I will leave you. Do try the deviled kidneys, my love. You are fond of them and the Renwicks' cook has a particularly good touch with them." She patted her lips with the trailing edge of the tablecloth, no napkins having been provided, and stood up. "I believe our hostess meant to do the flowers this morning. I will join her and see if I can be of use to her."

Sir Vincent nodded. He asked the footman for a fresh pot of tea. His first sip burnt his mouth and, swearing softly, he abandoned his breakfast as well as the tea and went to the game room. At this time of day, he might expect to find some privacy there while everyone else was occupied, either by regular duties or by the divertissements offered for a guest's enjoyment.

Perhaps, if he tried very hard, he could manage to talk himself into a mood proper to telling that dratted Tory he was thankful to have been rescued from France and that he appreciated Lord Merwin's part in seeing it came about. That was his honest intention as he stepped through the door, but, instead of giving himself a proper lecture, Sir Vincent fell into a self-pitying mood in which he managed to convince himself that Napoleon was to blame for the intolerable situation in which he found himself by failing to be the man he was supposed to be!

While Sir Vincent mumbled and grumbled to himself, his daughter wandered disconsolately through the oldest rose garden. The blooms were coming on beautifully and the scent wafted on the warm breeze, surrounding her in a delightful manner. The sun shone. Somewhere high in the sky a lark sang.

It is all very beautiful, so why, wondered Artemisia, *can I not feel joyful? Why, when I have finally managed to tell my father I mean to wed Alex, am I so very unhappy?*

But she knew. It was obvious why. She was, once again, worrying about her mother. About how lonely she would be. How bored with only her father to keep her company. Was there nothing one could do? Nothing that would help? Artemisia decided to find her mother and talk to her, see if there wasn't something that could be done to change her father's mind.

She turned toward the house and stopped. She had been so deep in thought she'd not heard footsteps approaching behind her. "Lord Renwick," she said. "Are you and Sahib enjoying the roses?"

"I haven't a notion if Sahib enjoys them, but I do. My aunt planted the gardens when I returned from India, blind and exceedingly sorry for myself. I owe her a great deal for making my life as a blind man as comfortable as she knew how."

Artemisia held her fingers out to Sahib, who came to sniff them. "Alex told me how she found your wife for you."

Jason chuckled. "She didn't know she'd found me a wife. She thought she'd merely found me a secretary to help with my writing. He dropped his hand to the tiger's head but discovered his pet was not there. "Sahib made us understand we were meant for each other."

"Yes. Alex told me Sahib has played cupid for four of you."

"You sound wistful, my dear."

"Hmm. I wish there was some magic that would solve *our* problems. Those Alex and I have."

"I believe," said Jason, "that there is an arbor at the end of this path. Will you join me there and trust me enough to tell me your problem?"

Artemisia stared at Sahib, who stared back. She drew in a deep breath. "Yes. I think I will."

They adjourned to the arbor where, her eyes locked with the tiger's golden gaze, she explained her dilemma. ". . . so you see, either Alex and I are unhappy forever and ever or my mother is left bereft of my company forever and ever. It is not a conflict I can resolve. Whatever I do, it is wrong. All thanks," she said, her bitterness unhidden, "to my father's stubborn insistence he'll not have a Tory in the family."

"It is a problem. One sees that. Is there no one who could come live with your mother? Be a companion to her? It would not, of course, replace you in her life, but at least she would not be alone."

Artemisia drew in a deep breath. "Her dearest friend was widowed not long ago. Why did I forget that? They have been bosom bows forever. And I do not think Mrs. Carter was left so very well off. When she was forced into her marriage, her husband was a very rich man but, over the years, he made bad investments and frittered his substance away in his attempts to gain a foothold in the *ton*."

"Ah. A manufacturer, perhaps?"

"An India nabob. His people were respectable but made no pretense of being tonnish. He was a rather rough man and his wealth alone insufficient to make the hostesses accept him. I believe he belonged to one or two clubs, but that only added to his problems."

"Gambling?"

"I believe so. Something my mother once said . . ."

"So," suggested Renwick when she didn't finish, "Mrs. Carter might like living with your mother?"

"And Mother would certainly like it. Lord Renwick, thank you. It is not the solution I would prefer, but it will ease things a trifle."

"I am always glad to help my friends."

"But why me? *I* am not . . . ?"

"Oh, my dear," he interrupted, "as soon as Alex decided to wed you, then you became one of us. Did you not know? An instant circle of friends who will do its very best to support you and love you and help you in any way we can." Lord Renwick grinned. "There is a problem, of course."

"A problem?"

"You are expected to aid and abet us as well!"

"I cannot see that that is a problem," she said, smiling. "Sahib, you are a glorious animal, but would you mind moving just a trifle? I wish to tell your master adieu and go find my mother. If you have no objections, of course."

The big cat stood up, turned in a circle, and slid to the ground on Lord Renwick's other side.

For a moment Artemisia didn't move. Then, tentatively, she stood. "Well, then, adieu . . ."

Lord Renwick chuckled. "We are always surprised and a trifle shocked when Sahib appears to understand what we say to him. I have never quite managed to believe he *does* understand, but it has happened so often I also find it difficult to scoff at the notion." He dropped his hand to Sahib's head and the cat leaned into his leg. "He is an amazing animal. I believe I owe him even more than I owe my aunt. During those first years of my blindness, before I accepted I was blind forever and found ways to compensate, he helped me stay sane."

"He is very beautiful. If you will forgive me, Lord Renwick, I will go find my mother."

"You are excused, if that is what you wish me to say. We will meet again later, Miss Bigalow."

" 'Til later, then." Artemisia smiled. "Good-bye, Sahib."

Lady Bigalow was in the front hall positioning a large bouquet on the table that also held a silver tray for visiting cards and a pair of candlesticks. A mirror on the wall behind the table reflected the bouquet and her ladyship could not quite decide which side should be forward and which to the rear. "Artemisia, come help me. How would you place it?"

Artemisia turned the bouquet a trifle, studied it, turned it a bit more, and backed away. "There. I think that will do."

"Hmm. I see. It was that long, trailing flower bothering me and I did not know it. Now it is perfect."

"Mother, if you have finished helping Lady Renwick, could we have a little talk?"

"Of course." Lady Bigalow looked around. "Perhaps it would be best if I found a parasol and we strolled in the garden?"

"I know a very nice little glade not too far away." Artemisia, ever since she and Alex enjoyed a *tête-à-tête* in it, had had a fondness for the glade! "Shall we go there?"

Fifteen minutes later the two women were seated on the bench near the bubbling spring, the water running off over small rocks, burbling and chuckling and making other interesting noises.

"It is so peaceful here," said Lady Bigalow, lowering her parasol and laying it aside.

"I have enjoyed our stay with the Renwicks," said Artemisia.

"Yes. I will miss them when we leave."

"Mother . . . I apologize for dropping that brick at breakfast. I should have found a more tactful way of informing Father I mean to wed Alex. And I should certainly have warned you I meant to talk to him."

"I knew it was coming," said Lady Bigalow gently.

"I worry about you. If Father does not relent, will not allow us to see and talk to each other . . ."

"I will ask Mrs. Carter to come to me. I thought of it when I received my last letter from her."

Artemisia put her arms around her mother and hugged her. "How silly of me. Here I have been trying and trying to come up with a notion and you had the solution all along. I was talking with Lord Renwick about it and he suggested you might have someone live with you, and only then did I think of Mrs. Carter."

"It isn't as if I needed someone to take care of me, dear. Merely that I will need company."

They sat silent for a long time. "Mother?"

"Yes, dear?"

"I will miss you, but I need to marry Alex. I must."

"I know, dear."

They sighed. Artemisia slid her hand to one side. Her mother's hand moved a trifle. Then each moved just a bit more and their hands clasped tightly.

Sir Vincent wandered out of the game room and down the hall toward an exterior door. He couldn't make up his mind what to do with himself. "What I ought to do is make those women pack themselves up and take us all away from here," he muttered.

The door just behind him opened and Sahib stuck his head out.

Sir Vincent continued his muttering. "If we went away I wouldn't have to talk to that man."

Sahib came into the hall, his eyes on Sir Vincent.

"I would never have to see him again."

Sahib tipped his great head.

"Going away," said Sir Vincent, "would save my Arta from that monster!"

Sahib padded down the hall behind Sir Vincent and, just as he reached to open the door, squeezed in front of him. Startled, Sir Vincent froze. Sahib roared and the baronet jumped back. Sahib followed. Sir Vincent backed several steps. Sahib stalked him.

The two continued as far as the door from which Sahib had come into the hall where Sahib herded Sir Vincent into the room.

"Who is there?" asked Lord Renwick, dropping his hand to the side of his chair where Sahib usually lay. "Sahib?"

The cat growled softly.

"What is it?"

"Your . . . your . . ."

Lord Renwick recognized the sputtering voice. "Sir Vincent? Is that you?"

"Yes!"

The man didn't sound exactly comfortable and the tiger was acting strangely. Jason thought quickly. "Sahib, have you brought me company? How nice. Do come in, Sir Vincent. You can find a glass of something on the side table." Lord Renwick gestured toward the tray that Reeves had stocked with three decanters and several glasses.

Sir Vincent hesitated, glanced at Sahib, who growled softly, and then, hurrying a trifle, moved to pour himself a glass, choosing randomly from among the decanters. He turned, discovered Sahib was lying at Renwick's side, and relaxed a trifle.

"Don't know what got into the beast," he said with false joviality. "There I was. Just going out for a stroll. The animal jumped in front of me and nearly frightened me to death!"

"Sahib! I'm ashamed of you. That isn't the way we treat guests." Renwick was wondering just what his pet was up to. "I don't believe he's ever before done such a thing."

"Ah well," responded Sir Vincent, glad enough to have an audience—even the rather intimidating Lord Renwick—since he always liked to hear himself talk. "Just telling myself that I and my womenfolk should be taking ourselves off. Not bother you anymore, don't you know?"

"I don't believe you are any bother," said Renwick carefully. "I know my wife enjoys the feminine company your wife and daughter provide."

"Yes, and *they* enjoy that scalawag's company as well, no doubt," said Sir Vincent more than a trifle testily.

"Scalawag?" Renwick repressed a smile, but made a mental note to tease Alex, ask him when he'd become a scalawag.

"Yes, yes. That . . . that . . ."

"I presume you refer to Lord Merwin. I have known him for a great many years now. I do not believe I ever before heard him called anything like a scalawag."

"He thinks to wed my daughter!"

"I know he loves her very much," said Renwick, nodding.

"Now the silly chit says she'll go against my wishes and wed him without my blessing!"

"I am sure she would regret the necessity."

"No necessity! No need. Should just forget the . . . the . . ."

"Nonpareil?"

"Non . . . ?"

"Nonesuch?"

"None . . . !"

"Paragon?"

"Now you listen here," said Sir Vincent. "He's a *Tory*. Can't be any of those things."

"I am a Tory myself. I don't see anything wrong with it."

"If you are all Tories," asked Sir Vincent, "then why are you all members of Brooks? Members of Brooks have to be Whigs! That's what fooled me at first. Thought he was all right. Then I learned he's some sort of secretary in the Tory party!"

Renwick chuckled. "Oh, we were all very young when we joined Brooks. Young, and kicking over the traces. But one grows older and becomes more conservative, of course."

"Didn't myself," said Sir Vincent.

Renwick's brows arched. "So you didn't. Well, we need Whigs as well as Tories, do we not? Couldn't have an opposition if there were none, could we?"

Sir Vincent's tone was belligerent when he asked, "What if we were all sensible and became Whigs?"

"Oh no! Think how very boring politics would be if we all thought just alike," said Renwick, a smile forming wrinkles at the corners of his eyes.

Sir Vincent eyed his host, wondering if the man was laughing at him. He decided that couldn't possibly be the case. "Don't know how it is," he said. "Can't seem to think what makes a man want to be a Tory. Never been Tories in my family. Never. How can I allow my Artemisia to wed one?"

"You want her to marry a good man? One who will care for her and pamper her and keep her in luxury? Keep her happy and content?"

"Don't know that I do," was the stubborn response.

"Want to see her with a man who will see she be-
· haves, see she don't embarrass me or my name."

"But she won't have your name, will she?"

Sir Vincent frowned. "No. She won't, will she?"

"So what matters it if she embarrasses her husband?"

Sir Vincent's eyes widened. "She'd be embarrassing
that Tory if she weds him like she says she will. *That's*
a good thing." He sobered. "But then, don't remember
her ever embarrassing anyone. Probably wouldn't."

"Then she needn't wed a man who would keep her
in line."

"True." Sir Vincent sighed again. "It is very difficult being a parent, you know."

"Yes. I am already discovering that. Even though
my daughters are still very young, they have already
become persons in their own right. Trying to form
their characters but keep their spirits from breaking
is a very great responsibility. I believe you and your
wife have done very well by your daughter."

"Great little gal, my Artemisia." Sir Vincent tossed
back the last of his wine. "Yes, great girl, a great
girl." Rather wistfully, he added, "Always thought I'd
wed her to Loomerbye. Be a great thing to be able to
call my best friend brother."

"But you wouldn't call him brother. You'd have to
call him son."

"Son?" Sir Vincent's eyes bulged.

"He wouldn't be your brother," explained Renwick.
"He'd be your son. In law, you know." Renwick listened to the utter silence. He almost laughed, knowing
from the stillness that his words had given his guest
a shock. Evidently Sir Vincent had never given
thought to what the legal relationship would be.

"Can't have that," the baronet burst out, his words
half strangled. "No, no. Not a proper thing at all!"

"Ah. Then Miss Bigalow need not accept Lord
Loomerbye's suit?"

"Didn't think it through. Can't have it. No, no. Won't do at all."

"Excellent. I doubt Loomerbye would make a woman happy."

"What is all this nonsense of making your women-folk happy? Woman is put on earth to serve man. Needn't worry about things like if they are happy!"

"But even servants work better if they are happy, so wouldn't one's wife be a far better wife if she were happy?"

"Hmm. Never thought of that."

It seemed to Renwick that Sir Vincent had thought of very little. "Your daughter is an excellent woman. She will make Alex an excellent wife and we will welcome her as a friend."

Sir Vincent rose to his feet. *"Don't want her marrying that Tory!"* He turned on his heel and stalked from the room.

After some moments Sahib seemed to sigh. Jason dropped a hand to his pet's head. "You had something in mind when you brought Sir Vincent here?"

Sahib bounced the hand on his head. Jason dug his fingers into the flesh at the back of the cat's neck and scratched.

"Sorry if I failed to bring about the result you wanted, Sahib." Jason was silent for a moment. "But why," he muttered, "am I apologizing to a tiger?"

TWELVE

Several days later a carriage pulled by four ill-chosen job horses came to the Renwicks' door. Reeves sent a footman out to hand the occupant into the house.

"Lord Merwin," said Mrs. Marchcomer, rushing up to Reeves in a most unladylike manner. "He is here, is he not? I must see him. It is imperative that I see him at once. He must help me!" She reached for the embarrassed butler's hands and squeezed them tightly.

Sir Vincent stood at the top of the stairs, listening. He grasped the banister and leaned well over it, but even so could not catch Reeves's soft reply.

"Please." The woman looked over her shoulder. "I doubt I've much time. Lord Merwin will know what to do. Oh, please . . ." Releasing Reeves, she wrung her hands.

Again Sir Vincent missed the butler's reply, but Mrs. Marchcomer followed the footman down the hall toward the breakfast room and Reeves strolled unhurriedly into the Renwicks' private wing. A door opened somewhere behind him and Sir Vincent started, a guilty reaction to the fact he'd been eaves-dropping. He hurried down the stairs and he, too, went toward the breakfast room, but unsure where the lady had disappeared, he entered the first room he came to and stood, waiting, peering through the barely opened door.

Some minutes later he was rewarded. Lord Merwin strode by, looking neither right nor left. Sir Vincent poked his head out. He carefully noted which room Merwin entered, and, pulling back, searched his mind concerning it. A lady's sewing room, he recalled. And it had a door connecting to the music room just beyond!

Checking that he was not observed, Sir Vincent entered the music room. He tiptoed across to the inner door, eased free the latch, and pushed the door open a mere fraction of an inch. Then he put his eye to it. Sir Vincent suppressed a sigh. He could see nothing. He put his ear to it—and smiled. He *could* hear.

". . . cannot do it!" The lady's voice grew shrill. "How can anyone ask me to suffer in such a manner?"

"My dear Mrs. Marchcomer—"

"Mrs. Renwick!"

"—have you consulted a doctor? Perhaps there is a remedy . . ."

"Would it not be talked of if such existed?" she interrupted. "There are many who suffer so. Would not everyone have such knowledge to hand? *No* one should suffer as I suffered. And they wouldn't, if there were a potion . . ."

Sir Vincent shut the door. "Suffer?" he asked himself. "Remedy?" He cogitated a bit longer but could come up with no possible explanation other than that the woman was with child and must instantly have Lord Merwin's help in the matter. And what sort of help could *he* give? Why, the only possible *remedy* was to marry the woman!

Which meant—Sir Vincent beamed—that the blasted Tory could *not* marry Artemisia.

Sir Vincent went instantly to find his wife. He passed on his conclusions and insisted they pack and leave. At once. Lord Merwin would not be allowed to embarrass their darling Artemisia. He would be allowed no conversation with her and no time alone with her. Such a blackguard must not come within yards of their daughter!

Lady Bigalow frowned. Could it be possible? Arta had had fears concerning Mrs. Marchcomer. She had even been unwise enough to give Lord Merwin the opportunity to develop a relationship with Edith Marchcomer. Had he fallen into the woman's trap? Had he, even briefly, made her his mistress?

Lady Bigalow doubted it. "I think I should talk to Lord Merwin."

Sir Vincent looked up in alarm. "You will do no such thing!" He wasn't about to have his neat little solution to a thorny problem proved wrong. "You'll have nothing to do with the scalawag." Sir Vincent remembered Lord Renwick's reaction to that. "Not just a Tory scalawag, as I thought, but a blasted *rake!*"

"But dear, is it truly fair to condemn the man when you admit you overheard only a tiny bit of the conversation? I fear you have misinterpreted something. Or heard something out of context which, if put in its proper place, would mean something entirely different."

"And what possible situation could need a remedy only Lord Merwin can supply?" asked Sir Vincent, blithely ignoring a number of overheard hints and clues which might answer that question. He was particularly careful to forget Mrs. Marchcomer's insertion of the name Renwick. "Well? Can you think of one?"

"I don't know, do I? Which is why I believe we should ask."

Sir Vincent actually stamped his foot. "We leave within the hour, so I suggest you save your energy for work and get to your packing. Thanks to your ill-managed escape from France," he blustered, "you've little enough in your wardrobe and Artemisia not much more, so you should manage in the time. I will order a groom to the nearest inn where he will hire me a carriage and team. We can be off instantly."

Lady Bigalow searched her mind for a means of delaying their departure until she could speak to Lord Merwin. "My dear! You have not thought! There are conventions one must obey. How can I oversee our packing, speak to our host and hostess, see to leaving proper vails for the servants and—" She threw up her hands. "Leave within an hour? Nonsense."

"I will do everything but the packing. And I will send Artemisia up to you. At once. She is to have no more to do with that . . . that *rakehell*."

All was accomplished—if not quite within the hour, then not too long thereafter. Sahib didn't know the Bigalows were departing until Lord Renwick walked out to see them off. Suddenly the beast stiffened his legs. His tail whipped back and forth and he roared. Loudly. Which frightened not only the horses but also the driver who, attempting to keep one eye on the tiger, had more than a little difficulty soothing his team!

Lord Renwick grasped a handful of skin at the back of Sahib's neck. "Be still," he ordered. He felt the tension drain from Sahib, found his hand shaken loose, and felt the animal turn and move away. "Eustacia?"

"He is going into the house," she whispered. "His head is hanging and tail drooping."

Lord Renwick nodded and, the horses back under control, he waved as the carriage moved down the drive. "Now, I'd best see to Sahib. What got into him?" He remembered how Sahib had herded Sir Vincent into his presence and been upset by the result. "Eustacia, I fear Sahib is growing more than a little erratic. Do you think I should fear he is growing dangerous?"

"I don't think it. That roar sounded angry, but his behavior was not at all vicious." Eustacia took her husband's arm and led him into the house. "Reeves, where did Sahib go?"

"He went toward the breakfast room, my lady," said Reeves. "If I may be allowed to say so, the beast looked a trifle down-pin."

The Renwicks went to see what they would see. "He is lying outside the sewing room door," whispered Eustacia.

Reeves, who had followed them, exclaimed and then said, "That is where Lord Merwin speaks to Mrs. Marchcomer."

"Mrs. Marchcomer! But when did she arrive?"

"Something over an hour ago. Perhaps I am wrong and they have finished their conversation, but if so, why does Sahib lie just there?"

Sahib lifted his head at the sound of voices. Now he rose and padded up to Renwick. He raised his head and opened his mouth in that silent roar, looked over his shoulder, and sighed an obvious sigh.

"Has anyone any notion whatsoever what is going on here?" asked Lord Renwick a trifle testily. Only rarely did his lack of vision bother him, but when it did it made him irritable.

"Do you suppose Sahib is worried about Alex and Artemisia?" asked Lady Renwick, hesitating slightly in her speech as if unsure she wished to voice such a thought.

Sahib roared. Aloud, this time.

The door opened and Lord Merwin poked his head out. "What is the uproar? That is the second time in a very few minutes that Sahib has raised his voice!"

"The Bigalows just left and Sahib appears upset by the fact."

"Gone!" Alex came out into the hall. "Artemisia?" Mrs. Marchcomer followed him. "Without speaking to me?" he finished, stepping on into the hall. "But why?"

"Oh, dear, it must be my fault!" Mrs. Marchcomer wrung her hands. "Somehow. Some way. I know it is my fault!"

"Surely not. No one knew you were here, Mrs. Marchcomer," said Lady Renwick.

The lady drew herself up. "Not Mrs. Marchcomer. I am Mrs. Renwick. I wed Trey by special license as soon after reaching London as we could manage the trick. We have been exceedingly busy ever since. Seeing my solicitor. Ordering new clothes. In fact, we have been so very busy we had no time to discuss the future." Her features fell into tragic lines. "Until last night. And then he told me he expects me to travel to Naples, which is his home now."

"So? You will like Naples, I believe," said Lord Renwick. He frowned.

"You don't understand."

"Exactly," he said tersely. The pressure of his wife's hand on his arm made him realize that was rather rude. "Will you not explain?" he asked in a less curt tone.

Edith, the new Mrs. Renwick, blushed rosily. "The *sea*. I will be forced to go to sea."

"You do not care to sail? I found it a delightful way to travel when we had to go north a year or two ago," said Lady Renwick.

"Delightful!" Edith's color faded. "I feel ill even thinking about it!" Edith's hand moved to press against her stomach. "Oh dear. Yes! Even *thinking* about it!"

"She does look a trifle green," murmured Eustacia to Lord Renwick.

His lordship did his best to repress a grin. For Edith, he guessed, suffering *mal de mer* was no joke!

And just about then still another carriage pulled up at the front of the house. Edith, hearing it, squeaked and grasped Lord Merwin's arm. "Please. Do something. Save me once again, as you did in the past! I cannot step foot on another boat. I cannot!"

"Now," said Eustacia in a soft voice to Jason, "she looks white as a sheet!"

The brand new Mrs. Renwick fainted into Lord Merwin's arms.

"Oh dear. Reeves!" Reeves had returned to the front door at the sound of arrivals. "Do come here! At once!"

Reeves returned and was apprised of the problem. While the rest adjourned to the front hall, he spoke quietly to two of the footmen who took the lady from Alex. They carried her up to the room to which Reeves ordered her taken, while a maid rushed into the back of the house to find the housekeeper who must go and tend to her.

The others found a neighbor lady and her simpering daughter. The family had just returned from a brief stay in Brighton and had heard that one of Lord Renwick's unmarried friends was visiting. Since Miss Wheeler was well beyond the age of feeling she could wait for her prince riding a white horse to arrive at their door, the two had come in pursuit of a likely suitor.

Lady Renwick, obviously suppressing irritation, invited the two ladies into the salon even as Alex spoke, *sotto voce,* to Lord Renwick. "Jase, I must follow her."

"Yes," replied Lord Renwick in normal tones, "but not at once. Reeves says they had only a pair and will be forced to travel slowly until they reach an inn where they can hire a proper coach and four. You've plenty of time, since you will ride, and Alex, you cannot leave until you sort something out about that woman."

"Woman?" asked Mrs. Wheeler, turning on her heel, her sharp gaze full of curiosity. "What woman?"

Lady Renwick caught her guest's arm and turned her back toward the drawing room. "Merely a lady who has asked Lord Merwin's advice in a small problem. That is all. Now do come tell me all about

Brighton. Did you enjoy yourself, Miss Wheeler? Did you order new gowns? Do tell . . ."

The door closed behind the three women and Alex heaved a sigh of relief. "Phew! Remind me to thank Eustacia. Jase, do you have to have such impertinent neighbors?"

Lord Renwick chuckled. "Come along to my study, Alex. You'll avoid the ladies and can decide what must be done about our newest guest."

"You are wrong," said Artemisia for the umpteenth time.

"You were not there. I tell you there is no other answer."

"There is."

"My dear . . ." began her mother sorrowfully.

"But Mother, you *know* there is. When they left Tiger's Lair, Edith meant to wed Mr. Renwick. My guess is that she *did* and only now understands that he wishes to return to Naples."

"Oh. Married? A sea journey? Oh dear, I had not thought of that! Oh, that poor woman!"

"What nonsense is this?" asked Sir Vincent, his voice querulous. He had been looking from one to the other and growing more and more alarmed. *Was* there another explanation to what he'd heard? Impossible.

"Father, just what *did* you hear?"

"She is a woman. She needed an instant remedy! What could she mean but that she is with child and needs a husband?" blustered Sir Vincent.

"Oh, Vinny," said Lady Bigalow, even more sorrowfully than before. "Arta is correct. Poor Mrs. Marchcomer—" She frowned. "—or perhaps I should say Mrs. Renwick—is merely frightened of going to sea!"

Renwick. Hadn't the blasted woman intimated her

name was Renwick? Sir Vincent sighed. Then recovered. "Well?" he said, his bluster at full measure. "How could I know the silly woman only wanted someone to save her from a sea journey? Besides," he grumbled, "that must be nonsense. No one is that afraid of sailing!"

"You wouldn't know, dear, because you never suffer when at sea. Nor could you have any notion how very ill she was merely crossing from France, but I *do* wish you'd allowed me to ask Lord Merwin what, exactly, was the problem."

Sir Vincent recalled that in one respect he had managed to do as he wished. "No, no. No need. No need. Glad you didn't have any opportunity to discuss anything with that blasted rake."

"*Not* a rake, dear," chided his wife. "Merely a gentleman to whom those in distress know they may turn."

"Bah!"

Silence fell. While Sir Vincent figuratively patted himself on the back for escaping from the Renwicks' with his daughter's honor intact, his wife brooded on what she might have done differently while remaining within the bounds of wifehood which she had set herself.

And, while her parents were preoccupied with their own thoughts, Artemisia plotted ways and means of returning, immediately, to Tiger's Lair and Alex's side.

The carriage pulled up to the posting house, where they were to change over to a better rig, a team instead of a pair, and, with any luck, far better horses. Sir Vincent helped his wife and daughter down and sent them into the inn to wait while he discussed with the head hostler exactly what he wanted. And Lady Bigalow, with Artemisia trailing along behind, entered the common area where they immediately ran into Mr. Renwick.

"Ah! Sir!" said Lady Bigalow by way of greeting.

Renwick bowed. "My lady. Miss Bigalow."

Artemisia's eyes narrowed and she chewed thoughtfully on her lower lip.

"I believe," continued Lady Bigalow a trifle coyly, "that we can guess your errand!"

"Then my wife *is* at Tiger's Lair?" he asked, his voice polite but the look in his eyes a trifle hard.

Lady Bigalow sobered. "Sir, may I speak with you? Privately?"

"She ran off to Lord Merwin, did she not?" he asked, ignoring her request.

"Please? Won't you speak with me? We've little time and there is something you need to know."

"Concerning that rake?"

Lady Bigalow sighed a whoosh of exasperation. "He is *not* a rake. Now do you wish to know why your wife ran away from you or do you not?"

Artemisia caught his gaze. "Go with Mother. Please. Mrs. Renwick did indeed have cause for panic." He went, his mouth a firm, hard line, and Artemisia instantly went in search of the landlady.

Ten minutes later she peeked into the commons where her father was discussing the condition of the roads while he drank down a heavy-wet. She continued on until she found her mother and Mr. Renwick in a smaller public room. Looking back to assure herself that Sir Vincent was occupied, she whisked herself into their presence.

"Mother? Have you convinced Mr. Renwick that his wife suffers greatly when at sea?"

"I am convinced," he replied, "and I don't know what to do for the best. We really must go to Naples. My home is there and I've business interests there. My little vacation has already lasted longer than I expected."

"Perhaps a larger ship? Are they not more stable?"

"I will discover what her experience was on the ferry which she took to Europe. And perhaps Lord

Merwin, who is active in the government, has contacts and can arrange passage for us on one of the larger naval ships. I will see what can be done. Also, there are potions. I do not recommend them except in the most desperate of cases, of course. Opiates, you know."

"Well, I am glad that is settled. And now you may settle another problem." Artemisia explained her plan.

Mr. Renwick and Lady Bigalow listened to her, looked at each other, and, Lady Bigalow biting her lip, turned back to Artemisia. "Mother," warned Artemisia before her ladyship could speak, "I mean to return to Alex one way or another. I believe that traveling with Mr. Renwick while chaperoned by a maid from this inn is the least objectionable I can imagine."

"I wish, dear, that you had simply done it." Lady Bigalow sighed. "I cannot permit you to do it. It goes quite contrary to your father's wishes and *I* cannot be a party to such a thing! Now, I must take myself off to the necessary and you, as your father would wish, should resign yourself to remaining here. Good-bye, Mr. Renwick. I believe you will have departed before I return." Lady Bigalow hugged her daughter a trifle desperately and left the room.

"She means me to go with you," said Artemisia softly.

"She does?"

"She could not say it, but her actions tell me it is so."

"In that case—" Mr. Renwick bowed. "—shall we go?"

They quickly collected the middle-aged maid the landlady had given leave to attend Artemisia and, with no one observing them but one very young and not very bright stable boy, they entered Mr. Renwick's carriage and set off for Tiger's Lair.

An hour or so later, Mr. Renwick handed his hat

and cane to Reeves as Edith, halfway down the stairs, stopped and stared at him. Her hand went to grasp Alex's arm. "Ah. You *did* come here. I thought you might," said Trey Renwick, his teeth bared. "Merwin? Should I feel insulted that my wife runs to you for advice and comfort?"

"I thought," said Artemisia, who was half-hidden behind Mr. Renwick, "that we had explained that. We did. What is more, you understood. You are merely teasing."

Alex, seeing Artemisia, removed Edith's hand from his arm and ran down the stairs where, at the last moment, he recalled it would be against all convention to pull her into his arms. Instead he grasped her hands.

"Alex, will you still have me?" asked Artemisia softly. "In my shift, as it were?"

"You mean it?"

"With Mr. Renwick's help, I escaped my father. You are my only hope." She smiled mistily up at him.

Sahib, coming into the hall with Lord Renwick trailing behind, saw the two. Once again he raised his voice in a roar, but this time it sounded very much like one of triumph.

Unfortunately, it frightened Mrs. Renwick and, once again, she fainted. With something of a sigh, Mr. Renwick asked Reeves where he should take her and, once again, Edith was carried up to her room.

That evening Artemisia came down for dinner and found Alex awaiting her in the blue salon. He looked her up and down, walked all the way around her, and smiled. "What a pretty shift," he said, teasing her.

Artemisia blushed delightfully. "Oh well, perhaps I exaggerated a trifle when I suggested you would have to take me in my shift. But only a trifle!"

"If you mean your father will refuse me your dowry

and very likely disinherit you, do you think I care? But I *might* become rather upset if you do not instantly explain how you managed to come back to me with your wardrobe intact! I remember that gown, you see, and it is not something you have borrowed from Eustacia."

"It is quite simple when you think about it," said Artemisia demurely.

"Simple, hmm?" Alex's brows pulled into a sharper vee as he cogitated. "If you did not pull your trunk from your father's carriage, which I doubt you could have done, then your gowns must not have been in your father's carriage. In that case—" A smile lighted his eyes. *"—Moonbeam! You meant to return!"*

"I had not come up with a scheme for doing so, but, yes, it was my intention. I fear my trunk, when my mother opens it, will be found packed full of Lady Renwick's comforter and a pillow or two. I must remember to apologize to her when we have a moment alone."

Alex nodded. When he continued it was on a thoughtful note. "I have not been particularly friendly to Jason's cousin, but I see I must do my best to repay him for his good efforts on your behalf. Worrying about you, I fear I had not truly put my mind to Mrs. Renwick's problem. Now whom do I know who might know a cure for seasickness?"

Artemisia smiled but then sobered. "I shouldn't find your question amusing. Edith was extremely ill, you know."

"Yes, but Miles's *Nemesis* is a small ship and it was a stormy passage. Unfortunately, after such a terrible experience, I fear it will be difficult to convince Mrs. Renwick that a larger ship and good weather would make sailing easier for her."

Together, they sighed. And then, catching each other's gaze, they smiled.

Just then Jason, Sahib at his side, entered the salon.

"Jase—" Alex cued his friend to their presence. "Do come and help us think of someone who can solve the problem of Mrs. Renwick's *mal de mer!*"

"But I do not know a soul who would be of help. Eustacia and I have discussed that very thing."

"Perhaps Ian knows." And, having decided to consult their Scottish friend, Alex changed the subject. The newlyweds and the McMurreys arrived together and the conversation became general—mostly concerning what was known of Napoleon's continued preparations for war, which was very nearly the only topic of conversation anywhere in England just then!

While the Renwicks and their guests ate dinner, Sir Vincent stalked from one end of the inn's private parlor to the other. When he had discovered his daughter missing and that no one could inform him of where she had gone—the baronet not thinking to consult the distaff side of the inn—he had exploded into a flurry of activity which had a large portion of the small town engaged in a search for Artemisia.

The attempts to locate her failed and her father stewed and fretted.

Lady Bigalow, her lower lip caught between her teeth, watched him. A frown etched ridges in her forehead. For hours she had debated telling her husband that their daughter had asked for Mr. Renwick's escort back to Tiger's Lair. For those same hours she had forced herself to remain silent. She was well aware that if she gave even a hint that she had guessed Artemisia's intentions and had not warned her husband, she would find herself in deep waters. So, even though she hated seeing him so agitated, Lady Bigalow could not bring herself to speak of it.

Instead she said, "Vincent, it will not help Arta if you do not eat. Please come sit at the table and try this goose pie. The landlady has made it just as you like it and her hand at pastry is surprisingly light. Please?"

Grumbling about insensitive mothers who could put food in their mouths when their daughters were heaven only knew where, Sir Vincent sat. He accepted the dollop of meat pie, nodded when Lady Bigalow lifted a spoonful of haricot beans and then added a slice of ham to the plate. But when she dipped into the conserved cherries he shook his head.

"Too tart. Makes my mouth pucker."

Lady Bigalow settled back and watched her husband nibble a bite, then another and, to her satisfaction, settle in to finish off his food with good appetite. In fact, having finished his goose, he asked for more.

"There," she said when he finished, "do you not feel better now?"

Sir Vincent scowled. "No."

Lady Bigalow felt a smile forming and quickly hid it. "My dear, I am surprised to find you so agitated. Can you explain it?"

"My daughter is missing and you wonder I am fretting! Where is she? What is she suffering? What utter villain has her in his power?"

"Has it not occurred to you that perhaps she has returned to Tiger's Lair?"

Sir Vincent slumped into his chair, his elbows splayed over the arms and his hands hanging loosely. "It occurred to me that . . . that . . ."

"Lord Merwin.."

". . . that he followed and stole her away, but I have found no one who saw his carriage, anyone resembling him, or his servant's livery." He shook his head. "I fear the worst, Penny." He sighed. "I fear that we will never see our precious daughter again."

Lady Bigalow again debated telling Sir Vincent what she knew. Again she did not. "Then I hope very much that she *did* manage, somehow, to make her way back to Lord Merwin." She spoke gently. "That would be far better than the fate you envision for her."

"If only it might be so, I would be only too thankful." He scowled and pounded the table with his fist. "Even if it still meant we would never see her again!"

"My dear, do not, I beg you, continue with this foolishness."

"Foolishness? *Foolishness!* That she would be dead to us if she were to wed that . . . that . . ."

"That exceedingly eligible young man."

"A Tory will never be an Eligible in my eyes!"

"Very well, Vinny." Lady Bigalow had finally lost patience. "In your eyes she will be dead. I, however, will be exceedingly thankful to discover she has found love and happiness in the care of that very caring man."

"Bah!"

"You are a very stubborn creature, Sir Vincent. You would cut off your nose to spite your face, which is your right, but I resent that you would cut off mine as well."

With great dignity, Lady Bigalow turned and left the room, going up to their bedroom. When Sir Vincent came up some time later, she pretended to be asleep.

The next morning was no better. Again Lady Bigalow wondered if she should tell her suffering husband where to find his daughter and, again, decided it was better for both Artemisia and herself if she pretended to know nothing. Sir Vincent picked at his breakfast in a fashion quite foreign to his nature and then, not quite knowing what to do, wandered into the yard. A gig pulled in and a middle-aged maid descended with the help of a stable hand who greeted her like a long-lost cousin.

Sir Vincent's mind was not working all that quickly, but something about the man and woman remaining in the gig niggled at him until, suddenly, he recalled the fellow was an undergroom at Tiger's Lair.

"Hey there!" he called, ignoring the maid who, after handing a sealed letter to the landlord, hurried inside. "You. In the gig!"

"Yes sir? Ah. Sir Vincent." The groom handed the reins to his wife and descended to the yard. "What may I do for you?" he asked.

The question rather stumped Sir Vincent. "Don't think you can do anything at all. Not for me. Just seemed odd. You being here, I mean."

"We returned Meg Johnston to her work here," said the groom politely. "His lordship has given us permission to visit my wife's mother, who is not well."

"Hmm. Oh. Well. Hope you find she is better," said Sir Vincent and turned away. His mouth turned down and a somewhat hangdog air about him, he wandered back into the inn.

Lady Bigalow hurried toward him. "News?" he asked, seeing her excitement.

She waved her letter which the landlord had brought to her. "Arta sent us a message, my dear. She is safe and happy and apologizes for any concern she may have caused us."

Sir Vincent's prominent eyes bugged still more. "Safe? She is safe?"

"Yes. Quite safe."

That fact percolated around in Sir Vincent's mind, settled in, and, as might have been expected—and had been by his wife—anger replaced his former stewing. "Blasted chit! Where is she? What is she doing? Why did she run off that way?"

"But dear, surely that is obvious."

It took a moment for him to put two and two together. "Tiger's Lair! She has run back to that blasted man!" Concern returned. "But didn't she understand? He will send her away! He will deny her!"

"Are you so very certain of that, Vinny?"

Sir Vincent, as was his way, blustered. "When I heard with my own ears that that Marchcomer woman needed him to wed her, how can I possibly be the least little bit uncertain?"

"Very easily. I believe she is a Renwick now, dear, and she cannot marry two men at the same time! But if you are still worried on that score, then we had better go and retrieve our daughter, had we not?"

"Go back there!" Sir Vincent sighed, his shoulders drooping. "Suppose we must. Silly wench. Putting us to all this trouble. Stupid girl . . ."

He wandered back out into the yard muttering more of the same and Lady Bigalow, shaking her head half in exasperation and half fondly, watched him out of sight. Then she returned to their room where she completed the packing she had begun after breakfast in anticipation of just what had ensued.

THIRTEEN

Artemisia and Alex were walking in the small rose garden near the front entrance to Tiger's Lair when they heard a carriage and four coming up the drive. They wandered toward the sound just as Lord Renwick and Sahib came around the other end of the house accompanied by Ian McMurrey who, with his wife, meant to leave for Brighton later in the day. The carriage pulled up and a groom, still panting slightly from racing around from the stables, opened the door. He handed out Lady Bigalow who, seeing her daughter, smiled.

"Oh fiddle," muttered Artemisia.

"If that is all the better you can do," said Alex in a low voice, "I must spend an idle hour teaching you a few far more appropriate words!"

"I had hoped Father would wash his hands of me and go on to London."

Sir Vincent stuck his head out of the carriage, saw his daughter, and hopped down. "You fool. You utter idiot. You . . . you . . ."

"Perhaps," murmured Artemisia, "you would be better occupied teaching *him*."

"Wouldn't be half so much fun." A muscle jumped in Alex's jaw. "Well, my dear? What do we do now?"

"Run?"

"Hmm. Maybe it would be more interesting if we wait and discover what Sahib is about."

Artemisia, her mind and gaze occupied with her parents, had not noticed the tiger's slow approach.

"Artemisia," called Sir Vincent, "you come here right this moment." He stabbed his finger up and down toward the ground at his feet. "You get away from that . . . that . . ."

"On second thought, perhaps he *would* pay for teaching," murmured Alex. "But do watch Sahib."

Ten or so yards from the carriage, Sahib had dropped to his belly and begun slinking forward. His eyes were glued to Sir Vincent.

The baronet stalked a few steps toward where his daughter refused to budge from Alex's side. "If I have to, I will pick you up and carry you to the carriage!" threatened Sir Vincent.

Since Artemisia was a healthy young woman and a good inch taller than the pudgy baronet, she rather thought he could not. Still, she did not wish him harming himself in the attempt. "Hello, Father. Mother? Did you worry?"

"Not so very much," said Lady Bigalow. She winked. "I *suspected* you had found a means of returning here. Your father, however, fretted more than a trifle. He actually had difficulty eating his breakfast this morning."

"Oh dear. I truly did not mean to upset you to that degree," said Artemisia contritely. "But, Father, you must have known I would not believe the lies you told me."

Sahib reached a position just behind the baronet.

Sir Vincent shook his fists. "Not lies. True. Every word!"

"What did he tell you?" asked Alex, for the first time rather curious.

"That you would be forced to wed Mrs. Marchcomer, having put a bun in—"

Alex covered her mouth, cutting off the crude comment.

Artemisia pulled his hand away and amended her comment. "—having gotten her in the family way."

"It *is* a lie, you know, that I ever had anything of the sort to do with her." Alex held her gaze.

"I knew that," said Artemisia softly.

"I tell you I heard them talking!"

"Sir Vincent, was this just before you left Tiger's Lair, taking my betrothed with you?" asked Alex.

"Betrothed? *Betrothed!* No such thing. Never let her wed a philanderer. Never let her marry a Tory, for that matter. That's even worse. Lots of men are philanderers and none the worse for it, but not for *my* daughter." Sir Vincent stalked nearer, his intention obvious. "Now, my girl . . ."

But as he reached for Artemisia, Sahib jumped between the father and daughter, holding up one paw and, very obviously, in his mute way, telling Sir Vincent he was to come no closer.

"You see, Father? Even Sahib knows I am to wed Alex."

Sir Vincent, his eyes popping, backed away from the tiger. "Get that animal away from me!" Sahib took a step toward him. "Get him away!"

Lord Renwick, who had held Ian back thinking the Bigalows and Alex must settle this on their own, realized Sahib was not at his side. "What is going on?" he asked, his mild tone hiding some concern. Sahib had seemed to dislike Sir Vincent from the beginning. Renwick didn't wish to discover just how far his pet might go when defending those he *did* like.

Lady Bigalow quickly moved to Renwick's side. "Nothing about which you need worry, my lord. My husband is a trifle excitable, I fear, when it comes to his daughter, and Sahib, it seems, feels she needs his protection."

"Sahib, behave yourself," said Renwick firmly.

The tiger glanced toward his master and then back toward Sir Bigalow. His tail lashed once and then he turned and—there was no other word for it—*herded* Alex and Artemisia back into the rose garden and away from the others.

"Tell me what is happening," said Renwick, speaking to Lady Bigalow.

"Tell you!" exclaimed Sir Vincent. "I will tell you. That blasted beast is forcing my daughter and that . . . that . . . *Tory* to go off together. I want a gun. I'll shoot him. Vicious, that's what he is. Vicious, I say, and I'll shoot him!"

"Nonsense," said his wife, although she too was a trifle worried about her daughter's situation. "The tiger is not vicious. He has never harmed a soul." And then unsure that was true, she turned. "He hasn't, has he, Lord Renwick?"

"No. Never. I've a suspicion what he is up to, but cannot prove it. I suggest we go inside and have some refreshments while our housekeeper readies your room for you."

"My room! I don't want a room. I want my daughter!"

"I am certain," said Lord Renwick soothingly, "that we can straighten everything out to everyone's satisfaction but not instantly."

"Only thing that will please me is to have my daughter in that carriage and away from here," insisted Sir Vincent.

"Nonsense," said Lady Bigalow. "For my part, my lord, I would very much like a cup of bohea and, if your cook will not be put out by the request, a sandwich or two. Vinny ate no more than a mouthful this morning. He is always cross when he fails to eat a proper breakfast." She put her arm through Lord Renwick's and turned him toward the house. He flicked his long cane back and forth ahead of them and, speaking softly of this and that, they moved to the steps and up them.

Ian motioned to Sir Vincent, silently suggesting they follow.

The baronet hesitated. He looked toward where his daughter had disappeared, back toward the carriage, then at the house. He sighed. Disconsolately, he nodded at Ian and followed in his wife's wake.

Sahib, meanwhile, made quite certain Sir Vincent was nowhere near before he allowed Artemisia and Alex to settle into the seat under an arbor covered with roses. Neither wished to speak of the scene they'd just endured.

"I don't believe I will ever forget the scent of Tiger's Lair," said Artemisia. "Every time I smell a rose it will bring back this time with you."

Alex nodded. "I, too, will find roses evocative of this period of our life, my Moonbeam." He was silent for a moment before moving restlessly, shifting his weight slightly and then back again.

"What is it?"

Alex sighed. "It is the same old thing. I cannot help but fear that you will regret it if you go against your father's wishes and he forbids your mother to have anything to do with you."

"I will regret it if I do not."

The simplicity of her statement startled Alex to stillness.

She picked up his hand and played with his fingers. "It was when I realized that I could not bear to lose you that I decided I could not wait until Father gave in to the inevitable."

"What gave you that awareness? Not that you *would* have lost me, of course."

"You will, I fear, think me very foolish, Alex."

"Could I possibly? I think not. Tell me."

"It was while we were in Vienna. When you showed interest in Mrs. Marchcomer—"

"Mrs. Renwick, now, and I have *never* . . ."

"—and I was silly about it," continued Artemisia

as if he had not spoken. "You had no *personal* interest in her, but at the time—" She blushed. "—I felt insecure. Afraid. I had no . . . no . . ."

"No hold on me? Legal hold, I mean, since you surely knew you had a moral and ethical hold?"

"It sounds so awful when you say that."

Crinkly lines appeared at the side of his eyes when he smiled. "If it made you conclude we may wed, then I cannot think it awful."

"You are laughing at me."

"Only a very little and very lovingly. Do you mind?"

"I told you you would think me foolish!"

"In this particular case I am very glad you were!"

Artemisia did something she almost never did. She pouted. And then, thinking about their situation, the pout disappeared. "It may have been foolish, but I am glad as well." She leaned against his shoulder. That wonderful feeling of closeness which was both comforting and, in an odd way, exciting, flooded into her. "Alex?" she asked, her tone wistful.

"It is broad daylight," he scolded, not pretending to misunderstand what she wanted, "and we are out in the open where anyone might see us."

Artemisia nodded against his shoulder. "I know."

He chuckled, looked all round, and, very quickly, tipped her chin up and placed a quick, hard kiss on her lips.

"Not enough," she muttered.

"No. Definitely *not* enough. How old are you?"

"How old? Do you not know?"

"Would I ask if I were certain?"

"*Why* do you ask?"

"If you are of age, then I may purchase a special license and we may be married when and where we will. Soon, I hope."

Artemisia compressed her lips and glared out over the rose bed. "Fiddle."

"You are not of age?"

"Not until my next birthday. I am very sorry, Alex."

"Not until September?"

"Not until September."

"But that is months!"

She nodded.

"Fiddle," he said.

She giggled.

He frowned down at her.

Her tongue firmly in her cheek, Artemisia said, "I really must take a few minutes and teach you a word or two—something which would be far more effective than *fiddle*."

For half a moment Alex looked put out. Then he recalled his saying much the same thing to her not many minutes earlier. He chuckled. "I wonder if we would teach each other the same words!"

"Someday we will compare notes. Alex, did you mean we cannot wed until September?"

"If your father does not relent, then that is exactly what I mean."

"But that means more than three months. I will have to return to living under his roof!"

"We will hope he relents," he said a trifle grimly.

Sahib, who had been lying quietly at their feet, rose to his haunches. He roared. Not one of his silent roars, but not one that was frighteningly loud.

"Alex," said Artemisia, her eyes on Sahib, "why do I have this strange feeling my father *will* relent."

"Hmm." He, too, stared at the tiger. "I, too, feel there is a very good chance he'll do just that."

Sahib growled.

"Or do I mean," amended Alex, "that there is *every* chance that he will?"

Sahib pushed his chin against Alex's knee, staring up at him.

"Moonbeam," said Alex, his gaze held by Sahib's,

"it will be no time at all before we are wed! Sahib has decided it is so and so it will be!"

"Sahib," said Artemisia, her hand going to rest on the tiger's head, "you will find arranging this match the hardest you've yet put a paw into!"

Sahib leaned slightly against her hand and Artemisia scratched behind his ears. He moved so that she could do a better job and she put both sets of fingers to work. Within moments the strange sound the Renwicks insisted was a tiger's purr erupted from the great beast's throat.

Alex looked at Artemisia and she looked back. "Is it foolish of us to think Sahib actually plays a part in arranging marriages?" she asked.

"It is difficult to *disbelieve* when you know Sahib's solutions to my friends' problems!"

"Sahib, I begin to believe that Prince Ravi has the right of it. You are magic!"

The big cat reached over his shoulder and licked it, for all the world as if, modest creature that he was, he were denying any such thing.

"Ah! That must be Captain Surewood now," said Lady Renwick a few days later. She and Artemisia had been sitting under a tree not too far from the house. Now she jumped up from the blanket from which they watched her ladyship's children play under Nanny's watchful eye.

Artemisia looked toward where a modest carriage had stopped before the front door and wondered who Captain Surewood might be. She, too, rose to her feet and strolled off. She was well behind Lady Renwick, who didn't appear to hurry but covered the ground with surprising quickness.

Alex appeared where the front doors stood open, smiling at the gray-haired man whose shaky hand rested on an ivory-topped, ebony cane and who made his way slowly up the steps.

"Captain! How good of you to come. We could have visited you, you know."

"Far too good sailing weather to sit at home," claimed the stranger gruffly. "Glad of a chance to haul sail and drop anchor in another port for a bit."

"Well, it was good of you. You understand what we want?"

"Aye. Dealt with many a new boy who suffered mightily their first few days at sea. If nothing else, can reassure the lady her problem will come to an end." Surewood had reached the wide, flat terrace just before the house and, waving off the footman who offered an arm, stood for a moment catching his breath.

It was just long enough for Lady Renwick and Artemisia to arrive. "Captain Surewood, how glad we are to see you!"

The retired naval captain looked at Lady Renwick from under craggy brows. "Don't think I've received such a sincere welcome in many a year, my lady. Why do I suspicion your sufferer has become something of a problem to you?"

"Hush!" Lady Renwick looked all about. "We would not wish Mrs. Renwick to suspect we are desperate to find a solution for her problem."

The captain sobered. "Better tell you right now. There is no solution if you mean keeping the lady from *all* sickness. Can ease the matter. Can't get rid of it entirely."

"She was exceedingly ill when we came over from France in Seward's *Nemesis*. Rough weather, of course, but she says she was also ill when she crossed to the continent on a ferry out of Dover. Although that, too, was likely to have been stormier than now," finished Alex, thoughtfully, "given the time of year. I didn't think to ask her."

"Let us not stand here on the steps," said Lady Renwick, urging everyone into the house. "Reeves," she added, seeing the butler hovering, awaiting orders, "we require refreshments in the blue salon and send a message to Mr. and Mrs. Renwick to join us. And Lord Renwick, of course."

Artemisia bit her lip. "Eustacia," she whispered. "I believe my mother and father are in the blue salon . . ."

"My dear, you cannot avoid them forever," said Lady Renwick softly.

"No," said Artemisia doubtfully. "Nevertheless, I planned to inspect the conservatory today since the gardeners worked in there all day yesterday. I have looked forward to enjoying the fruits of their labors—and will certainly enjoy it far more than taking tea with Father!"

"The conservatory? I believe I will join you," said Alex.

"No, you will not. If anyone can convince Mrs. Renwick that she can board a ship and not suffer so very badly, then you are that man," said his betrothed. Her eyes twinkled even though her expression also spoke of a ruefulness she preferred not to voice.

Alex pressed his lips together. "You know," he said softly, "that I would far prefer to be with you?"

"I know. But it would be as well if my father sees you urging her to go off with her husband and discovers that the help she required of you was how she was to go about doing so!"

"He still believes that I indulged in a liaison with her?"

"Of course he does! How else is he to justify his desire to take me away from here?"

"Would not his old cry of 'that dastardly Tory' do?"

"We will hear it again, I am sure. Ah! Here are Mr. and Mrs. Renwick. Edith, perhaps Lady Renwick's visitor can soothe your fears of sailing. Do go on in, Alex. I will see you all later."

Artemisia disappeared down the hall to the rear where the conservatory could occupy her time until the captain left and Alex could come find her.

Alex, forestalling the footman, opened the salon door and waited until Edith and Mr. Renwick entered before following them in and closing it. He surveyed the room. Lady Renwick and the captain were chuckling about something. Sir Vincent alternated his expression between one of rue and a thundering irritation. Lady Bigalow was doing her best to hide her amusement at her husband's discomfiture. Obviously, Lady Renwick had just explained the captain's reason for calling and the baronet had finally been forced to admit he'd been in error.

"Ah! Edith, do come meet Captain Surewood. He retired last year after many years at sea and, if anyone can do so, he can give you advice concerning your aversion to sailing."

"You know it is more than a mere aversion," said Edith a trifle tartly.

"Yes," said Lady Bigalow soothingly, "it is far more. But please, do listen to the captain. He has some sensible things to say and some encouraging words. Come, Edith, and sit beside me, will you not?"

Lord Renwick arrived just then, Sahib at his side. Sahib pressed gently against Jason's leg, which was the way he asked about strangers. "Eustacia, my dear, will you introduce us?"

The captain, at sight of Sahib, had risen to his feet with the aid of his cane. "I met the beast as a cub, of course," he said, "when we sailed from the East, but I did not believe the tales that he roamed free." He eyed Sahib. "A beautiful animal," he added with only a hint of reserve.

Eustacia did the honors and Sahib, always polite, drew near to sniff the visitor and then, much to the captain's obvious relief, stalked back to Lord Renwick's side and slid to a prone position there.

"Now," said Eustacia—only to be interrupted, again, by the arrival of the tea tray. Once tea was dispensed and plates of fairy cakes and cut sandwiches passed, she tried again. *"Now,"* she began—and this time managed to finish.

Captain Surewood gave Edith a commiserating look. "I've known many a lad to suffer so when first at sea. It is not the least bit humorous, so please believe that I understand. But, child, I was many years at sea and I learned ways of alleviating the problem. You do understand there is no getting away from it altogether until you've been to sea for three or four days?"

Edith's eyes widened and her mouth dropped open. She closed it, and then, speaking hesitantly, asked, "You mean that after some days it goes away?"

"I've never known a case in which it did not."

Edith drew in a deep breath. "I will listen."

The captain discussed several points at some length and then summed up. "So, if you remain on deck, if your keep your eyes glued to the horizon, and if you can stomach just a small tot of hot rum every so often, you will not be desperately ill. Too, a larger ship and the happier weather will help you feel more the thing."

Edith had listened carefully. Now she drew in a deep breath. "And after a few days you swear I will feel well again?"

"You'll find your sea legs, madam, and enjoy the rest of your journey."

Edith turned to her husband. "You will hire me a maid who *knows* she does not suffer from the sickness? Someone who can stay with me and help me?"

Mr. Renwick came to her, knelt before her, and took her hands in his own. "We will find someone. A nurse, perhaps, who understands what it is to be ill. Or perhaps the captain knows a seaman's widow who has had experience of sailing, who would know how to care for you." He turned to look at the captain, his brows arched.

Captain Surewood pursed his lips, his eyes almost hidden by lowering brows. "Well, now, I'm not certain—" Suddenly his expression lightened. "—ah! But I *do* know. Mrs. Goodie. A trifle rougher than you'll be used to, madam, but a good woman. Wouldn't do for a personal maid, mind. Wouldn't know a silk from a satin or what to do with either, you see. But if you promise to send her home again, then you'll have a bluff, good-hearted woman to look after you during those first days of your journey. Could very likely send her back from Gibraltar," he added thoughtfully.

"If you would be so kind as to write us a letter of introduction . . ."

The captain interrupted Mr. Renwick. "Wouldn't do you the least bit of good. The dear lady can't read. Tell you what. She lives along the coast not far from my own place. Why do we not go now? I'll lead the way and introduce you and you can make your arrangements."

Alex, a feeling of relief filling him that Edith Renwick might soon be on her way to Naples, eased himself from the room and ordered a footman to run to the stables. They were to send around the captain's carriage and one of Lord Renwick's for Trey and Edith.

". . . At once," he finished with a wink before he slid back into the salon in time to see that the captain and the Renwicks were involved in further discussion and that Lady Renwick had joined Lord Renwick by the fireplace.

"Well, Jason," he said, approaching them, "your plan was a good one."

"I had forgotten all about Captain Surewood until just the other night. He'd picked up a debilitating disease and was sent home on the same ship that brought me home from India. Since I was not at my best on that journey—" Lord Renwick spoke with sudden dryness. "You will forgive me, I know, for putting the man from my mind?"

Alex chuckled. He then turned, holding out his hand to the captain. "You are leaving, then?"

All the proper things were said and the captain, the newlyweds' carriage following, tooled off down the lane. Alex escaped the party and went directly to the conservatory—where he found his future mother-in-law as well as his future wife. "Lady Bigalow. Moon-beam?"

"What did he call you?" asked her ladyship.

Artemisia blushed furiously. "It is his pet name for me. Because of my name," she finished.

"And because of her moon-washed hair," said Alex with a smile in his eyes.

"I like it," said Lady Bigalow, her head tipped to one side. She smiled at Alex. "You will be good for my Arta," she said.

"I certainly want the opportunity to try!"

"You refer to my obstinate husband and his stubborn refusal to acknowledge you as a proper suitor for our daughter."

"Yes. I should not have mentioned it, however. It was grossly impolite of me to do so."

"You have been uncomplaining for a very long time, Lord Merwin. I am not surprised if you have begun to lose patience."

Alex grinned. "It is not so much that I have lost patience. Far more that Moonbeam has finally agreed to wed me and still we cannot do so! Having *her* agreement, you see, makes me yearn for *his* as I did not while she still believed she could not go against his wishes."

The door opened and the object of their discussion, Sir Vincent himself, strolled in. He paused when he noticed the three standing together near the base of a grapevine that had been trained up one wall and was beginning to grow across the ceiling where a catwalk provided a means of pruning and future harvesting.

"Here now!" blustered Sir Vincent, his eyes shifting from his wife to his daughter to Alex and back to his wife. "What do you mean by it, hmmm?"

The baronet started toward them just as the door opened again and Sahib slunk in, his gliding steps following behind Sir Vincent's stomping approach.

"And you!" His gaze shifted to Artemisia. "Do I have to lock you up in a tower to keep you from this man?"

Sahib pushed between the two and turned to face the irate father. He growled.

Sir Vincent paled slightly but held his ground. "I swear it! I'll shoot the beast!"

"You'd very likely miss if you tried," said Lady Bigalow. "And besides, it would be grossly improper of you to shoot your host's pet."

"Miss? Miss!" Sir Vincent ignored the other half of his wife's comment. "I'd not, then!"

"But Father, what of your promise to your grand-mother that you would never shoot at anything but a target."

"Oh. Forgot," said the harassed man. Then he recollected when last they had discussed his shooting. "And I will thank you not to mention that! It was all play-acting, that talk about deathbed promises!" Another thought struck him and he pointed his finger at her. "Which you very well know! *You* made it up! Artemisia Theodora Felicia Bigalow, you will go too far one day and I swear I *will* lock you in your room with nothing but bread and water to eat. And I'll keep you there until you promise to be good."

"I think you forget my age, Father. I am far and away too old for such treatment. In fact, in a very few months I will be of age."

"Of age! So soon?" Sir Vincent, a horrified expression crossing his features, glanced at Lord Merwin. "I must marry you off to the first Whig I see! Not Loomerbye," he quickly contradicted himself. "That won't do, but any other Whig, and at once so you will be out of the way of *that man*." He pointed at Alex and Sahib reared up, pawed the air, and roared. Sir Vincent involuntarily backed away two steps. "I swear . . . !"

"Don't swear to something you'll regret. Has it not occurred to you that Sahib only roars when you insist I'll not wed Alex?" asked his daughter sweetly.

"He does?"

"Think back."

Sir Vincent put his mind to it. "Seems like maybe he does. But what does that say to anything?"

"It says that Sahib approves our marriage." Artemisia stalked off down one of the brick paths but turned. "Oh, and another thing for you to think about. You cannot marry me off against my will. Women have attained that much control over their lives, or so I've been told, so you may forget your notion of marrying me to some man of your choosing. I will marry Alex or no one." She continued on down the path and went out of the conservatory by a garden door.

"I cannot?"

"You cannot force her to wed where she will not," said his wife. "It is the law and one every girl should know."

Sir Vincent digested that. "Silly chit. Knows too much, to my mind," he muttered.

Alex moved away in the other direction and was soon lost in the shrubbery. With Alex and Artemisia gone, Sahib slid from his haunches to lie flat, putting his great head onto his crossed paws.

"My dear," said Lady Bigalow softly, "can you not see your way to accepting Lord Merwin's very flattering offer? Our daughter will be so very unhappy if you do not."

"Nonsense. Mere infatuation. Girlish fiddle-faddle. She'll come to her senses any day now."

"It has been nearly three years now."

"Three years? Three . . . years? Can't be. Not possible. Infatuations don't run on for three years."

"Exactly."

"Exactly?"

"Since it has run on for so long, it is *not* an infatuation."

Sir Vincent had to think about that one. Logic was not a thing that came naturally to him. "Oh," he said at last. And then, once again blustering, he added, "Well, makes no odds. I'll not have her marrying that Tory!"

At which point Sahib sat up and roared, making the baronet jump almost out of his skin. "Forgot the beast was still here," he said and eyed the cat. "You know, Penny, that blasted tiger has a one-track mind." And with that comment, Sir Vincent turned on his heel and strode back into the house.

Lady Bigalow looked down at Sahib. "Do you think it possible he'll come around in the end?" Sahib got to his feet and came to her, politely sniffing the hand she rather shyly held out to him. "What a fool I am, asking the opinion of a wild beast." She eyed him thoughtfully. "And yet, sometimes you seem to be much more than that. I have to wonder if that prince hasn't the right of it. Are you magic?" she asked.

Sahib blinked, seemed to Lady Bigalow to smile, and then turned away and disappeared into a small portion of the conservatory, which had been allowed to grow into a wild tangle of greenery.

Lady Bigalow, watching him, bit her lip. "Well, Sahib," she said softly, "I truly hope you *are* magic, because I see no other solution to this little problem of ours."

Somewhere, lost in the tiny man-made jungle, Sahib chuffed.

"I am not to worry?"

The sound came again.

Lady Bigalow nodded and left the conservatory. And then, all the way up to her room, she silently scolded herself for being nonsensical.

Hours later the Renwicks returned. Trey asked for an interview with his cousin and Lord Renwick, knowing the inevitable *tête-à-tête* had arrived, something he had so far avoided, led the way to his study. Once they were seated, Lord Renwick dropped his hand to Sahib's head and asked, "Well?"

"I know you have wondered why I returned to England."

"To be frank, I assumed you wished to ask me for an allowance."

Trey laughed a trifle bitterly. "Actually, if you were to ask it of me, I could give one to *you*. I do very well with an import-export company. I returned to England merely because I was homesick and wished to see it again. But then, when I arrived—" His lips compressed into a hard line, then relaxed. He shrugged. "—my welcome was not all I could have wished. That old scandal! It will never be forgot, will it? Jason, I did not kill her. If I were the sort to murder anyone, then I would have murdered her mother. The woman was a harridan, possessive—in a word, impossible. It was she who insisted I killed her daughter, you know. There had been not the least notion in anyone's head it was anything other than an accident. Which it was!"

"I have always kept an open mind, Trey. I am sorry you have not enjoyed your trip home as you should have done."

"Ah well. What is, is and must be endured. Edith and I have decided to take a wedding journey before leaving England. We will avoid places where people might be found who knew me and simply enjoy the beauties of our island since it will be many years before we, either of us, return." Trey rose to his feet.

"Our first stop will be Portsmouth. Captain Surewood
gave us a letter that should get us a place on an out-
bound ship. We will arrange our passage so that we
will know how long we have for our little holiday.
Since I doubt we will return here to Tiger's Lair, I
wished to thank you for giving me houseroom and for
not casting accusations and threats at my head!"

Lord Renwick nodded. "Sahib did not object to
you. I trust his instincts when it comes to judging
people. By the way, I believe you did not kill your
wife, if that is of interest to you."

Jason heard his cousin heave a huge sigh. "It is. I
am glad. Do I," he said, returning to the slightly cyni-
cal tone that had become part of him after the scandal
broke, "thank you or the tiger?"

Jason chuckled. "Sahib, of course. Blind as I am,
I do not trust my own judgment at all!"

"Sahib, I thank you," said Trey solemnly. Sahib
chuffed softly. Whether in response to the thank you,
or because of a dream, neither man knew. After a moment he added, "We leave early tomorrow morning
so I will say good-bye now."

"Be happy."

Trey sounded a trifle surprised when he responded.
"You know, Jase, I think I will. Edith isn't to everyone's taste, I know, but I have found it fun showing
her the world she should have known so very long
ago. And she'll have far less difficulty adapting to
society in Naples than might have been the case for
a properly brought up young lady of British birth and
breeding. And she has a great deal of curiosity about
just about everything and that has given me back an
interest in life I had thought lost forever."

A few more words and Trey left Jason seated behind his desk, his hand on Sahib's head. "You know,
Sahib, that is the most I have heard Trey say all at
one time since he arrived. I wonder if I should feel
guilt that I did not do more to rehabilitate him with

the *ton*, or if I should think it was fate that brought him here just now when Edith needed a husband!"

Sahib bounced Jason's hand and, obligingly, Jase scratched the tiger just as he liked best.

FOURTEEN

Prince Ravi, escaping his studies for a time, found Artemisia huddled into one of the rose-covered arbors that dotted the Renwick gardens. "Shall I go away?" asked the youth politely.

"What? Oh. Prince Ravi. No, of course not. Please join me."

"You are sad."

"Yes."

"It is because your father will not permit you to wed Lord Merwin?"

Artemisia wondered how the youth knew so much about her business but she nodded. "Yes, my father continues to stubbornly deny that I may wed Lord Merwin."

Prince Ravi smiled, his teeth very white. "But Miss Bigalow, truly, you need not concern yourself. Sahib has your affairs in hand. He will see that you have your heart's desire!"

"I hope it may be so, Prince, but you do not know my father."

"You must have patience. Sahib is magic. He will succeed. I am aware you who live here in England and have not had the advantages I have had cannot understand how that may be, but it is so. When I was younger I would become upset that no one here believes in Sahib's magic, but I am older and wiser now. I see that you are to be pitied for your blindness."

Artemisia very nearly smiled, but Prince Ravi was so very serious she knew she must not. She struggled to hide any hint of humor. "I wonder," she said, "if it is still true that no one believes in Sahib's magic. It has seemed to me that, although they will not come right out and say it, there are several who hold private views about Sahib that our churchmen would find unpalatable!"

"Unpalatable?" Prince Ravi repeated the word carefully, the upward inflection at the end making it a question.

Artemisia complied with his unvoiced request and defined the word. "So you see, Prince, it is quite possible that, although you will never hear them say it, some, at least, believe Sahib is a magic beast."

"I see. It would be against all they have been taught so they will not put it into words." He nodded. "I will explain this to Sahib. His feelings are hurt, you know, that no one believes in him."

"Tell him I believe and that all my dependence is on him. There is, I know, no one else who has a chance of changing my father's mind!" Artemisia rose to her feet. "Thank you, Prince. I was feeling rather hopeless, but you have restored me to optimism."

The lad bowed from the waist. "I am pleased I could be of service," he said, his tone formal. "May I escort you back to the house?"

Prince Ravi offered his arm in proper fashion and, although she had not thought to leave the gardens just yet, she could not bring herself to chance upsetting the boy's adolescent feelings by refusing. She set her fingers on his bright blue satin sleeve and strolled beside him back to the house. There he told her he must return to his schoolroom and, with all proper decorum, he took his leave.

Eustacia had arrived in the hall just in time to observe Ravi's leave-taking. She joined Artemisia as he disappeared upstairs. "The boy who arrived here a few short years ago is growing up," she said. "Despite all the problems the spoiled brat gave us, I am almost sad to see him disappear in the young man!"

"I am never quite certain which Prince Ravi I will see," agreed Artemisia. "One day it will be the mischievous lad and the next an exceedingly formal young man. I always feel I must be very careful to determine his mood before I dare to say anything. It is quite ridiculous, is it not?"

"Quite. Artemisia," continued Eustacia a trifle abruptly, "I have been meaning to tell you that, if your father does not relent as we all hope he will, then you are welcome to remain here with us until you come of age. You need not return to Sir Vincent's house unless you wish it. No," she added, raising her hand, "do not say anything, but be aware you have a home with us for as long as you may need it. Jason and I have discussed it and are agreed."

"I am under age," said Artemisia.

"Yes, that is what I . . . Ah! You would say your father could *force* you to return to London and your home there." Eustacia nodded. "I know. But would he?"

Artemisia tipped her head, her gaze going out of focus as she considered the question. Then she shook her head. "I do not know. If he acted from logic one could predict his reaction, but he does not and—" She grimaced. "—that is something I should not say aloud! My mother would scold me for such unfilial thoughts, let alone the voicing of them!"

Elsewhere in the house Lady Bigalow was scolding her spouse for exactly that, his lack of logic. "My dear, how can anyone follow the machinations of your mind when you allow it to jump here and there and to contradict one day what you have said the day before?"

"Nonsense. Doesn't matter what I said yesterday. It is what I say right now that is important."

"And then tomorrow when you say something else?"

Sir Vincent's expression changed to one indicative of confusion. "But why should I say something else?"

"When our Arta was missing, you said you hoped she was with Lord Merwin because the alternative was not to be thought on. So, now you find she is with him, and you wish to tear her away! It is not logical that one day you approve of him and the next you do not."

"Phoo. Bah. Nonsense. He's a *Tory.* How can I even think of giving her to a Tory?"

"But my dear, *don't* think of giving her to a Tory. Think of giving her to the foremost catch now gracing the *ton!* Think of it! Our daughter wedding the man every matchmaking mother, for years past, has tried to snabble up for her own daughter and it is *ours* who caught his eye!"

Sir Vincent's eyes narrowed and he chewed on his upper lip. "Good thing that, marrying her to the prize of the Season?"

"A very good thing," agreed Lady Bigalow, wondering if she had finally gotten through to him.

"But—" The stubborn look returned. "—he's a Tory." Sir Vincent turned on his heel and made for the door . . . only to stop short when Sahib rose to his feet and growled.

"Here now! What is it this time?" The baronet stared at the tiger. "Can't a man have any peace in this house? Everywhere I turn that blasted tiger is right there staring at me. Growling at me. Even roaring at me. I don't like it, Penny. I don't like it at all!"

"It is only that Sahib believes our daughter should wed Lord Merwin and he is as stubborn as you, my dear. I wonder which of you will hold out longest."

Sir Vincent turned on his heel and stared at his wife. "Are you feeling quite the thing, my dear?" he asked.

"I am in perfect health. Why do you ask?"

"I don't remember any insanity in her family," he muttered but not so softly that Lady Bigalow was unable to hear it. She grinned. He looked up. "Wasn't your Aunt Betty that was put in the tower room with a keeper, was it?"

"No, dear. That was your great-aunt on your mother's side."

"Sure?"

"Very sure."

"Oh. Well, that's all right then." He glanced at the tiger and back at his wife. "But you are *certain* you feel all right?"

Lady Bigalow no longer felt like smiling. "If," she said sternly, "you wonder that I impute thoughts and feelings and intentions to Sahib, then perhaps it behooves you to discover more of the animal's history." She turned on her heel and left the room, Sahib making no objections to *her* going.

Sir Vincent stared at the tiger. Sahib stared back. "Need to know more about you, hmm?"

Sahib tipped his head.

"So who do I ask?"

Just at that moment, Prince Ravi crept by the door, looking back over his shoulder.

"Aha! Prince! Just the one I need. Have you a moment?"

Ravi looked into the room, swept a quick glance back over his shoulder, and then, shutting the door carefully and quietly, he joined Sir Vincent. "Yes sir? You wished to speak with me?"

"Not to say wished. Need to."

"I see," said an obviously confused Prince Ravi. "And what is it about which you need to speak?"

"Not easy to explain," said Sir Vincent.

The prince had spent no time with Artemisia's father and had no knowledge of the convoluted way his mind got from point *a* to point *b*. "Hmm, could you say what it is you wish to speak *about?*" he asked cautiously.

"That is easy enough. That blasted tiger, that's what." Sir Vincent gestured to where Sahib lay stretched across a warm patch of sunlight that streamed through one of the windows.

"You must not be insulting when speaking about Sahib, Sir Vincent. It is not proper. Not at all."

Sir Vincent's eyes bulged. "Not proper? Not *proper!* He's a beast. An *animal!*"

"A very special animal. A magical animal."

"Nonsense."

"You do not understand because you are English. It would be perfectly clear to you if you were from my country."

Sir Vincent struggled with several different thoughts, trying to sort out what it was he most wished to say. What he wanted to say most was that that must be nonsense, but there was something his wife had said to him and it was *that* which he was supposed to be saying to Prince Ravi. "Ah! His history. I am supposed to learn something of the blasted tiger's history. And you are just the one to tell me."

Ravi nodded. "It is because of childish behavior on my part that Sahib was given to Lord Renwick, so certainly it is I you should ask this question. I see that. First I must explain to you about white tigers. They are very rare. They appear only once in a very great while and when they do it is momentous. There will be great changes and our world will turn upside down and all sorts of things will happen that our astrologers are, even now, attempting to sort out and explain to my father, who sent me here to England to learn how an English prince behaves." Prince Ravi nodded. "If Sahib had not been found and given to Lord Renwick, then I would never have come to England, would not have had an English tutor as I do now and . . ."

Ravi continued talking until the baronet's head spun. He shook his head, attempting to clear it. "But what has all this to do with that blasted tiger?"

"But I am explaining, am I not?" Ravi looked bewildered. "Sahib is magic. He knows what is right and wrong. He has determined that it is right that Miss Bigalow wed Lord Merwin, and he will not rest until the two are one."

"Right that my daughter wed a blasted Tory? Can't be right."

"But it can. Sahib has said it."

Sahib roared.

"There. You see?" said Ravi. "What I say is true."

"Nonsense!" But Sir Vincent looked a trifle perplexed. "Magic?"

"Magic." Ravi nodded.

"Ain't no such thing as magic," asserted Sir Vincent.

"There is," asserted Prince Ravi just as firmly.

"There is?"

"Of course."

Sir Vincent drew in a deep breath and let it out. "I don't understand a word of it. Tigers don't make matches. Fathers make matches. Why won't my daughter see that?"

"This match is fated. It is nonsense to interfere."

"But he is a Tory," said Sir Vincent, his voice very nearly a wail.

Just then there was a soft knock at the door.

"Come in," called the baronet, glad of any interruption that would make it unnecessary to try to puzzle through the dilemma in which he was mired.

"Ah. There you are, Prince," said Ravi's tutor. "I wondered where you were." There was a half-stern quality to Aaron McMurrey's tone and half amused. "You did not finish that Latin essay I set you."

"Latin," said Ravi a trifle angrily, "is nonsense. For me, I mean." He was very much on his dignity as he continued. "I understand that I must learn English and learn it well, but that I learn any more Latin than I already know is a very great waste of time."

"And when the English come to you and wish you to sign their contracts and half of it is in Latin, how will you know what they are really asking of you?"

Ravi's half boyish and half adult features fell into lines denoting frustration and sadness. "But I do not like Latin. It is a bore . . . I know!" He brightened. "I will hire myself a Latin scholar and he will read these contracts and will tell me what it is the English traders wish me to sign!" He pointed toward his tutor. "I will hire *you.*"

Aaron nodded. "I will be happy to serve you in any capacity which suits, my prince, but not for all of my life." There was a commiserating tone as he continued. "We have discussed this, have we not?"

Ravi nodded glumly. "Yes. When I return to my father's palace, you will come with me. You will stay, if my father allows it. You will stay until you wish to return home—" He reeled that off as if by rote and seemed to grow more glum as the words passed his lips. "—and you will leave me and I will be the only one in my kingdom who has lived in England and the only one who understands the English and I will be very lonely and very much alone. It is too bad of you," said Prince Ravi, glaring at his tutor. He stalked from the room, turning up the hallway toward the stairs that would take him to his schoolroom.

"Well, well," said Sir Vincent. "You really mean to go off to India with that lad when he goes?"

Aaron nodded. "I am engaged to a wonderful woman. We will wed and travel with the prince and stay with him for a year to two. I am certain it will take Prince Ravi no time at all to forget his English manners and become the despot his father expects him to be, but there will be a period when the boy will feel confused and lost between two cultures." Aaron sobered. "I fear he will never be totally comfortable in his own country as he is not completely comfortable here. I fear it was not an altogether good thing that his father sent him to Lord Renwick."

"Not?" Sir Vincent blinked. "But a very good thing to be English. Best thing in the world!"

"Still, he is *not* English and his homeland is not England. It will be difficult for him."

Sir Vincent couldn't see why anyone would care where he was if only he were that best of all possible things—in other words, English—but he was too polite to say so. Besides, he had his own problems and wasn't about to waste time trying to understand those that faced the prince! "Well, well. Young yet. You'll see. He'll do quite well."

Aaron nodded. He was too well-mannered to contradict the baronet although he wished to do so. "I must return to the schoolroom. The prince is contrite at the moment, but it will not last." He grinned. "The boy in him will soon have him rebelling against his schoolwork. And today I rather agree! It is far too nice to sit in a schoolroom, so perhaps I will suggest we go riding before we take out his mathematics."

"Very good notion." *And,* thought Sir Vincent, *you just take yourself off and do it.* When the young man bowed and left him in peace, the baronet wondered if he had spoken aloud. He glanced toward Sahib, who watched him. A scowl settled on his brow and he exchanged stare for stare with the big cat.

"Harrumph," he said and stalked to the door. Sir Vincent was outside it and standing in the hall before he realized Sahib had not objected to his leaving!

In the meantime, Lady Bigalow had tracked down her hostess. "My dear Lady Renwick," she said when Eustacia was found sitting in the blue salon with Artemisia, "I've a favor to ask."

"Of course. Anything I can do," said Eustacia, laying her handwork in her lap, but not setting her needle.

"I have had a little talk with my husband concerning Sahib. I believe someone should tell Vincent the stories Arta told me of Sahib's interference in the lives of your friends."

"Ah! Easily done, but do you think that will help the situation?"

Lady Bigalow bit her lip. She glanced at her daughter, then across the room and out the window, and back to her hostess. "I should not say this. It is disloyal—" She drew in a deep breath and let it out in a whoosh. "—and I have done my very best to be loyal to my husband. At least in public." She smiled a quick, flashing smile. "Within the privacy of my room is something else again!"

"We are discreet. You know, Mama, that we would say nothing to hurt you."

"Yes, dear, I know, and I must say it if I am to make Lady Renwick understand why I believe telling your father tales of Sahib might be of help. You see, he is a very suggestible sort of man. I have inserted into his mind the notion Sahib is magical. He poohpoohed it, of course, as any sensible person would do, but if we can convince him it is true, and that Sahib always gets his way—" She glanced from one to the other. "—well, surely, you see that he might then give in, thinking it was inevitable?"

"Or he might stubbornly decide to be the exception to the rule!"

"Artemisia," scolded Lady Bigalow, "you are not naturally a pessimistic sort of person. You will instantly apologize for doubting Sahib's omniscience."

"And his omnipotence?"

"Still more important, of course."

Lady Renwick chuckled. "You, my lady, are a complete hand!"

Lady Bigalow nodded. "So my irrepressible daughter informed me on another occasion. An odd phrase, but I believe I took her meaning."

"If you took it that I thought you a perfect, a consummate manipulator, then yes, you understood," said the irrepressible daughter pertly.

A pinkish glow filled Lady Bigalow's neck and cheeks. She smiled, or perhaps grimaced—it was hard to tell which. "Well," she said, "I must admit that I have, over the years, felt it necessary to—to *manage* Sir Vincent to one degree or another."

"We will see if we can *manage* to convince him of Sahib's infallibility," said Lady Renwick, laughing. "I will discuss it with my husband and see if he can come up with a plan. Perhaps," she said, her tone thoughtful, "it would be better if it were done indirectly . . ."

"You've a plan? Already?" asked Artemisia when Lady Renwick's voice trailed off and a funny little smile gradually widened to what could only be called a grin.

"I do. I do not think I will explain it to you until I have talked to Jason. And perhaps to Alex. Alex is very good at organizing plots. He is very careful of detail, you see, and allows for every possible contingency." Lady Renwick folded her handwork, laid it in the workbox at her feet, and stood up. "In fact, I will see what I can do right now. The sooner, the better, do you not agree?"

"Yesterday might have been *almost* soon enough," said Artemisia.

"Hmm. Or last week, perhaps," agreed Lady Bigalow.

"Or even one or two years in the past! Poor Alex. Poor Artemisia. It has been a very long courtship and it is more than time it ends!" On the words, Lady Renwick nodded sharply and exited the room.

"Do you think it will answer?" asked Artemisia.

"I have known your father a very long time, my dear, and even so I cannot say if it will do the trick. He is difficult to predict."

Artemisia nodded sadly. "I know. Where logic plays no part in one's thinking, then it is impossible to know which way that person will jump."

"Hmm. Most likely straight up," said her mother in a dry tone. "If he gets the slightest hint he is being tricked, I mean."

"Alex will know that. And just in case he has forgotten, I will remind him!" Artemisia went to Lady Renwick's workbox and took out the shift her hostess had been sewing for the charity box at the church. She threaded a needle, bent her head, and slowly, carefully, began setting tiny stitches in the half finished hem.

Lady Bigalow watched her daughter for a long moment. She shook her head, worried about Artemisia's mood. Then she sighed. Softly. She, too, went to the workbox and found another shift which had been seamed front to back but nothing more. She set to work making a rolled hem around the neck opening.

While the Bigalow women sewed in the blue salon, Lady Renwick found Alex sitting with her husband in Jason's private study. She asked if she could join them, was told yes, and took the seat Alex held for her. Sahib rose to his feet and came to sit beside her, looking up into her face. Lady Renwick smiled. "You, Sahib, have a role to play. I hope you do not muff your lines."

"What is this?" asked Jason, bemused. "You would turn Sahib into an actor?"

Lady Renwick chuckled. "But he is very like an actor, is he not?"

"I believe Sahib is merely Sahib and unique," said Alex, grinning. "But I scent a plot. What do you have in mind, Eustacia?"

Lady Renwick explained. . . . so you see, if you can convince Sir Vincent that Sahib will somehow manage to get his way in this, Sir Vincent might actually decide it is foolish to hold out any longer and allow the wedding!"

Or, thought Alex, echoing Artemisia's thought, *become still more stubborn, determined to thwart not only Artemisia and myself but Sahib as well*. Out loud he said, "It is worth a try."

"I think it is more than that. It is a dashed good plan!" enthused Jason. "Come, Alex, we must put our heads together."

Sahib looked from one man to the other. He opened his mouth in one of his almost silent roars.

"There!" said Jason, grinning. "Sahib agrees. My dear, why do you not go away so that we may lay our plans in peace?"

Lady Renwick harrumphed. "I can take a hint. I know when I am not wanted!"

She rose to her feet but Sahib got between her and the door and gently pushed her the way he wished her to go. When she stood beside Lord Renwick the big tiger put a huge paw against her back and, still gently, forced her to bend down to her seated husband. Lady Renwick turned a quick look toward Alex. He studied the nails on his left hand and whistled softly, but even so her skin heated to a glow as she bent just a trifle farther and kissed Lord Renwick's cheek.

His lordship put up his hand, moved her slightly, and kissed her back . . . right on the mouth.

"Sahib continues to show us the way, does he not?" she said softly.

"Had he a hand in this? A paw, I mean? I must remember to thank him!"

"An extra dollop of meat at his next feeding, perhaps."

Jason chuckled. "It does seem very nearly the only way of rewarding him, does it not? You go on now. We are, I suspect, embarrassing our friend."

"Assuming Sahib is agreeable, I will go. Sahib?"

The big cat moved out of her way. Lady Renwick was rather startled by what appeared to be an expression of smugness on his muzzle. She eyed the cat for a moment, shook her head at the thoughts running through her mind, and left the study to the men. She closed the door behind her and, still musing over Sahib's behavior, stood still for a very long moment. Only when a maid came from one of the rooms did she give a start, her thoughts interrupted by the oblivious servant.

Some moments later she found her new friend alone in the salon, still sewing, "Artemisia," she said, "I have had the strangest thought. What if Sahib *is* magical?"

Artemisia's brows arched. She went to her friend and put a hand to her forehead. "Eustacia, are you sure you are quite well?"

Eustacia chuckled as she drew Artemisia's hand away. "Do I sound deranged? It is just that for the umpteenth time Sahib has done something unaccountable and it makes me wonder." She described Sahib's insistence she kiss Lord Renwick before leaving the study. "It was as if Sahib knew I was irritated that I was not wanted for their discussion and that he was insisting I forgive Jase for telling me to go!"

"I agree. That is so eerie it is rather unnerving! Does he do this sort of thing often?"

Lady Renwick related one or two stories. Then Sahib's behavior the night he pushed her into his lordship's bed, forcing Lord Renwick to insist she wed him, popped into her head. She blushed hotly. "So, um, you agree, surely, that he behaves very strangely," she said in a hurried fashion, hoping Artemisia would not ask why she blushed. "Sahib appears to believe the shortest way to a goal is the correct one. For instance, when I first came to Tiger's Lair, he decided Jason and I should be married and—" Eustacia realized she'd mentioned the very thing she had wished to avoid. "—and well, he . . . um . . ."

"Alex told me Sahib played a part in your marriage.

You do not have to tell me the details," said Artemisia, speaking quickly.

"Of course I do not, but I find I want, to." Lady Renwick drew in a deep breath. "It is just that this particular story is rather embarrassing. Jason used to suffer really terrible nightmares. Because of his blindness, you know. One night, Sahib woke me and insisted I go to Jason. When I reached the bedroom, Sahib . . . well—" The blush had faded to a rosy glow but turned scarlet again. "—he pushed me right into Jason's bed and, well, once the night was over, Jason insisted we must wed. Not that it wasn't something we both wanted, but you see, Jason felt his blindness precluded his ever proposing to any woman and I, well—" Lady Renwick raised her fingers and covered the small, heart-shaped birthmark on her cheek. "—I had been told by my stepmother that this mark precluded anyone ever wishing to wed me!"

"So Sahib put his paw into the situation and your marriage resulted, is that what you would say?"

"Hmm. And now he has a paw in your affairs, does he not?"

"You would say I am not to worry, that Sahib will see Alex and I are wed?"

The door, which had opened during Lady Renwick's story, closed softly. Sir Vincent, frowning mightily, stood just on the other side in deep thought.

Is that blasted tiger truly magical, then? he asked himself.

FIFTEEN

Sir Vincent spent several minutes convincing himself that it was nonsense to believe any such thing. Sahib was a beast. A rather nasty beast, in fact. Reaching this conclusion, the baronet went to the billiards room. He sent a few balls around the table, but soon tired of it and took himself across the room to where a small but cheery fire blazed in the grate. Several comfortable chairs were judiciously placed for lounging.

Their comfort appealed to Sir Vincent and, squirming slightly, he settled into the largest of the leather-covered chairs, moved a pillow to support his head, and drifted off to sleep. The sound of balls clicking against each other woke him and, still groggy, he wondered who had disturbed his nap.

"Nonsense," he heard Alex's well modulated tones. "Sahib is nothing more than an intelligent animal. To suggest he has magic powers is ridiculous. Is it not, Sahib?"

A soft snarl reached Sir Vincent's ears.

"You see?" said Lord Renwick, a laugh in his voice. "Sahib agrees with *me*."

"Nonsense," said Alex, chuckling.

The big cat snarled more loudly.

"Or—" This time there was a questioning note to Alex's tone. "—maybe not?"

"I have told you."

"Tell me again."

Lord Renwick said, "Sahib understands every word said to him. Remember when we had to rescue my wife? When her stepmother's new husband stole my dearly beloved away and tried to force her to sign papers giving him authority to do as he pleased with the inheritance left her by her grandfather? Well, then," he said when Alex nodded, "you will also remember that when we opened the door to rescue her, Sahib attacked the man. When told he must not harm the fellow, Sahib merely controlled him. And then stood guard until we decided what to do."

"You consider that proof of magic?"

"Sahib could have torn the fellow to bits. He did not when *told* he must not."

"So what else do you consider proof?"

"How about when Tony and Libby were first married? Do you not recall how Sahib was continuously forcing the one into the company of the other until they came to their senses and admitted they loved each other? Once they had done so he didn't bother them anymore. Of course, at that point no one *had* to force them into each other's company!"

"Ah! There does appear to be method to his madness, does there not?" asked Alex. "I seem to recall that Libby found him rather frightening."

"Not after she and Tony realized why he did it."

"No. Not then."

"And what of Jack and your cousin?" Jason demanded of Alex. "Remember how Sahib would not allow anyone into the hall that day?"

Alex chuckled. "You mean when they were kissing and cuddling beneath the mistletoe? After they concluded they would wed?"

"Sahib makes an odd-looking cupid," said Jason, "but he does know, does he not, just who should marry whom?"

Alex sighed. "He at least seems to understand that

my Artemisia and I should wed. Sahib, can you not do something to see we may do so?"

The tiger roared.

"You can?"

The roar sounded again, still louder.

"I wish you would do it soon," said Alex, a note of sadness in his tone. "I am so tired of waiting for her and even if she agrees to wed me without her father's blessing, I know she will be very unhappy to have done so. And lonely for her mother. Why must the man . . ."

"Hush," said Lord Renwick with a glance toward the chairs and fireplace. "Do not say something you will wish unsaid. My stomach says it is nearing time to dress for dinner and I believe we've neighbors coming in to dine and for an evening of cards, so I think I will go to my room. Coming?"

"I suppose so. Just let me hang up my cue stick."

After a long, silent moment, when Sir Vincent was certain the others had gone, he rose to his feet. Sahib snarled. Sir Vincent stared. Sahib snarled again. "Er . . . ?"

Again the snarl.

"What do you mean by it?" asked Sir Vincent, blustering.

Sahib raised his paw and pawed the air.

"Wish you could talk. Maybe I'd know what you want."

Sahib made a swipe at the air, his claws extended.

"Drat it!" Sir Vincent scowled. "If you want me to say they can get married, I'm blessed if I will!"

Sahib roared.

"Dammee, it ain't the thing to be telling a father what is best for his daughter!"

Sahib sat on his haunches and put both front paws in the air. "You'd fight me for the right? Nonsense. You got claws and teeth and it wouldn't be a fair fight at all."

Sahib snarled.

"Oh, all right. I'll think about it. Fair enough?"

Sahib stared at him.

"I will! I promise I will!"

Sahib snarled, again pawed the air while continuing to stare, and then dropped to all fours and padded from the room.

Sir Vincent mopped his brow. "Did I really have a conversation with that animal?" He shook his head. "Nonsense. Just a beast."

Sahib stuck his head back into the room and snarled.

"Er? *Not* just a beast?"

With a sound oddly reminiscent of agreement Sahib nodded, backed out of the doorway, and again disappeared.

Sir Vincent, staring at the empty doorway, gulped. Now Sahib was gone he discovered he was trembling. "Don't like that animal," he whispered. "Don't like it at all." He stared another long moment, shook his head, and seemed somehow diminished in stature. He sighed a long, mournful sigh. Concluding he had no choice—after all, he *had* been threatened by a tiger, had he not?—Sir Vincent decided to get it over and done.

Still shaking ever so slightly with fear of the great beast, Sir Vincent went in search of his daughter.

The next day, Alex and Artemisia strolled through the garden and into the glade at the edge of the woods. Once there, Artemisia turned into Alex's arms. "I cannot believe my father has agreed. I will never understand it."

"Thank Sahib."

"Hmm?" Artemisia was too busy exploring the planes and angles of Alex's face to really listen.

"I said," he repeated patiently—once he'd removed her hand from his cheek—"that you must thank Sahib."

"What did he do? What *could* he do?"

Alex grinned. "You'd have to ask Sahib, but I do know your father checked the room very carefully before we had our little talk about settlements and all that. And he locked the door. Once, when he objected to a suggestion, Sahib roared. Your father instantly backed down and said that *of course* we could be wed here where so many of my friends have been married."

"I wonder why Sahib roared."

"I asked Jason that question."

"And?"

Alex grinned. "Jase couldn't be sure. He said he had been discussing a section of his new book with Eustacia when suddenly, for no reason he knew of, Sahib roared. Maybe," suggested Alex, his tongue firmly in cheek, "Sahib didn't like Jason's prose."

Artemisia smiled but was silent for a long moment. "I wish there was something we could do to thank Sahib. Do you suppose he is lonely? Do you think he would like a friend of his own?"

"Another tiger?" asked Alex, half laughing.

"I had in mind something smaller. A kitten, perhaps. One he could raise himself."

Alex sobered. "My dear girl, Sahib is so big and a kitten so small. Are you seriously suggesting the tiny creature would not come to harm?"

"Sahib would be careful. Think how he is with the Renwick children."

"Hmm. Yes, he allows them to crawl all over him. I saw Elizabeth pull his tail the other day and he merely turned and nudged her away and then pulled her around in front of him. It was, I swear, as if he were giving the tot a talking-to."

Artemisia chuckled. "What is more, she *listened*."

"Hmm. I will suggest to Eustacia that they give

Sahib a kitten. I think it is worth a try. But why, my dear, did you suggest it?"

"Oh, I don't know. Yes I do. I was trying to explain that unexplained roar. If he had been in the same room as my father, then one might think it was in response to his stubbornness. Since he was not . . . ?"

"Moonbeam," said Alex suddenly, "why are we discussing Sahib as if he were a rational being? He is a *tiger*. And—" He put her hand, which he still held, back against his cheek. "—I've far better things to talk about than Sahib."

His gaze held hers as he lowered his mouth to her lips . . .

Lady Bigalow sat with Lady Renwick in the blue salon. The women laid their plans for a wedding which would take place no later than it took for all of the six and their wives to arrive at Tiger's Lair along with a few other friends and relatives. "I will write our friends if you will write yours," said Eustacia.

"The children insist they do not wish a large wedding. We've a few relatives I *must* invite and there are *several* friends who would never forgive me if I did not. Even so, the task should not take long."

Eustacia then described the habit they had fallen into of decorating the altar with flowers for weddings. "It looks very well and adds a happy, celebratory note to the ritual. If you do not object I will discuss with our gardener the availability of blooms."

"I have never seen it done before. Your vicar does not object?"

"He was a trifle shocked the first time, but then he grew accustomed and now he likes it very well."

"Hmm. It sounds delightful," said Lady Bigalow a trifle doubtfully.

Eustacia smiled. "Oh, it is. Vicar says that God makes the flowers bloom and a marriage should blossom in much the same way! In fact, he is likely to say just that during his homily. You will see. Now, the wedding breakfast . . ."

The discussion lasted until everyone arrived in the salon at pretty much the same time just before dinner. It was observed by Jason, when talking to his wife, that now he had given in, no one would have ever guessed that Sir Vincent had ever made any sort of objection to his daughter wedding Lord Merwin!

Of course, everyone did their best to avoid any mention of anything that in any way might rouse Toryish thoughts in Sir Vincent's Whiggish head!

SIXTEEN

The wedding took place two weeks and three days later, the banns first called the day after Sir Vincent gave his reluctant permission for the marriage. Alex had been ready to ride to Canterbury to buy a Special License, fearing Artemisia's father would change his mind, but everyone talked him out of it. Except Artemisia, who was nearly as worried as Alex that something would interfere, but they finally agreed they should do things in traditional manner.

"It is better to be conventional," said Lady Bigalow soothingly. "Your poor father's sensibilities are rubbed rather raw as it is. Let us not make bad worse."

"You do not think he'll find reason to object?"

"Now he has said yes you think he'll say no?" Lady Bigalow chuckled. "Oh, my dears, you do not understand him at all. What he has said publicly he will not retract. Which is why it took something like Sahib's roars to convince him he should do what he very well knew he should do. He had to have some way of convincing himself he was right, but was forced by circumstance to go against his own wise decision."

"You would say he pretended to be frightened of Sahib?"

Lady Bigalow frowned. "No. I fear he has truly convinced himself the tiger is a magical beast and that there is no way he could go against the animal's wishes. Sahib wishes to see you two married, so he had to give in, do you see?"

Alex and Eustacia looked at each other. "Oh yes," they said in chorus, Eustacia recalled when she and Artemisia discussed Sahib's role in the Renwick marriage. Alex, thinking of the carefully laid plot he and Jason had concocted and carried through in the game room one evening, added, "We understand!"

The church altar was thick with blossoms. Prince Ravi contributed an exotic-looking, silk-clad honor guard, which, fully armed, stood along either side of the church. At Tiger's Lair the wedding breakfast was ready to be served and, last but not least, the guests had arrived.

Alex was rather sad that Jack and Patricia and Tony and Libby were unable to come. The first couple had moved from Vienna to Brussels while the other pair had followed Libby's brother across the Channel, but he wouldn't allow his disappointment to interfere in this very special day. He stood near the vicar, his hands clasped before him, awaiting Artemisia's appearance at the back of the church.

Everyone waited.

And waited.

Alex glanced at Sahib, who lay sprawled near Prince Ravi. Sahib tipped his head, eyed Alex for a long moment, and then silently got to his feet. Just as silently, he padded toward the back of the church. He looked up at Prince Ravi, who followed him, silently asking that the door, which had a knob rather than a latch, be opened for him.

The outer church doors stood wide and, framed in them, were Artemisia and her father. Her father had tears running down his cheeks. "I cannot . . ."

"You must. Father, believe me, it is not so bad. No one will notice . . ."

Sahib, stopping only a few feet away, snarled.

Sir Vincent gave a start and turned. "I *fell,* you dratted beast. I didn't change my mind, I say. How can I go in there with a great splotch of mud on my trousers?"

"It is *not* a great splotch, Father," said Artemisia. "It is a very small, dark patch and does not show up in the least." She, too, was very nearly in tears.

Sahib walked around Sir Vincent, who looked over his shoulder to keep the beast within sight. Sahib seemed to stare at his trousers for a moment, looked up, and snarled.

"You are certain it is all right?" asked Sir Vincent anxiously.

Sahib growled softly.

"Very well then," said Sir Vincent, sighing. He offered his arm to his daughter and started toward the church door.

Sahib and the Prince ran on before them, flung open the inner church doors, and, walking swiftly but sedately, Prince Ravi and Sahib returned to their places. Ravi actually winked at Alex. Alex's brows flattened and the lad nodded.

Alex relaxed. He turned his gaze to the back of the church, and, moments later, was rewarded by the sight of his bride, who wore a new gown in her favorite blue with three flounces to the narrow skirt and several narrow ruffles edged with her mother's tatting decorating the top of the bodice.

As the service started, Alex whispered, "I feared you'd been made off with."

"Father did not wish to walk down the aisle with mud on his trousers," she whispered back. "Now hush!"

Alex squeezed her hand, but, as she wished, turned his attention to the vicar, who was preaching a homily on marriage and life and duty.

Not a word, thought Alex, *about love!*

He said as much later when he and his bride rode back to Tiger's Lair, a long line of carriages following theirs. They carried not only the close friends and relatives Eustacia and Lady Bigalow had invited, but every local person who could manage to believe they, too, had received an invitation—or, if they could not quite do that, could convince themselves that their invitation had been lost and that Lady Renwick would be insulted if they did not appear.

Much later, when Alex and Artemisia were finally alone in a special suite Lady Renwick had had cleaned and made up for them, and after they had, at long last, found each other in every way possible, Alex turned onto his back and cleared his throat.

"The minister wants you to go to Brussels," said Artemisia into the dark.

Alex stifled a laugh. "I was worrying myself to death, wondering how I was to tell you. How did you know?"

"That exceedingly official-looking packet Reeves gave you when we returned from the church. You were amazingly nervous after you read it. How was I not to know? We will leave as soon as you are ready," she said, her voice firm since she rather feared Alex was going to tell her he would not take her with him.

"We?" he said, proving her intuition was correct. "But that is the problem, my love. I fear there is to be war. Well, I *know* there is to be war. Every word we receive from the continent is about Napoleon's preparations and how the Allies are rushing to meet the challenge. I don't want you there."

"You would go into danger and leave me here to fret and worry and wonder what was happening to you?"

"As I would worry about you if you were there."

Artemisia felt her temper rising and, remembering something the vicar had said only that morning, took several moments to choke it back. "Alex, is there not some compromise? What if I come now while everything is calm but go away when you think Napoleon is about ready to cross the border?"

Alex, about to say no in no uncertain terms, recalled something the vicar had said only that morning. "May I think about that? And read the latest reports which were sent me this morning along with that letter? For some reason, I have not gotten around to them."

Artemisia giggled and snuggled into his arm and shoulder. "And then you will say I may go until danger nears!"

He laughed. "You are a minx."

"And you are wonderful."

Such words led to them forgetting all about Brussels and Napoleon and war and everything that might interfere in their far more important discovery of each other.

So it was that a week later the newlyweds left for the continent, where Jack Princeton had located rooms for them in a city that was already overpopulated with foreigners. Alex, leaving his Moonbeam to unpack and organize their temporary home, went immediately to Allied Headquarters to announce his arrival.

Charles Stewart was there and in uniform. "Merwin! Have you come to enlist? We can use every man!"

"Then I must not be a man. I am here as one of the minister's watchdogs."

"Another one? How many does the man need? Ah well, let me see when I can fit you into Wellington's schedule for a briefing."

Charles turned, but was halted by Alex's hand on his sleeve. "Charles, may I ask a favor of you?"

Charles tipped his head. "Depends, does it not?"

"I brought my brand-new wife with me. Neither of us could bear to be parted so soon after the ceremony, as it were, so against my better judgment, I allowed her to come. But now . . ." He frowned, his brows forming a deep vee. "Charles, I cannot help but fear for her."

Wellington's aide-de-camp nodded. "You want word in time that you can send her home, is that it?"

"Yes."

Charles grinned. "I'll add you to the list."

"The list?"

"Have you any notion of just how many men have wives here that they wish seen to safety if there is the least chance of Napoleon overrunning Brussels?"

Alex grinned. "You would say I'm not the only fool."

"Something of the sort. Now, I've no time for more banter. You would not believe the work Wellington has piled on his family. We are swamped."

Alex nodded. He knew that *family* was Wellington's way of referring to his aides-de-camp. "Send me word when you can fit me in." He wrote down his direction and left, jumping out of the way of a busy officer coming in on official business, the gentleman obviously proud of his brand-new regimentals and terribly young and very earnest.

Alex wondered how many of the beardless young men would survive the coming conflict. Sobered, he strode to his horse and returned to where Artemisia, her impatience carefully hidden, awaited his escort around and about Brussels.

She didn't fool him for a minute. He grinned. "All ready for a nice, long nap, are you?"

She pouted—but only for half an instant before she realized he teased her. "No," she countered, "but I see how tired you are and that you only want your bed." Alex seized her by the arm, turned her sharply to the right about, and led her into the hall, where she dug in her feet and refused to move. "I need my hat, my parasol, and a shawl!"

Ten minutes later they were on their way. Twice they had to push back against the building behind them to leave room for a troop of soldiers marching by. The first were grenadiers. The second were Scots in full kit, their kilts swinging at their knees. Both units were huzzahed by the watching crowds.

The more they saw of military preparations, the more slowly Artemisia walked. When they reached a park where tents had been raised over the whole of it, she stopped. "I don't believe I quite accepted that we are again going to war until just now. Alex, why? Why must men fight?"

"I don't know, Moonbeam. I don't believe anyone knows."

They walked on.

Nearly an hour later they were about to turn a corner when Artemisia, a horrified look on her face, stopped Alex. He glanced down at her, saw she was straining to hear something, and he listened as well to the words drifting from the open window above their heads. . . .

"So you see, my lord, all we need do is force Renwick to bring that blasted tiger of his here and the tiger will see to everything."

"My father," whispered Artemisia.

"And doing what he does best," said Alex, laughing softly.

"Who do you suppose lives in this house?" asked Artemisia.

"I'll ask." He walked along the street to where a unit of the First Foot were temporarily bivouacked A few moments later he returned, grinning. "We will wait for Sir Vincent. The gentleman he visits speaks hardly a word of English. I have met him in London where, when it was official business, he had an interpreter at his elbow every moment. Socially, he doesn't let on that his English is so poor!"

"How did my father meet him? How did he get inside?"

"We may never know, but the Grandee is polite to

the point of inanity. You need not worry he will do anything more than complain bitterly of Englishmen who do not know when to go home. In Spanish, of course."

Ten minutes later, Sir Vincent came out of the house looking quite pleased with himself. "Ah! Artemisia!" He ignored Alex. "Did I know you were in Brussels?"

"Of course you did. And Mother?"

"Stayed with your grandmother and that friend of hers." Sir Vincent grimaced. "Know how I feel about your grandmother," he said in what he thought was a whisper. "Came along here to do my duty."

"If that was to suggest the Allies turn the war over to Sahib, I fear you have made a mistake, sir," said Alex in a confiding tone. "Sahib is a peaceful beast. He only concerns himself with love and marriage. He'd have no idea at all what to do in a war!"

"He wouldn't?" Sir Vincent looked very near to tears. "But that is terrible. I have just been telling my Spanish friend all about Sahib, explaining how he will make everything right and tight and settle all without a shot fired. Oh dear, I hate to go back in there and disappoint the gentleman. He will be so very unhappy."

Artemisia looked at Alex, whose brows were pulled into a quick, deep vee. Alex's lips were tightly compressed—very obviously against the laugh that wished to escape. "Why do I not explain, sir, while you take your daughter on to that café you see across the street from the park there. It will save you the embarrassment of facing our friend again and I will be certain to explain to him you were unaware of Sahib's limitations. I will join you in only a few minutes."

"You'll do that for me?"

"Come along, Father. Alex will see to everything."

"You know, Arta," said Sir Vincent when they were some yards down the street, "perhaps your . . . your . . ."

"Husband."

"Yes. Perhaps he isn't so completely bad after all."

Artemisia spent the twenty minutes Alex gave them convincing her father he really must return to England and their mother. "With me gone, she will be missing you," finished Sir Vincent's daughter a trifle inaccurately. "She will be *needing* you," she added, knowingly compounding her error.

"You are right. I had not thought of it. I will arrange to leave at once! A diligence departs for the port each afternoon and I can make it if I hurry." Sir Vincent looked around, saw Alex approaching, and rose to his feet. "I'll say good-bye now. You say all that is proper to that . . . that . . ."

"Husband?"

"Yes, yes. Your—" Sir Vincent grimaced. *"—husband."*

Alex arrived as Sir Vincent disappeared down the street. "Couldn't face me?"

"I convinced him he should leave instantly for England. I said Mother would be missing him."

"My dear!"

Artemisia sighed. "I know. It was terrible of me. But he needed an excuse to go now that he understands that Sahib cannot stop the war. Alex, you were wrong that he couldn't face you. He even managed to admit you are my husband!"

Alex stared. Then he blinked several times in rapid succession. "Artemisia, I do believe there may be hope for your father yet!"

She laughed. "Oh, no. You are premature. The next time he must say it, he will find it impossible. No, I fear you are to be that . . . that . . ."

"That?"

"That is what he says whenever he must refer to you."

"And how do you refer to me?"

"As my dearest, most wonderful husband and the

love of my life," she said promptly. She cast him a speculative look. "Alex," she added, lowering her voice and speaking just a trifle urgently, "I have seen enough of Brussels for now. Shall we return to our . . . our rooms?"

He looked thoughtful. "I believe you knew better than I earlier. I *am* tired."

"And I," she responded demurely. But then she stopped short and jerked urgently on his arm. He bent to her. "Alex," she whispered, "are we actually proposing to behave in such a truly depraved fashion?"

"Here now! Nothing depraved about it!"

"But it is the middle of the afternoon!"

"My dear," said Alex, patting her hand where it lay on his arm, "love knows no time. And we, my Moonbeam, are very much in love."

Artemisia's eyes opened wide. "Why, so we are. So we are."

"So, my dear, come along now and behave in a manner every bit as depraved as you'd like. I assure you—" His eyes sparkled with love and joy. "—I will abet you to the very best of my ability!"

And, as Artemisia had already discovered, his best was very good indeed.

Dear Reader,

I had great fun with Alex's story. I hope you enjoyed reading it as much as I enjoyed writing it.

Miles, whose story is next, is the wildest, the least tame, of the Six. With the war ended and Napoleon unlikely ever again to slip his leash, boredom strikes. Miles goes looking for trouble—and finds it in the form of a woman very nearly as adventurous as himself!

Thérèse Marie Suzanne is the granddaughter of the Comte de Saint Omer. Her grandfather and grandmother perished under Madame Guillotine's blade, but her father was hidden away by kindly fisherfolk in a village north of Calais. The new comte has not enjoyed his life among the poor, but Thérèse has imbibed the best of both worlds, absorbing all her father could teach her and, at the same time, learning all she could of the sea.

Miles feels annoyance for a wily smuggler who escaped him again and again when the British government had him working to prevent smuggling by both the English and the French. With nothing else to do, he is determined to capture the man and does—only to discover that *he* is a *she!*

Thérèse escapes. And turns the tables. When she kidnaps Miles, he discovers *why* she turned to smuggling—and is impressed at how she helped her people.

A reluctant friendship develops between the two. Whether either would have admitted it was *more* than friendship is doubtful—until Sahib takes a hand. Then there is no question the two will find happiness. Together.

Smuggler's Heart will be in the bookstores in April 2002.

Happy reading!

Cheerfully,
Jeanne Savery

P.S. I love to hear from my readers.

JeanneSavery@Yahoo.com will reach me or you can send mail to P.O. Box 833, Greenacres, WA 99016.